CW01574657

The [illegible]

by

JOANNE PHILLIPS

This novel is entirely a work of fiction. The names, characters and incidents portrayed in it are the product of the author's imagination. Any resemblance to actual persons, living or dead, or events or localities is entirely coincidental.

Mirrorball Books
An imprint of Bostock Publishing
Bostock Hall, Shropshire
SY13 2RN

www.bostockpublishing.co.uk

Paperback Edition 2013
ISBN 978-0-9573094-1-8

Copyright © Joanne Phillips 2013

Joanne Phillips asserts the moral right to be identified as the author of this work. All rights reserved in all media. No part of this publication may be reproduced, stored in a retrieval system, or transmitted, in any form, or by any means, electronic, mechanical, photocopying, recording or otherwise, without the prior written permission of the author and/or publisher.

Typeset in Sabon, printed and bound in the UK by Lightning Source
Cover design by Blondesign

The Family Trap

by

JOANNE PHILLIPS

Mirrorball Books

Praise for *Can't Live Without*

"If you're looking for something with more substance than chick lit, something thoughtful, funny and very well written, try CAN'T LIVE WITHOUT." *Linda Gillard, author of House of Silence.*

"I love that Phillips creates in Stella, a character in her late 30s with many flaws, but ultimately the heart of an angel, someone all readers will rally around ... CAN'T LIVE WITHOUT is all about finding out what really matters in life." *Cindy Roesel, Chick Lit Central*

"Joanne Phillips has an incredibly wonderful easy to read writing style. I absolutely did not want the book to end. I'm sure that Joanne Phillips will be giving some of the big names in the chick lit world a run for their money." *Kim the Bookworm*

For Louisa-May Phillips

Chapter 1

'Get it out of me. Get. It. Out.'

My daughter is only sixteen, but today is possibly the best and the worst day of her life. Even though she's still my baby – will always be my baby – right now she's trying to squeeze out her own baby into the waiting arms of a red-faced midwife. While discovering the hard way that some young bodies just aren't designed for childbirth.

Her gasps of pain bring back the memory of her own birth with a force I hadn't expected, and I almost find myself reaching for the gas and air in sympathy. They say you eventually forget the torture of giving birth – why else would any woman go on to have more than one child? We're brave, not masochists. Well, I only had one, and I can tell you right now: a woman never forgets.

They also say nothing is more painful than giving birth. Wrong again. Watching your own child in labour is far more painful. Right now I wish it were me lying there on the bed and not her.

What is it they also say? Be careful what you wish for?

Sometimes I wish *they* would just shut up.

I'm standing away from the business end, holding my daughter's hand and mopping ineffectually at her forehead while she screams and swears at the midwife. My feelings aren't important right now, are they? This is about her, and that little life fighting its way down her underdeveloped tubes, every beat of its heart monitored carefully, every movement another stab of agony for my girl.

I push away the tiny, ashamed-to-show-its-face part of me that is also thinking: See? You didn't listen, did you, when I told you how awful it would be? You weren't careful, you didn't take precautions, and now look at us. A slip of a girl, high on Pethidine, showing off an astonishingly varied vocabulary, attended by her own single mum who still hasn't gotten used to the fact that any minute now she will become a grandmother.

A grandmother! At thirty-eight. There is so much wrong with this picture I don't know where to start.

Here comes Robert with fresh supplies of ice and chocolate, his face showing the strain of watching Lipsy suffer. Robert is one of those people who seem to be all one colour: his fine hair is the same pale biscuit shade as his skin; even his clothes are beige. He looks young for thirty-one, but his hairline tells of problems to come.

That my daughter chose to fall in love with a man nearly twice her age tops off the craziness just perfectly, in my opinion.

'Stella?' says Robert, handing me the ice wrapped in a flannel. He's only just stopped calling me Mrs Hill, despite the fact that I've never been a Mrs in my life. This is about to change in two weeks' time, of course, but I won't be Mrs Hill.

I take the flannel and apply it to the back of Lipsy's neck. She's on all fours now, panting like a marathon runner, her white T-shirt stuck to her back. Her long dark hair is matted at the crown like a fallen-out beehive, her lips vivid against her fair skin.

I know why I'm angry, why I'm blaming Lipsy and dragging up all the stuff I thought I'd buried months ago. It's because I'm scared. No, terrified.

If I allow my mind to process what's happening in front of my eyes – if I let the fear in for a second – I'll be no use to my daughter at all. So I huff when she asks me for a glass of water, and I tut when Robert tenderly places a square of Bourneville in her swollen mouth.

'I need the toilet,' Lipsy croaks, her voice hoarse from shouting.

'Oh, for God's sake,' is my response. It's how I'm dealing with it. Don't shoot me.

We shuffle her off the bed and move as one towards the toilet cubicle in the corner of the room – all of us, including Robert and the midwife, who has to drag the heart rate monitor and the drip stand across the floor. Somehow we manoeuvre this circus into the cubicle without anyone tripping up or pulling the line out of Lipsy's arm.

'Piss off then,' my daughter says. We stare at her, mouths open.

'I'm not doing a poo with you lot all watching me,' she tells us defiantly. 'Aren't I allowed any privacy?'

It's right then, in that precise moment, that all the love I've ever felt for my little girl, and possibly all the love I ever will feel, hits me with the force of ten hurricanes. She is a separate individual. She's about to become a mother. She's not my baby anymore – she hasn't been my baby for some time, in fact.

And I'm bizarrely proud of her for telling the woman who's been looking up her nether region for the last four hours to give her some privacy. It's ridiculous, it's completely pointless, and it's very, very Lipsy.

Robert is allowed to stay after some hissed negotiations – 'You might fall over,' he points out, 'and you can't actually sit down or stand up again without help' – so the midwife and I shuffle backwards out of the toilet and take up our former positions.

'She's a feisty one,' she says. I notice her silver name

badge reads *Maggie*. I smile to myself: Maggie is my mother's name. I take this as a good omen.

'Yes, she is. I think she takes after me.'

Maggie rolls her eyes. 'It's a shame she hasn't inherited your child-bearing hips though, eh?'

Suddenly I don't like this midwife very much at all.

*

Lipsy's baby is born in the toilet. Well, of course it is – nothing ever turns out the way it should in this family. Bearing down with all her strength, thinking herself mightily constipated, Lipsy finally managed what the midwife had been trying to achieve for hours. Thankfully Robert realised what was going on pretty quickly, and Maggie managed to dive in and ... well, I'll leave it there, shall I? There is such a thing as too much information. The first I heard about it was when Robert shouted, 'It's a boy', and ran out of the cubicle to hug me, before promptly collapsing at my feet.

'Hi, Mum.' Lipsy smiles at me weakly as I peer around the cubicle door. She's propped up against the far wall, surrounded by blankets.

'It's a boy,' she says, gazing down at the bundle in her arms, mesmerised. All I can see is one tiny pink fist, clenched as if in triumph. When Lipsy looks up at me again she is crying, the tears mingling with the sweat on her cheeks. Her face is swollen from all the fluids they've pumped into her and her skin is blotchy with broken veins. There's nothing beautiful about childbirth, that's for sure. But the sight of her hopeful expression breaks through my defences and I sink down by her side.

'I thought it was going to be a girl,' she says. 'I was going to call her Estelle.'

'Really?' Estelle is my name, although I've always preferred Stella. I tear my eyes from Lipsy's face to look for the first time at my not-to-be namesake.

And instantly I'm being dragged back through time – same hospital, same maternity ward, different midwife and very different circumstances, but this baby is surely the identical twin of the one I gave birth to nearly seventeen years ago. Same big blue eyes, same spiky, matted black hair, same rosebud mouth with a slightly larger top lip. And the exact same soppy expression on my face, no doubt. Love and wonder, and complete devotion.

I hadn't expected this either. I hadn't expected to fall in love with Lipsy's baby the way mothers fall in love with their own. Maybe it's my hormones. Maybe it's the uncanny resemblance. But whatever it is, I just lost my heart to my grandchild. Despite everything I've said, I just know I'll be a very proud lady the first time someone calls me Grandma.

'So what do you think, Grandma?' asks Lipsy.

Or maybe not.

OK, I'm not loving the Grandma label. But I guess I'll just have to get used to it.

'He's absolutely beautiful,' I tell her sincerely. 'And so are you,' I add, not quite so sincerely as she looks a complete fright, but the poor child doesn't need to know that right now.

Lipsy hasn't always been so bothered about her appearance – no more than any normal teenage girl, anyway. But oh boy, once she started to grow a bump she became obsessed with her looks. I've tried telling her she'll get her figure back in no time, and that everyone's skin tone changes when they're pregnant, and that looks don't matter anyway – Robert loves her just the way she is – but generally she just glares at me like I'm offering up a future of unthinkable torture, then returns to her beauty magazines.

There'll be no beauty magazines now, I think, as I

haul up off the floor to help the midwife move mother and baby back to the relative comfort of the hospital bed. It'll be all parenting magazines and mumsnet and NCT groups. Unfortunately, I won't be there to suffer it along with her. In two weeks' time I'm changing my name to Mrs Paul Smart and moving to deepest darkest Derbyshire with the love of my life.

Which is really quite the worst timing I can think of. But, as Paul keeps reminding me, it's only a three hour round trip, not the other side of the world.

Anyway, I've got other problems to dwell on right now. While Lipsy and Robert pose for the photo the midwife insists on taking (Lipsy will make me burn that later, I just know it), I finger the slim box in my pocket. Soon I'll head off to do my designated duty and let the rest of the family know that all is well. Paul will be waiting by the phone, and my mum and dad are probably on their way here right now, unable to bear it any longer. And once I've worked my way down the list, then it will be time. I wanted to wait. Finding out beforehand didn't seem right, somehow.

'Mum,' calls Lipsy, 'come over here. We want to introduce you properly.'

I join them by the bed, where Robert is leaning over my daughter and looking very proud of himself. Not that he actually did anything ... Well, maybe that's a bit unfair. But only a bit.

'Have you thought of a name already?' I ask, smiling. They've got dippy looks on their faces, the pair of them, and Lipsy looks fit to burst with excitement. The midwife is still in the toilet, hopefully clearing up the devastation.

'Yes,' Lipsy says with a grin. 'And you'll love it.'

'Well?' I look from Lipsy to Robert and back again. 'Tell me.'

'Mum, we'd like you to officially meet ... Phoenix.'

For about ten seconds I cannot speak. It's a long time – count it. Here in the maternity suite, surrounded by bleeping instruments and bloody sheets, ten seconds feels like a lifetime. And then I hear a cough and a suppressed chortle coming from the toilet.

That woman has a nerve. First she insults my hips, then she laughs at my grandson's name. Outrageous.

'Phoenix! How wonderful!' I exclaim, plastering a smile on my face and making my voice joyous. As I'm very, very tired I probably only manage happy, but that's enough for Lipsy.

'You like it? Oh, I'm so relieved. I thought you'd hate it. You know how you've always said symbolic names are really naff. But we thought it was cool because he was conceived on the night of the fire – and the whole phoenix rising from the ashes thing?' She smiles up at Robert, and then at me. 'Thanks, Mum. And thanks for being here for this. You were a star.'

Murmuring that it was nothing, really, I look down at baby Phoenix. Oh, the poor child. Yes, I have often said that symbolic names are naff. Because – they are! Rising from the ashes? Is the girl insane? A house fire caused by a faulty washing machine – a disaster compounded by zero house insurance – is hardly an event you'd want to mark by naming your child after it. Or maybe that's just me.

Phoenix turns his head slightly and appears to look directly into my eyes. I say appears to because it's a well-known fact that babies can't focus on anything so soon. Or maybe the scientists have got it wrong. Because as baby Phoenix looks up at me, I'm absolutely certain I see him roll his eyes just a little. Oh great, he seems to say. And this pair are my parents? That's just wonderful.

*

It's nearly time for us to leave the maternity suite and head up to the ward. Visiting hours are relaxed for new fathers but not for new grandmothers, and I want to see Lipsy settled before I go home. But first, there is something important I must do. It's a task I've been putting off for weeks, but it can't wait any longer.

I stroll nonchalantly over to the toilet cubicle, now mercifully spotless thanks to the hospital's crack cleaning detail, and carefully lock the door. Then I take the slim box out of my pocket, pull out the white pen-shaped stick, and do the necessary. I don't need to read the instructions, I've already committed them to memory. Blue line means no baby, blue cross means shit hitting fan at one hundred miles an hour. And so I wait, perched on the loo like a teenager waiting to have her future mapped out. The way my own teenager must have waited all those months ago.

If it comes to it, I just hope she's as understanding of my news as I was of hers.

As I watch, every cell in my body wishing for a blue line, the little window very clearly – and you could say proudly – starts to show a clearly defined, bright blue cross.

There is a loud cry from outside the cubicle – baby Phoenix trying out his new and perfectly formed lungs. And inside there is a helpless whimper. That's me. Today – the day I've become a grandmother for the first time and an expectant mum for the second time – is possibly the best and the worst day of my life.

Chapter 2

I really can't take it in. It shouldn't have come as a surprise, I guess. Haven't I been noticing the signs for weeks now? Sore boobs, that extraordinary tiredness like someone's sucked all the strength out of your bones, and of course the missed period. Or maybe two missed periods – they haven't been regular for a while now so it's hard to tell. Which was, I had tried to convince myself, the first sign of the menopause. Wishful thinking, I'm afraid. Surely accidentally getting pregnant at thirty-eight is worse than being menopausal?

I tuck the little white stick into my pocket, bury the empty box deep in the waste bin, and finally emerge from the cubicle, unnoticed by Lipsy and Robert who are deep in thrall to baby Phoenix. As I turn to close the door behind me, I wonder if ever a toilet has seen so much drama in one day.

'You've got a few sleepless nights ahead of you,' the midwife says, parking a wheelchair inches from my feet. For a moment I'm confused. Is the wheelchair for me? I might be pregnant but I'm not ill. And how can she tell about the baby just by looking at me? Is this some kind of secret midwife skill?

But then I realise she's talking about Lipsy, about Lipsy and Robert and the baby and me all living together under one roof, and that the wheelchair is for my daughter, not me. Well, duh! I'm not thinking straight, is all. It's my hormones.

'I think Paul's here,' Lipsy says, noticing me hovering in the corner. 'Aren't you going to go out and say hello?'

Oh, hell on a stick. Paul. Less than an hour ago I phoned and asked him to come to the hospital. Now I'm wishing I hadn't been so hasty.

Since Paul and I got together last year – after almost two decades of pretending we didn't have feelings for each other – things have been just peachy. He's a wonderful boyfriend, soon to be a wonderful husband. Caring, thoughtful, funny – and damned sexy too. But the one thing we have never discussed is having children. I guess we just assumed at our age there wasn't much point.

How on earth will he react when I tell him I'm pregnant?

Seems like I won't be long finding out – the hordes are about to descend upon us. I can already hear voices outside, and now Maggie is helping Lipsy into the wheelchair and Robert is placing Phoenix into her arms, and any second now we're going to burst out of that door and face the world. Would it be completely crazy for me to look around for somewhere to hide? I'm not ready. I can't see them yet. What if they can tell? My mum – surely she'll know just by looking at me, even if the midwife doesn't? Granted I'm not showing yet, but don't mothers have a sixth sense for this kind of thing?

Then I think back to how gobsmacked I was when Lipsy dropped her own baby-bombshell last year and I realise this is nonsense. No one will know unless I tell them. And right now is definitely not the time. Not with Lipsy all glowing and proud, and the family overjoyed and rallying together properly for the first time in ages. This is not the time for me to drive a tank through the middle of them and say, 'Hey, forget about all that – now it's all about me again.'

And there's the wedding to think about ...

'Mum? Hello? Earth calling.'

Lipsy and Robert are waiting by the door, Lipsy's free hand outstretched. I walk over and grip it tightly. She smiles up at me, my little girl, the purpose of my life for the past sixteen years.

Never mind Paul, how is Lipsy going to react when I tell her?

There will be no easy solution to this problem. The fire last year, and the rebuilding of my house and my fractured family – not to mention the problems Paul and I had getting together – all this will fade into insignificance compared to the fallout from the news that I'm going to be a mum all over again. Lipsy might never forgive me. My life will never be the same again, and neither will Paul's. My parents will think I'm crazy, not to mention irresponsible.

But as I catch a glimpse of baby Phoenix's dark blue eyes, wide and amazed at this big new world, a strange calmness washes over me. Maybe I can make this work. Maybe the fallout won't be so bad. A new baby is not a calamity, after all. It's a cause for celebration.

Placing a protective hand on my flattish tummy, I fix a smile on my face and follow Lipsy out to meet the rest of the family. No matter what happens, I'm going to love this baby. This is my second chance. My chance to do it right.

*

When we emerge from the maternity suite, it's like I've spent days in there, not hours. I grip hold of Lipsy's hand, blinking against the bright sunlight that slants in through the high windows. The midwife trills her fingers goodbye and pads away along the corridor in her red Crocs, her behind wide and swaying. (And she had the nerve to talk about my child-bearing hips!) Hard to believe I've just spent ten hours in her company, and off she trots without a word.

Mind you, I'll probably be seeing her again in about seven months' time.

My mum is the first to rush forward, with Dad not far behind. No sign of Lipsy's dad, but that's no surprise. John Dean popped back into her life briefly last year, after leaving me high and dry when she was just a tiny baby herself. He stuck around only long enough to cause trouble for Paul and me, and to build up Lipsy's hopes that she might finally have a father in her life. But when his plan to get back together with me fell on deaf ears, John Dean crawled back into the loser-shaped hole he came out of and we haven't heard from him since. Good riddance.

And then I see Paul. He hangs back until Lipsy is surrounded, then walks slowly forward and takes my hand. Holds it to his cheek. Kisses it, and then kisses me on the lips, very gently.

Paul is effortlessly good-looking: the kind of guy who doesn't know the effect he has on women. Wavy blonde hair that curls around his ears when he forgets to get a haircut, a well-built frame just on the hunky side of sporty, and a mobile, kissable mouth.

'Are you OK?' he asks, so softly it feels as though I'm hearing the words inside my head. I nod, but suddenly find I can't speak. He pulls me close and holds me. I'm enclosed safely in his arms, my face pressed to his chest, inhaling his scent which is spicy and clean, and there is nowhere on earth right now I'd rather be.

Until I remember.

I leave my head where it is for a moment and rehearse what I'm going to say. What I'll do is whisper it to him now, then ask him to keep it to himself for a few days. Maybe even until after the wedding. At the very least until I'm ready to tell the rest of the family. By this I mean Lipsy.

Paul, I'm pregnant. No, that's too direct.

Paul, darling, in about seven months we are going to have a wonderful surprise – a beautiful, darling little baby. No, no, no! That's too *Sound of Music*.

Maybe I should go for a jokey tone: Hey, Paul, I've got a present for you. It's in my tummy. No, I haven't eaten it! It's a baby!

This isn't going to work, is it? I need more time, need to think this through. How best to tell the love of your life that a wonderful thing has happened, but as you've never even discussed babies – and you're just about to get married and move in together without having discussed babies – you have no idea how they are going to react?

'Stella?'

I move back and look into his eyes. In the light from the high windows they are impossibly blue. The sunlight picks out the faint lines around his eyes, and highlights dust motes hovering in the air. When I was a child I used to call it fairy dust. It had magical properties, and there was a lot of it in my childhood home; my mother derived great pleasure from beating cushions.

I could do with a sprinkling of magic right now.

But hang on – this is Paul. The man I've loved since I was in high school, my best friend, the nicest, kindest, most sensible man I've ever met. Surely he'll be overjoyed at the news, if a little surprised at first.

I take a deep breath. 'Paul,' I begin, 'there's something I need to tell–'

'Mum? Are you coming?'

Lipsy, finally freed from the ferocious hugging, is waving for me to follow them up to the ward. I shrug helplessly at Paul and hotfoot it down the corridor behind my daughter.

I never said I wasn't a coward.

'I'll catch up with you later,' I call over my shoulder, but to my surprise Paul is right there behind me.

'I'll walk up with you,' he says. 'There's something we need to talk about.'

We're practically jogging now, side by side, behind Robert and Lipsy and Mum and Dad. I try to tell my dad to slow down – why he's almost running up the corridor I do not know – but I'm too out of breath to make myself heard. Paul's wittering on about Hannah and her birthday next week, and I'm envious as usual of how fit he is. He can jog and talk at the same time. For me, that's multitasking taken too far.

Our convoy turns a corner at ten miles an hour, and I hold up my hand to Paul and lean against the wall, trying to catch my breath.

'She'll follow you up,' Paul calls after them and I nod gratefully.

'You really should get more exercise, Stella.'

He means well, but I do want to give him a slap all the same. He knows how I feel about the E word, and besides, I'm completely exhausted after being up all night. I can't remember when I last ate anything, and I am, in fact, pregnant ...

I say nothing. He starts talking again, and this time I manage to listen.

'So Hannah said she'd really like to go away for her birthday. Serves me right for asking, I suppose, but I've managed to book a caravan in Wales – remember that outdoor pursuits place I told you about? Of course, she's even more excited about the trip now there's the possibility of us all going. I know it's a whole week, longer than we'd planned, but I do think it will be easier with two adults keeping her occupied. What do I know about nine-year-old girls, after all? Anyway, what do you think?'

I think it sounds like Paul's daughter is wrapping him around her little finger as usual, but this I keep to myself.

I put on a fake frown of disappointment. 'Paul, you know it's not great timing for me. Lipsy needs me at home – she's only got me for another fortnight as it is, and I really want to get her and the baby settled before the wedding. I can't just go away and leave her to it, can I?'

And I'm thinking that a week in a caravan with Paul and his nearly nine-year-old daughter is not exactly my idea of February fun, whatever the situation.

Then I see his face and wonder what I've said wrong.

'Stella ... you haven't been listening, have you? It's my fault, I shouldn't be telling you all this today, you're bound to be preoccupied.' He bashes his head with the palm of his hand and smiles contritely. 'I'm really sorry. The thing is, I wasn't talking about *you* coming with us. What I was trying to tell you was, Sharon's health farm thing has been cancelled at the last minute and Hannah sort of asked if her mum could come along with us, and I didn't know what to say. But I knew you'd be cool with it because you know it's no big deal, right?'

It's a good few seconds before I can speak. Hannah was supposed to be staying with Paul for a few days over half-term while her mum was away. Now they're going to Wales for a week, and ...

'You're taking Sharon on holiday with you? In a caravan?'

Why the fact that it's in a caravan makes it worse, I have no idea. But it does.

Paul has the grace to look sheepish. 'It's a pretty big caravan,' he tells me, as if this makes it any better. 'There are separate bedrooms. Sharon and Hannah can share.'

Oh, well. Silly me. That's all fine then.

'I couldn't say no, Stella. This means the world to

Hannah. It was all she wanted to do for her birthday, you know how sporty she is. And with us moving away and all … You do understand, don't you?'

Well, of course I understand. He only found out he even had a daughter six months ago; of course he wants to spoil her and take her away on holiday, and probably go fishing and kayaking and mountain biking – all the things I most definitely wouldn't want to do. And all the things I imagine Sharon will jump at.

But taking your ex on holiday? Isn't that a bit inappropriate – particularly the week before your wedding?

When I say this, his face crumples, and I know he doesn't have any answers that will make me feel OK about it. He won't deny Hannah this. And I shouldn't ask him to.

Still, it hurts. Paul knows I've always felt insecure about pocket-sized Sharon, with her zest for life and her yoga and Pilates – the woman practically has a sign around her neck that reads: *Paul's ideal partner*.

'You're the only woman I want to be with, Stella,' he tells me whenever I share my fears.

It doesn't make me like Sharon any better.

'Come on,' he says now, nudging me in the ribs. 'Don't be a grump about it. What's a week in a freezing cold caravan when we've got our whole lives together to look forward to?'

'As long as it's not so cold you're cuddling up to keep warm,' I grumble.

'You could come too, if you wanted,' he says with a grin. 'There's plenty of room.'

'Ha! Right. Like that's not my idea of hell.'

'Exactly. And you'll be so busy with Lipsy and the baby you won't be thinking about me at all, will you?' He puts his face to my hair and inhales. 'Whereas I'll be thinking about you every second.'

'You'd better be, Smart-boy.' I give him my best stern look and then relent and allow him to kiss me. His lips are warm and insistent; I could never get tired of being kissed this way if I lived to be a hundred.

A passing orderly hisses, 'Get a room,' and with a wry smile, Paul allows me to come up for air.

'Don't get so caught up in baby stuff that you forget to finish packing,' he says as I extricate myself from his arms. 'Two weeks tomorrow and it will be just me and you.'

Hmm. Not quite. My hand falls automatically to my stomach. But this whole Sharon thing has discombobulated me: I can't seem to get my head back into the right place for new baby news. There's this crushing sensation in my chest that I don't recognise. I guess I'm just really tired.

Paul watches a man wheel himself down the corridor and looks off, his expression faraway. 'Me and you going on our new adventure,' he says, and I smile to myself and reach for his hand.

One of the things I love about Paul is the way he takes the whole "what's mine is yours" thing so literally. The new adventure in Derby isn't really ours – it's his. The recession hit Smart Homes badly; many estate agents, especially small independent ones, have been struggling to survive. And in Milton Keynes, with the glut of cheap new houses being sold off by the bigger agencies, Smart Homes didn't stand a chance. By Christmas, Paul was already operating on a skeleton staff of one – himself – and searching for new ways to make money. When the offer came to head up a new rental agency in Derby, Paul considered it a lifeline. Smart Homes was his baby, the business he'd built from scratch. I knew the day he closed the door to the office for the last time would be devastating for him. How could I refuse?

This was just after he proposed, by the way, which made it even harder to for me to say no.

'It'll be a fresh start for us, Stella,' were his exact words, and the relief on his face told me more about the stress he'd been under than I necessarily wanted to know.

One phone call from an old college friend and Paul had it all worked out.

'We can rent to start with, but I'll sell my flat here as soon as the market picks up and we can buy something ourselves. Together. A little terraced house, perhaps. Something you can renovate, a little project for you. What do you think?'

He had me there. Last year I had big plans to get into property developing – my plans came to nothing, which is a whole other story, but now Paul was offering us both the chance to start again.

But once he'd demonstrated that driving from Derbyshire back to Milton Keynes only takes an hour and a half, and promised that we would make this journey each and every weekend, I jumped on board with as much enthusiasm as if the idea had been mine all along.

'We are still coming back here at weekends, aren't we?' I ask him now, thinking of Phoenix and that little rosebud mouth. Thinking of the new baby, and how I'll need my family around me too. 'Even though you'll be managing the new agency, you will still get time off, right?'

He sighs and shakes his head, dragging his attention back to me. 'We've been through this a hundred times, Stella. It will be fine. Lipsy is a big girl now, and she has Robert and your mum and dad to help her out. This is our time now. Just you and me. You have to start to let go.'

Well, he's right. Of course he is. But letting go is

always easier in theory, I've found.

Like letting him go now, knowing that tomorrow night he'll be sleeping in a caravan with the mother of his child. The mother of his *other* child ...

'I love you,' he says. His expression is the one I love best: besotted and completely soppy.

'I love you too. And I'll be here all ready and waiting for you when you get back.'

And so will the baby he still knows nothing about.

'Bye, nearly-wife.'

I go up on tiptoes and kiss him one more time. 'Bye, nearly-husband.'

'And you're OK about Sharon coming with Hannah and me?' he asks again.

I bite off the 'What choice do I have?' and nod instead.

'I hope you all have a lovely time,' I say. Which is an out-and-out lie. But the moment for my news has passed; there's no way I could suddenly announce my pregnancy now. It will wait. News this big can wait a week, right?

With a kiss and a happy grin Paul walks away, confident and impenetrable, not a single cloud on his horizon. I'm watching his back – OK, I'm admiring his back, which always has the power to stir me: broad shouldered, clad in a tight-fitting T-shirt, just yummy – when I suddenly have a horrible, stomach-wrenching thought.

I remember what happened between Paul and Sharon eight years ago. The reason they split up in the first place.

I turn away from Paul's retreating form and lean against the wall. My head is spinning, and not just from hunger and tiredness.

Why didn't Paul know he had a daughter until last year? Because he broke up with her mother when she found out she was pregnant, is why.

Which does not bode well for my current situation at all.

There's no reason to think he'd do the same to me, of course. No reason at all.

Chapter 3

'He's so beautiful. He's the most beautiful baby I've ever seen. Apart from you, I mean.'

I'm holding baby Phoenix in my arms while Lipsy snacks on toast and marmalade. She looks tired, but also radiant, the way only new mothers can. In about seven months' time it will be me sitting there looking tired but radiant.

Or maybe just tired, me being so much older and all.

I push the thought away and focus back on my daughter. I won't think about the next new mum-to-be. Now is not the time.

'I missed you last night,' I tell Lipsy. It's true – the house seemed empty without her. Robert came in looking like a ghost after visiting hours ended and crept straight up to bed. I should have basked in the solitude, but all I could do was fret. When I arrived back at the hospital this morning I expected to find Lipsy exhausted and in tears with the stress of it all. I underestimated her. She's taking it all in her stride.

'Yeah, right,' she says, reaching for a plastic cup of orange juice. 'I bet you were living it up, making the most of your last night of freedom before the house gets overtaken by baby things.'

I laugh at this. 'Last time I looked, the house was already taken over by baby things. I can barely move for soft toys and changing mats and boxes of clothes.'

'Speaking of boxes, how is your packing coming on?'

'Fine.' I look at Phoenix's face, watch his breath go in

and out, the little tremble of his lips. 'Lipsy, are you sure you don't mind me moving so far away?'

The words are hardly out of my mouth before she sighs and rolls her eyes. 'Mum! I'll be fine. I'm not a little girl anymore, you know.'

'I had noticed.'

She looks at Phoenix and then smiles at me. 'Right. Still, I'm glad he came on his due date. I wouldn't have wanted to go through that on my own.'

It's not lost on me that she seems to consider Robert's presence insignificant, but I let it go for now. I also don't bother to remind her that while Phoenix might indeed have arrived on his due date, everyone – doctors included – expected him to be at least a month premature due to her tender age. I thought I'd have a good six weeks with her and the baby before I had to move out.

But there is no way I would have missed it, wedding or no wedding.

'I would never have let you go through that on your own, Lipsy,' I tell her. 'Even if Phoenix had arrived late, I'd have stayed behind until you were ready for me to leave. Paul can move up on his own if necessary, you know that. If you want me to be around longer, all you have to do is ask.'

'Mum, I'll be fine. You and Paul are moving eighty miles up the motorway. It's not like you're going to the other side of the world, is it?'

Lipsy might be more perceptive than I've ever given her credit for, because when I fall silent at this, she says, 'You really miss Bonnie, don't you?'

I nod.

'And Los Angeles really is the other side of the world,' she adds with a rueful smile. 'Is there no way at all she can come back for the wedding?'

'Apparently not. Flights are expensive, and they're

saving up for their own wedding. Anyway, it's no big deal. I'll see her at Christmas. It'll just make it even more special.'

But now I'm wondering if I'll be able to fly out for Bonnie's wedding. According to my calculations, I'll have a three-month-old baby in tow by then. Not the best circumstances for transatlantic travel. When my best friend announced her move to America with high-flying Marcus, I took it in my stride, too loved-up with Paul to feel the full impact of being Bonnie-less.

I'm feeling it now.

'But Christmas is, like, ten months away, Mum. Aren't they coming back over the summer? What about Cory?'

Cory is Bonnie's stepson-to-be. Although younger than Hannah, he's used to his dad's international job expeditions.

At least Bonnie doesn't have to worry about Marcus dragging Cory's mum out to the States with them. She's more the hands-off type. Unlike Sharon.

'Bonnie said that Cory's flying out for the summer holidays. She also said Marcus only gets two weeks holiday a year. How crazy is that?'

'Vacation,' Lipsy corrects. 'They call it vacation out there.'

I just roll my eyes at this.

'Couldn't she come over on her own?' she asks.

'Money,' I repeat. 'Lack of. But don't worry about it, Lipsy. I'll be fine. You're still up for being my chief bridesmaid, right?'

She grimaces, and I give her a little kick. 'There's nothing wrong with that bridesmaid dress and you know it.'

'If I fit into it,' she says, prodding her stomach, which is practically shrinking before our eyes. Oh, to be so young and elastic. When my time comes I'll probably have a jelly belly for a decade.

Lipsy crams the last bit of toast into her mouth then holds out her arms. Reluctantly, I hand Phoenix back, smoothing a strand of wispy black hair off his forehead as I do. The hospital bed is high and wide, but visitors aren't allowed to sit on it. Instead I'm perched in a red plastic tub chair that is only just wide enough for my bum.

'Is Phoenix going to be OK sleeping in with us, do you think?' she says as she settles him for a feed. I'm both fascinated and a bit weirded-out, watching my daughter breastfeed. It's amazing to see my little girl being so grown up – feeding a baby with her own body! – but it also seems like a very private thing, intimate, like when I come across her and Robert sitting on the sofa, gazing into each other's faces as if they contain the secrets of the universe.

Some things aren't for a mother's eyes.

'He'll be fine,' I reassure her for the hundredth time. 'Besides, it's only for a fortnight. Then you can have your dream nursery, can't you?'

Phoenix's nursery-to-be is actually my bedroom. Once I'm gone, Lipsy and Robert plan to redecorate and install a proper cot bed with matching furniture from John Lewis. Actually, the cot bed is already in there, and the furniture is flat-packed and stacked against the wall next to my wardrobe. There are piles of boxes under the window and heaps of plastic bags shoved under my bed – it's wishful thinking that Lipsy is going to miss me. She clearly can't wait for me to vacate the premises.

Until then, Phoenix will sleep in his bassinet in the room Lipsy and Robert share.

'Have you had the windows open, you know, to air it?' she says.

'You're sounding like an old woman,' I tell her, laughing. 'Next you'll be telling me not to go out with my hair wet in case I catch a cold.'

She raises her eyebrows. 'You mean I sound like you, then.'

Touché.

My daughter and I get on so much better now; the imminent arrival of a baby certainly helped us bond again after I let her down so badly last year. The fire, while not directly my fault, was made a hundred times worse by my failure to keep up with the house insurance. But we managed. Together. Once she forgave me – and once she got fed up living with her grandma, which didn't take too long. Much as I love my mother, she does have a way of driving a person crazy. I'd rather live in a burnt-out shell than under my mother's roof for more than a week, which is exactly what I did do. You could never say I don't put my money where my mouth is.

Speaking of money ...

'Has Robert asked about a pay rise yet?' I say. Lipsy pulls a face.

'No. He says it's awkward, doesn't want to rock the boat.'

'But with the new baby and all ... Surely it's OK for him to just ask?'

'I don't really want to talk about it, Mum. Do you mind if we just leave it for now?'

I do mind, but I tell her it's fine. That's a mum's job, isn't it? To pretend things are fine even when they're not? But one thing I learned after the fallout from the fire fiasco was that it's essential to talk about the important things. And Robert and Lipsy's financial situation definitely comes under that classification.

But then I guess my baby does too. And I'm certainly not talking to Lipsy about that right now. So maybe I haven't learned anything at all.

Instead we chat about the coming weeks, planning a routine for her and the baby, with Lipsy listening intently to my stories of how I coped when she was born. In the bed across from Lipsy is a woman with twins. A nurse walks past and says, 'How are we this morning?' and the twin's mum says, 'If one more person says "double trouble" to me I'm going to kill them.'

Lipsy smiles at me and lays Phoenix down on the bed to change him.

'Should I hold his legs like this?' she asks. 'They feel so fragile. I'm scared I'll hurt him.'

This is so nice. My daughter is treating me like I'm a fount of knowledge, a person with important opinions. Long may it last.

'Mum?' she says after a while, interrupting a very funny story of how toddler Lipsy peed all over a grumpy man during potty training. Well, funny for me at least.

'Yes?'

'Could you pop down to the hospital shop? Get me something to eat?'

'Didn't you just this minute have breakfast?'

'I'm replacing all the calories I expended giving birth,' she counters huffily.

'I'll pick you up a new sense of humour while I'm down there, shall I?'

A nappy narrowly misses my head. But it's a clean one, so I figure she's not too cross.

I jump out of the chair and grab my purse, only to be struck by a wave of nausea that makes me feel as though I've just stepped onto a ship in a storm. I grab hold of the nearest sturdy object, which happens to be Phoenix's plastic crib. The nausea passes quickly, but it leaves my skin feeling both clammy and cold, like the aftermath of a fever.

'Mum? Are you OK?' Lipsy's voice is pitched high with concern. She makes to get off the bed, holding Phoenix tightly. I wave her back.

'I'm fine,' I lie. 'Must be the Chinese I had last night. I

think I'll pop to the loo on the way, just in case.'

'No rush,' she calls after me. 'See you in a bit.'

Outside the ward I stop and lean against the pale green wall of the corridor. A man with shoulder-length hair is pacing up and down, talking on his phone.

'When will you get here?' he says, and then, on his second pass, 'But when will you *get* here?' He glares at me and I look away embarrassed.

I scan for the nearest toilet and push myself off the wall. Another wave of sickness hits me and I quicken my pace. I picture Paul en route to South Wales, Sharon by his side and Hannah in the back, singing travel songs and playing I Spy.

And here I am, alone and about to vomit into a hospital toilet.

OK, Stella. Deep breaths. Nothing to get worked up about. It's just a bit of morning sickness, that's all. You've been here before – albeit nearly seventeen years ago. You know the drill.

Morning sickness? Starting sooner than I'd expected. Just how pregnant am I, anyway?

How long do I have before I need to sit my daughter down and tell her that her new baby is going to have a playmate soon – a stepbrother or sister younger than her mother's own grandson?

Thinking about it makes my head ache, and my stomach lurches again. Dropping all pretence of nonchalance, I grit my teeth and race for the loo.

I make it just in time.

Chapter 4

'Just remind me why *I'm* doing this?'

I'm standing in the middle of my kitchen, which has been transformed into the definition of chaos by the arrival home of Lipsy and Phoenix. Gone is the aura of calm I managed to create when I refitted it last year. My beautiful granite worktops have disappeared under a mound of baby paraphernalia, and the carefully distressed oak table is now properly distressed owing to the activity taking place upon it. (Think three different colours of poo, like stripy toothpaste. Not pleasant.) With one hand I'm holding two tiny legs out of the way while the other hand tries to wrap up the nappy from hell. Unfortunately I don't have a third hand or I could hold my nose with that one. This baby smells!

'Could you pass me a nappy sack, at least?' I snap at Lipsy, who is sitting as far away as possible, sipping tea. The tea I made for her, right after I'd unloaded the mountain of equipment I'd been instructed to go shopping for, which was right after I'd picked her up from hospital. I don't mind – really, I don't – it's just that I'd quite like to sit down myself at some point today.

'Hello? I'm in a bit of a pickle here.'

Lipsy leans forward, pulls a nappy sack from the bag and drops it next to Phoenix, never once making eye contact with me.

'Well, gee, thanks. You be careful now, Lipsy. We don't want you overdoing things.'

Oh, I'm a crabby one today, aren't I? It's not Lipsy's fault. Note to self: don't take your problems out on your daughter. I can see she's knackered, and I can remember only too clearly how it feels to come home to your parents' house with a new baby. Except when it happened to me I was alone. I didn't have a loving, caring, hands-on man like Robert to help me. Lipsy's dad had hotfooted it to God-knows-where by the time Lipsy was born.

Good riddance, of course. Except I didn't think that at the time.

Also, technically this isn't her parent's house anymore. As Lipsy and Robert reminded me this morning, in exactly eleven days this will be their house. Their chance to find out how hard it is to manage on one salary and run a household and look after a baby without the bank of mum at the ready.

I keep this to myself too.

I finally manage to get the offending article into the oddly sweet-smelling plastic bag, and then I grab a fresh nappy from the pile on the table and quickly fold it around Phoenix's bum. While I'm doing up the poppers on his cute little Babygro I think, Hey, I'm quite good at this.

And it is really good practice.

'I'm going to bed,' Lipsy announces, yawning, and I move from feeling sorry for her to feeling outraged all over again.

'What about Phoenix? Won't he need a feed soon?'

'That's what all this is for.' Lipsy gestures to the heap of plastic bottles and boxes of formula littering the worktop.

'But I thought you were breastfeeding,' I say, feeling my cheeks grow hot. Saying the word breast to my daughter feels acutely embarrassing for some unfathomable reason.

'Well, I was. But I'm not anymore.'

'What? That's a bit sudden, isn't it?'

'What do you care? You didn't breastfeed me, did you? So why are you so bothered about it?'

'I'm not bothered about it. What are you getting all worked up for?' I take a deep breath. This is how arguments used to kick off in the bad old days, when Lipsy was still in her sulky teenager phase and hated everything I did or said.

'You've just been out to buy all this stuff, Mum. What *did* you think it was for?' she says, sounding very much like a sulky teenager.

'I thought,' I say carefully, 'that it was for Phoenix. For in a month or so's time. Or maybe as a stand-by if you, you know, if your ...'

I want to say breasts again but just can't bring myself to. Wishing this conversation was over, I point in the general direction of Lipsy's chest (which is unnaturally large at the moment, something Robert is no doubt chuffed to bits with).

'You can remember what to do, can't you?' she says, tipping back her head to eyeball me. 'Feeding and all that. You're not nervous, are you?'

It's a challenge, is what it is. I'm old, she's saying. Past it. And the only way to prove I'm not is to take charge and look after Phoenix for her. Unless I can't remember what to do, because it was so long ago.

I've always been a sucker for slights about my age. They get me every time.

'Of course I can remember,' I tell her haughtily. 'And I'm not nervous. Didn't you see me change his nappy then? Like a pro?'

We both look at Phoenix, who is lying on the changing mat waving his arms and legs happily. His nappy, I notice, is on back to front. I grab him and hold him up to my shoulder before she can notice. 'It's not so very long ago I was changing your nappies, young lady. You're not that old. Old enough to have a baby though, eh? And what was it you said to me, all those months ago? That you could cope with a baby perfectly well on your own? That you didn't need anyone to help you?'

'Fine,' Lipsy says, hauling herself out of the chair. 'I'll take Phoenix up with me. Wouldn't want to put you to any trouble.'

Now I feel terrible all over again. My emotions are up and down like a bungee jumper today. 'I'm sorry,' I say, placing my free hand on her arm. 'I'm not in a good place today. You go on up and have a rest. I'll make up some bottles and give Phoenix a feed, then I'll put him down for his nap. OK?'

She smiles weakly and nods. She must be really, really exhausted because ordinarily Lipsy would ask me what's wrong. She used to be very nosey – before she became a worn out mum like the rest of us without the time or the energy to think, let alone speak.

Now, where did *that* come from? Phoenix is only two days old and already I'm talking like it's the beginning of the end for Lipsy. It felt like that for me, but things will be different for her.

Like they'll be different for me, this time around.

I pop Phoenix in his bassinet and shuffle Lipsy up the stairs to bed, tucking her in like I used to when she was still a little girl, then I creep back down to tackle the formula problem. Truth be told, I can't remember what to do at all. There was, I think, lots of sterilising and measuring and powder going everywhere. And then there was water to boil and cool, and more measuring. Lots of mixing.

Phoenix looks up at me from his bassinet, his nose a little wrinkled. I notice the nappy sack on the table beside him and quickly sweep it into the bin. But that won't help, will it? We'll need one of those special nappy bins with the scented cartridges and the sweep-around top.

The list of equipment is never ending. But at least we'll have it all ready for when the next baby comes along.

It's when I'm tidying up I notice the calendar. I've been counting the days – literally – until the due date, and now it occurs to me I need to start counting the days until the wedding. Robert and Lipsy are doing that for me, of course, but I can't blame them for wanting their own space. But now one milestone has been reached and passed, it's time for me to focus on the rest of my life. Let go of Lipsy: put some distance between us, both physically and metaphorically.

And then I realise that today is the fourteenth of February. The most romantic day of the year, so they say, and where is the love of my life? He's living it up in a field somewhere in deepest Wales with his nine-year-old daughter and Milton Keynes' answer to Gwyneth Paltrow.

While his fiancé tries not to nurse a grudge, and wonders how to tell him that his plan for just the two of us is soon to become just the three of us.

Even I can see that doesn't have quite the same ring to it.

*

At half past seven the phone rings. I've been staring at a half-empty bottle of dry white wine for forty minutes, wishing I was ignorant of current health care regulations regarding mums-to-be. When I was pregnant with Lipsy we weren't told to avoid alcohol and pâté and rare steaks and Brie. The last three I can live without, but wine?

Funny how before I peed on that little white stick it

didn't seem to matter if I had a tipple or two, even though I knew there was a possibility. Now I have the evidence in my handbag, I just can't bring myself to pour a glass.

Paul's voice is husky, which makes me feel all funny inside. Until I realise he's probably whispering so Sharon won't hear him.

'Happy Valentine's Day,' I say mournfully.

'Oh, sweetheart. Did you get my card?'

I sigh. 'Yes. It arrived this morning. Lovely, thank you.'

'I found the one you left at the flat. Thanks, Stella.'

'That was before I knew you were taking you-know-who with you. Cracked open the champers yet?'

'Still sore about it, huh?'

I stare into the phone. You think?

'So, anyway,' Paul says, wisely changing the subject, 'How's Lipsy? And, you know, the baby?'

'Phoenix and my daughter are both fine, thank you.' I don't mean it to come out so stiffly, but he's right, I am sore about it. I should have said no. No, Paul, you can't take her with you. No, it's not OK. Fine, go off on a jolly with your daughter to salve your conscience now that you're moving eighty miles away and getting married to someone other than her mother, but taking said mother along with you? A step too far, in my opinion.

There is an uncomfortable silence on the line.

'How is Hannah?' I ask eventually.

'Fine.'

'Weather any good?'

'Not really.'

Poor Paul. Always trying to do the right thing, always getting it slightly off. I take pity and ease the tension by telling him how Lipsy and Robert have popped out for an hour to celebrate, leaving me to babysit.

'You can't let them take advantage of you, Stella. Should they be going out so soon? Phoenix is only two days old.' This is more or less what I knew he'd say, but once he's said it I bridle.

'But Lipsy's only got me for another fortnight. I *want* her to take advantage.'

'What were you moaning about, then?'

Who was moaning? This is called sharing, I explain: a bonding exercise undertaken by two individuals with the purpose of cementing the understanding between them.

And if the two individuals are a man and a woman, it usually leads to a row. I keep this thought to myself, however.

'Have you been reading Robert's parenting books again?' Paul says with laughter in his voice.

'I can't wait to see you next week,' I tell him just before we say goodbye.

'I can't wait until next Saturday,' he whispers. 'Our big day.'

'And I've got something important to tell you,' I say softly. Too softly: Paul has already said goodbye and hung up. I say it anyway, into the empty space between us.

'I'm pregnant.'

It feels good to say it out loud. Even if no one is listening.

Paul will be the first hurdle to get over. Once I've told him, we can decide together whether to tell the rest of the family before or after the wedding. Maybe during the reception. A hysterical giggle bubbles up inside me as I think about the fact that I'll be getting married while up the duff. It's not the way we planned it, but it still feels just fine to me.

It took me at least an hour to get everything ready for Phoenix's first bottle feed, so I start ahead of time before he wakes up again, and this time I make up a batch for the fridge. I was nervous he wouldn't take to formula after being breastfed for two days, but I'd worried over nothing. This is one hungry baby.

We settle on the armchair in the lounge, and I prop my elbow on a cushion. Phoenix sucks on the bottle like he's never tasted anything so good, and I close my eyes and rest my head. I think about Lipsy and Robert at the pub, and I wonder if they are managing to talk about anything other than Phoenix. I try not to think about a certain caravan on a hillside in Wales.

Time slips away. It's quiet here on a weekday evening; my neighbours keep to themselves and I expect a new baby waking through the night will be the most excitement Chaplin Grove has seen for some time. Since the fire, in fact. I watch Phoenix feeding, his eyes closed tight with pleasure, and I smile to myself. It's been a hell of a few days. But here in my arms I hold my very own grandson, and inside another little life is starting to take shape. Yes, my daughter is an unmarried teenage mum, and yes, I'm soon to become an older mum – albeit a married one – but right now, with the warmth of this baby heavy in my arms and the sound of his gentle sucking filling my ears, I am totally and supremely happy.

*

'What a beautiful sight.'

A deep voice pulls me out of a dream. I've no idea how long I've been asleep; judging by Phoenix's contented sucking, not very long at all. I smile up at my dad, who is standing on the threshold holding an enormous wicker hamper. I really hope that hamper is full of chocolate now wine is off the menu. And maybe the odd olive to count towards my five a day.

'Come in,' I tell him, waving at the sofa. 'Take the

weight off.'

He shakes his head. 'I won't, if you don't mind. I'm filthy. I've just finished my shift, but your mum wanted me to drop this off for you. Just a few things to keep you going, you know what she's like. I'll pop it in the kitchen, shall I?'

'Sure, if you can find room.'

'Jesus! What happened in here?' My dad sticks his head back around the door. 'It's like a tornado struck a branch of Mothercare.'

'Lipsy sent me shopping,' I tell him. He nods knowingly.

'Ah. That explains it. Old habits die hard, eh?'

I'm not going to rise to the bait. My family have this idea of me as someone who loves to shop, but that was before the fire, before I had to lose everything to find out what really mattered to me. Now I'm a reformed shopper – if there was a twelve-step programme for shopaholics I'd be right there in the middle of the circle talking success. I positively hate shopping these days.

Mainly because I have no spare money, and shopping's just no fun if you can't buy stuff.

Eyeing the hamper, I ask, 'Didn't Mum want to bring it over herself? I'm surprised you managed to keep her away.'

We could, in fact, do with a little help here.

'She didn't want to overwhelm you, love. Thought she'd give Lipsy some space to get settled into a routine and all that.'

Typical. When you don't want her around she's all over you like a rash; when you need her she's nowhere to be seen.

The hamper's a nice idea, though. I struggle out of the chair holding Phoenix to my shoulder and take a peek. Home-cooked lasagne, French bread and pâté, packets of ham and pitta bread and Brie – and two bottles of wine.

And no chocolate.

Fantastic.

'How's her ladyship?' my dad asks.

'She's fine. Mainly because Mary Poppins here is in charge.'

He raises an inquiring eyebrow.

'She's out with Robert,' I explain. 'It is Valentine's Day, after all. Speaking of which, shouldn't you be taking Mum out somewhere? Or are you having a romantic meal at home?'

'Don't let her wear you out, Stella. He's her baby, not yours. You've got enough on your plate with the wedding and getting ready for the move.'

I smile. It's so funny how this conversation mirrors the one I just had with Paul.

'What?' he says. I just shake my head.

'So shouldn't you be getting on home?' I prod him with a free elbow. 'Won't Mum be expecting the whole red roses thing?'

He laughs and heads for the door. 'I'm on my way.'

'Via the petrol station, right? Last minute bunch of flowers and a box of Terry's All Gold?'

'No way, Stella. I've learned my lesson. She's had her card already and I've got a special surprise for her.'

'What is it?'

He taps the side of his nose. 'Not telling. You'll have to wait until after the wedding to see.'

I'm not a big fan of secrets when they're someone else's. But then it's not like I don't have a pretty big secret of my own.

I could tell him right now. There's just the two of us, and I know my dad will be one hundred per cent supportive of me. It might be nice to have someone on the inside. Also he could help with the fallout, because I know my mum and Lipsy will go ballistic. Maybe it would be good to get him onside ahead of time.

But shouldn't Paul be the first to know? It being his baby and all.

Dad starts talking again and the moment passes. Ah, well. All in good time.

'Looking forward to your last week at work?'

'Yes and no,' I tell him. 'I'm going to miss them all so much. I keep thinking – how will they cope without me?'

He's opened the door, but now he pushes it to and turns to consider me. 'There goes Stella with her omnipotence complex.'

'What do you mean?'

He sighs. 'You always do this, Stella. You get too involved in other people's lives, in sorting out their problems. It's an old folks' home, not MI5. They'll be fine without you – life will just go on exactly the same as it did before.'

I'm stung, but I try not to show it. Instead I come out fighting. 'You didn't mind my so-called omnipotence complex when it was Mum's problems I was trying to sort out while you were inside. Then it was OK for me to feel responsible, but not now?'

No sooner are the words out of my mouth than I wish I could bite off my tongue. The last thing I want to do is hurt my dad. I'd rather stick pins under my nails.

'I'm sorry,' he says, looking contrite. He rubs his hand over his scalp as if raking through the hair he used to have. The look on his face brings tears to my eyes. I still haven't forgiven myself for deserting him when he got sent to prison – wrongly, I might add – for tax evasion three years ago. We made up when the whole debacle got sorted out (long story) but I feel so protective of him I can't bear to see him upset.

'No, I'm sorry,' I say, giving him a one-handed hug. 'I'm just feeling tetchy, is all. No need to take it out on you.'

'Because Paul's away on Valentine's Day?'

I nod. It's as good a reason as any.

'And you're right about work. They will be fine without me. Besides, I can't wait to see the back of Velma. She has to be the worst boss I've ever had.'

'Be nice to have a bit of time off, hey?'

I nod again, but another lump forms in my throat. Dad and I had planned to go into business together, using his building skills to renovate houses and rent them out. But our plans came to nothing. He was a changed man when he came out of prison, risk-averse, with no desire to go self-employed again. Plus I figured the recession wasn't the best time to start a new business. So now he's working shifts at B&Q, and I've been employed as a care assistant at the Twilight Retirement Home for the past six months.

He says he's happy. I just hope it's true.

'Will we see you before the big day?' he asks, opening the door again. I tuck Phoenix's blanket around him more securely and shake my head.

'Unlikely. I imagine I'll be pretty tied up here once I finish work. You're still driving me to the register office, right?'

'You betcha. Happy Valentine's Day, Stella love.'

I wave goodbye and watch him walk to his car, the outside light throwing his long shadow ahead of him. His gait, like the way he brushes his hands through non-existent hair, is so familiar it hurts my throat.

This is the thing with parents, isn't it? You're always their baby, even when you've got a baby of your own. Even when your baby's got a baby of her own. To them, we never really grow up, and they never lose the right to tell you what's what, even if it's the last thing you want to hear. It's both a blessing and a curse.

But then one day you look at them and realise they're getting old. You realise that one day you might be the one taking care of them. And it makes all the hurtful things you've ever done or said rub at your soul like sandpaper.

Chapter 5

Four days later I'm on babysitting duties again. I've got the two till nine shift this weekend, so when Lipsy asked me to look after Phoenix so she and Robert could 'do lunch' I happily agreed. The clock is counting down to the time when I won't be able to see my gorgeous grandson every day; I need to stack up the memories while I can.

I'm settling Phoenix into his bassinet when Lipsy and Robert storm in. I'm surprised to see them back so soon – and you don't have to be good at reading body language to tell they've had an almighty row.

'I'm sick of you,' cries Lipsy, turning her back on Robert with an exaggerated huff. Her eye make-up is smudged and her lips are blurred from crying. She throws me a despairing look, plants a gentle kiss on Phoenix's head, and then runs up the stairs. I listen for the door to slam, eyeing the sleeping baby warily, but I needn't have worried. Maybe the histrionics are only for effect. With Lipsy, it's impossible to tell.

'Robert?'

He's still standing by the front door with his head bowed. I can see where he's going just a little bit bald on top; it makes him look vulnerable, like an old man with the weight of the world on his shoulders. But I guess a part of me has never truly forgiven him for taking up with a girl practically half his age, and getting her pregnant to boot. So I resist the urge to reach out a comforting hand, folding my arms around myself instead.

'She's planning on going back to work,' he says. His voice is flat, his face expressionless.

I shrug. 'That's what you've had planned all along, isn't it? She said you'd talked about it.'

'Well, yes. Eventually. She says we need the money. My job's not too secure at the moment, there's been talk of pay cuts across the board. There might even be redundancies.'

I didn't know this, and I feel my face pinking up. And there was me hassling Lipsy about Robert asking for a pay rise. I guess things will be pretty tight for them when I move out, but living here will be cheaper than renting a flat. At least I can console myself with that.

It also gives me a good reason to hang on to my house, of course. Not that I need one, but Paul is putting his flat on the market, and although he hasn't said that I should sell up too, I do wonder if that's what he's hoping for ...

But this is Lipsy's home, and for as long as she wants to stay she can. I think it's what Robert wants too, but he's one of those closed-off kinds of people. It's impossible to know what he's thinking.

Robert has moved over to the bassinet and is gazing down at his son. 'She's talking about going back in a matter of weeks, not months. She earns a pittance at that boutique, Stella,' he says, looking up at me. I can see that he's been crying too. 'It's hardly worth it anyway. And it's too soon for her to go back to work. Don't you think so?'

Damn right I do, but I'm not about to side with Robert over Lipsy. Not openly, anyway. Relations with teenage daughters are delicate at the best of times. Mums have to tread a very narrow and precarious line.

I leave Robert minding Phoenix and head upstairs to find Lipsy sobbing into the bathroom sink.

'He's so old-fashioned, Mum,' she wails the minute I walk in. 'He wants to keep me chained up here forever. I'm going to be one of those dreadful women with no life outside of their babies, getting fat and boring and talking about nappies all the time ... It's not fair, Mum. I hate him.'

Oh, Lipsy. How I could have predicted all this and more. How I hate being right.

Teenage pregnancy ends in happy ever after? Not in my lifetime.

'Sweetheart, you don't hate him. You've just had a baby, you're bound to be overwrought. Come here, give me a cuddle.'

For once, she complies. She smells of fried food and wine. Wine! At lunchtime. The luxury of it. I pull her into my bedroom and we sit side by side on the bed.

'Robert says you want to go straight back to work. Is that true?'

She nods and cries onto my shoulder.

'Are they putting pressure on you?' I ask. 'Is that why?'

Lipsy is a sales assistant at an upmarket boutique in the city centre; I can't imagine they are hassling her to go back any sooner than the standard six months.

She shakes her head. 'I don't get paid while I'm off, Mum. No more than the statutory maternity pay, which is rubbish, of course.'

'How about I help with the bills for a while?' I offer. I should probably discuss this with Paul first – what's mine is his, I guess – but I can't bear to think of Lipsy worrying about money.

'It's great of you to offer, Mum,' she says, sniffing, 'but it's not just about the money. I still want to go back to work. As soon as possible.'

'Why?' I ask again.

She shrugs, stretches out her shoulders, and looks up

at the ceiling. A mermaid mobile revolves slowly above her head. I hadn't even noticed it until now. This room is turning into a nursery by stealth.

'I just want to, I can't explain it any better than that. I want to be more than just a mum. Robert doesn't understand, and I don't expect you to understand either, but it's something I realised the minute Phoenix and I came home from the hospital.'

Which was, in fact, less than a week ago. 'It's early days, Lipsy. You've got to give it time, settle into the swing of it. Get into a routine – remember we talked about that? You need to get to know Phoenix and he needs his mum.'

'I'm not planning on going back tomorrow,' she snaps, rounding on me. 'But I'm not waiting six months either. Everything will have moved on without me, Mum. Can't you see that? Can't you see that I don't want life to leave me behind?'

A memory comes to me, unbidden. Lipsy is two weeks old and I'm walking her in the park by my parents' house in Shenley Church End. In the distance I see two of my old college friends. They are sitting on a bench with their heads close together, brightly coloured shopping bags at their feet. I'm excited – it's been ages since I've spoken to someone my own age, and I'm eager to show off my cute little baby in her pink and white fluffy jacket with bunny ears on the hood.

I start running across the park, holding the pram in front of me like a trophy. I call out when I get close enough, and they look up, as one. I'm still running, and I'm watching their eyes take me in, then move to the pram, then back again. They turn to look at each other, and the one called Serena raises her eyebrows and pulls a disgusted face. I'm slowing down now, confused, another greeting dying on my lips. But before I can reach them, they stand up, grab their bags, and hurry away in the opposite direction.

I could tell my daughter more about watching life move on without you than I hope she will ever have to know. But I could also tell her how fiercely protective it makes you, how you turn into someone who will sacrifice anything to keep your baby safe and happy.

Instead I pull her to me and hold her tight. I can't tell her anything; she has to figure it out for herself.

'Will you talk to Rob?' she asks, her tone half challenging, half pleading. I shake my head.

'No, sweetheart. That's for you to do.'

But she mistakes my hands-off approach for not caring and pushes me away.

'I knew you wouldn't understand. You didn't go back to work for years after having me. How could you possibly know how I feel. Just forget it, Mum. Just don't bother.'

I turn away from her, my eyes tearing up. But I'm not crying for myself; I've a tougher skin than that. I'm crying for her, for my strong-willed, fiery daughter, who will one day hate herself for hurting her mother the way I hate myself for being so hard on my dad.

And I'm crying for parents everywhere, who still feel they have to try so hard to get their children's approval.

*

The Twilight Retirement Home is a converted manor house in Bletchley, right at the very south of Milton Keynes' city limits. When I took the job last summer I didn't know I'd be leaving come February. If not for Paul's decision to embark on a new adventure in the wilds of Derbyshire, I'd probably end up working at Twilight for the rest of my days.

Which wouldn't necessarily be a bad thing, if it wasn't for Velma.

Velma Manley has one aim in life, and it isn't – as it should be – to keep the residents healthy, happy and comfortable. Velma's aim is to make me miserable. And as she's my boss, her situation is one that suits her very well indeed.

'Evening, Stella,' she says when I turn up on Saturday afternoon at five minutes past two. She's trying to be funny. Everyone in reception looks up at the clock. Velma smirks and tells me I'll have to stay late to make up the time.

Five minutes! She's the devil incarnate.

'How's Lipsy?' Jean, head of Twilight's cleaning team, rushes to my side as soon as Velma is out of the way.

'Do you have any photos?' asks Martha, leaning over the reception desk and resting her enormous bust on top of it.

I smile and pull out my phone. As there are about a hundred photos of Phoenix on there, this takes quite a bit of time, and I don't get away from their questions until two thirty. Now I really am late, so I run up the stairs to the staffroom, panting all the way, and change into my overall while looking longingly at the coffee machine.

Lipsy was mortified the first time she saw me in my pale blue tabard. 'What the bloody hell are you wearing?' were her exact words. In her eyes I could see I'd reached an all-time low – but at least, she said, it suited me better than the canary-yellow, midriff-exposing shirt I'd donned for my shifts at Cafe Crème.

'I've always worked hard for this family,' I reminded her somewhat huffily. 'I wasn't too proud to take a second job after the fire, and I'm not too proud to wear a uniform now.'

'You only had to take the second job because you forgot to renew the house insurance,' Lipsy reminded me right back, 'and you're only doing this job because you are too proud to ask Paul for your old one back.'

Quite. Isn't it wonderful how our children get right to the heart of the matter? And then cheerfully stick a knife into it.

If Paul was surprised or dismayed to find his new girlfriend suddenly working as a care assistant in a run-down retirement home on the fringes of the city, he kept it to himself. But maybe it's no coincidence that not long after I met him for lunch still wearing the tabard, he proposed and suggested I gave up my job.

I'm only a quarter of the way through my rounds when I hear someone hissing my name from the bottom of the main stairs.

'It's Lipsy,' Martha whispers. Her whisper could shatter glass, and I look around to make sure Velma isn't in earshot.

'What's the matter?'

'She didn't say. Just said you need to phone her right away. Grandma,' Martha adds with a wink and a hefty nudge when I reach the bottom step.

I speed over to the reception desk, breaking rules number one and two in the process: no personal calls and absolutely no running. Lipsy answers on the first ring.

'Mum, you have to come home.'

'Why? What's wrong? Is it Phoenix?'

'I don't know what to do with him, Mum. He won't stop crying.'

I can hear him in the background, exercising his lungs. 'Have you fed him?'

'Of course I've fed him, I'm not retarded. I've fed him, changed him, taken him around the block for a walk. He must be ill. You need to come home right now.'

'I only left an hour ago and he was fine,' I hiss, trying to quell my rising alarm. Phoenix's cries reach mammoth proportions and Lipsy lets out a sob.

'Where's Robert?'

'Gone out,' she says. 'He's sulking about our row.'

For goodness sake. What's the point of getting together with an older man if he ends up acting like a child?

I bite my tongue. Something you get very good at when you have a daughter like Lipsy.

'I'll be fifteen minutes, OK? Keep him warm, but not too warm, and give him lots of fluids, and ...' What else should you do with a sick baby? My mind's gone blank. And what if he really is sick? 'I'm on my way,' I screech into the phone.

Martha looks stricken as I wrench off my tabard and race for the staffroom.

'What am I going to tell Velma?' she shouts two minutes later as I run back past her, handbag and keys in hand.

'The truth, of course,' I tell her. 'My grandson is ill.'

Surely even Velma won't have a problem with that?

*

As soon as I enter the house I can tell something is wrong. There's no crying baby, for one thing. The house is eerily silent. I stand in the hall for a couple of seconds, catching my breath. All the way here, driving like a lunatic up the A5, I could hear Phoenix's cries in my head. I have the route to the hospital planned out, and I've rushed in ready to grab the car seat and go. The lack of panic alarms me more than anything I could have imagined.

'Lipsy,' I cry. 'Lipsy, where are you?'

Maybe they've got a taxi and gone without me. Maybe Lipsy called Robert and he got here quicker than I could. I search the kitchen worktops for a note, check the pin board, and then head back to the hall in case I missed one there.

Nothing.

I've just started up the stairs to check the bedrooms when I see Lipsy's legs descending.

'Where's Phoenix?' I say, backing down again.

She puts her finger to her mouth and shushes me.

'Is he OK?'

I let her pull me into the lounge and shut the door behind us.

'He's fine,' she says, laughing and shaking her head. 'I think it was wind.' Her face is calm, showing more than a hint of pride. My heart is still hammering in my chest. 'Mum, I was brilliant. I put him up on my shoulder, like this, and walked him all around. Then he just suddenly stopped crying, gave a massive burp, and went to sleep. It was amazing.'

All the life drains from my legs and I flop onto the sofa.

'So,' I say with a long sigh, 'it was just wind.'

'Yup.' Lipsy gives a little roll of her eyes, as if to say: What was all that fuss about?

What indeed.

She sits down beside me and starts to inspect her nails.

'So you dragged me all the way across the city, pulled me out of work, because he had wind.'

'I didn't know it was wind when I phoned you, did I? And you didn't know what it was, either,' she adds accusingly.

'How was I supposed to know your baby had wind from listening to him cry down the phone?'

'Grandma did.'

'What?'

Lipsy has this look sometimes: sullen and defiant at the same time. I guess teenagers the world over have the same look nailed to perfection.

'Grandma knew instantly what it was when I called her. She listened to him and said, "Have you tried winding him", so I did and he was fine.'

'And you called her when, exactly?'

'Right after I called you.'

'So, within a few minutes of calling me – and begging me to leave work and come home immediately – Phoenix was fine and you knew you didn't need me anymore. But you didn't phone me back to let me know?'

My daughter has another look, and this is one she employs when she knows she's in the wrong. It's kind of hard to describe, but it's a mixture of hurt and outrage, with a little bit of disgust thrown in for good measure.

'I can't believe you,' she says, jumping to her feet. 'You should be glad that Phoenix isn't sick, not having a go at me for dragging you out of your stupid job.'

'You know what Velma's like,' I say, standing too and towering over her. 'I could get fired for this.'

Silence follows. We stare at each other. I notice that Lipsy has somehow had time to redo her make-up, and that her hair is washed and straightened to within an inch of its life. When I was a new mum, I struggled to clean my teeth each day. I sure as hell hope I'm as together as her when my baby comes along.

Or maybe that's just one of the benefits of youth.

'Mum,' Lipsy says to me, speaking as if to someone very, very stupid, 'you can't get fired. You've already handed in your notice and you leave on Monday.'

There really is nothing worse than a know-it-all daughter. I sincerely hope next time I have a son.

Chapter 6

By Monday morning I'm fit to burst with anxiety about seeing Paul. I'm on the late shift at work – my last ever shift – so he's coming over at ten for breakfast.

This is my first real chance to tell him about the baby. He'll be full of his holiday, and not a little sheepish about the Sharon debacle, so I'm banking on a good reaction. Scratch that: I'm hoping for a great reaction. After all, this is fantastic news.

There's nothing to worry about. I keep telling myself this over and over. There's a Johnny Cash song on the radio, and his voice sounds like a warning, penetrating my calm. I get up and turn it off.

Phoenix is the only thing that can soothe me. He's lying in his bassinet, fists flung out to the sides, his feet treading against the white blanket as though he's dreaming of running. Do babies dream? Maybe their dreams are like memories: milk and warm arms and a mother's heartbeat.

Yes, I'm babysitting. Again. Phoenix is just over a week old, and so far I've looked after him for at least three hours a day. Often more. This is on top of my own job, and packing, and tying up all the loose ends before the move. And on top of the last minute details for the reception on Saturday, which is going to be pretty low-key but still needs organising. Lipsy is getting on with her life, as she tells me every time I complain I could do with a little help around here. I don't blame her, but I do worry how she's going to manage when next Monday rolls around and Paul and I set off into the sunset together.

'That's the understatement of the year,' I whisper to Phoenix. He stirs but doesn't wake.

I'm more than worried about next Monday – I'm terrified at the thought of leaving Lipsy and Robert and the baby all alone. In theory, it seemed like a fine plan; in reality, not so. And I'd be lying if I said I wasn't going to miss Phoenix. He's a part of me now, like some of his essence has been grafted onto my soul, and I know the best moments to come for me will be those Friday night journeys down the motorway to be by his side again.

Paul will reassure me. This was all his idea, after all, and he's pushed through my fears and anxieties so far. But I can't get rid of this niggling sense that all is not well in my world. I fry up some bacon and pop bread in the toaster, and I set the kitchen table. And all the while the knot in my stomach gets tighter and tighter.

When Paul arrives I'm a wreck, and his kisses don't transport me back to happiness the way they should.

'What's wrong, baby?' he says, pulling me down onto his lap and regarding me with serious eyes. 'It's not the Sharon thing, is it? Because I can assure you, you have nothing to worry about there. I think after six nights in the freezing cold in the middle of South Wales, Sharon is regretting inviting herself on that trip as much as I am.'

I smile and shake my head. Sod Sharon.

'It's Lipsy,' I say, stalling. 'She's talking about going back to work in a matter of weeks. And she's found this so-called friend of hers who wants to be a childminder, but she's a complete nightmare, Paul. I wouldn't leave her in charge of my dog let alone my baby.'

'You don't have a dog,' he reminds me.

No. But I do have a baby.

Paul listens patiently while I prattle on a little longer, then he takes my hand and presses it between his palms.

'Stella, Lipsy will be fine. She's a big girl now, she's got Robert, and your mum and dad nearby. Even if we weren't going to Derby, you wouldn't be living here, would you, after the wedding? She'd have to get used to you not being around all the time anyway.'

'But she's hardly looked after Phoenix on her own at all. She phones me every day, or she phones my mum. I just don't know how she'll cope.'

Paul shuts me up with a kiss. 'She's doing all that because she can, Stella. Because you're here. And she'll still have your mum, won't she? And she'll still have you on the end of the phone. We'll be ninety minutes away. It's not the other side of the world.'

'That's what she said,' I tell him. He laughs.

'So all this is coming from you? Lipsy's not pressuring you to stay, it's just in your head?'

Just because it's in my head doesn't make it any less important, I don't say. Instead I confess how much I'm going to miss Phoenix, and Paul comforts me the only way he can.

When I come up for air, I realise this is the perfect lead-in to my news. The time has come, but there is a little paving of the way to be done first.

'So, anyway, I've been thinking.'

'Argh,' he says in mock horror. 'Not thinking! You know what happened the last time you did that.'

'Funny.' I give him a little punch on the shoulder, coming off worse because his shoulders seem to be made of iron. 'Have you been working out?' I ask, massaging the muscles under his jumper eagerly. He gives me a sexy smile, full of promise.

'Down, girl. Can't you wait a few more days until I'm officially yours.'

Officially mine.

What's yours is mine. And what's in my tummy right now is yours.

I take a deep, preparatory breath. Go on, Stella. You can do it.

'Paul, how would you feel if I told you I've been thinking I'd like us to have a baby together?'

There are moments in life that define you – moments from which entire futures are carved out, where you can practically see the universe split into two. This is one such moment. I hold my breath, and wait for Paul to answer.

In one universe, he takes my hand, gazes deep into my eyes and says, 'I would be honoured to have a child with you, Stella Hill-soon-to-be-Smart. Shall we head on upstairs to make a start on that right now?'

In the universe I unfortunately inhabit, he drops my hand and rolls about on the sofa laughing.

'Oh, you kill me,' he says, wiping his eyes with the back of his hand.

I might yet, if you carry on laughing at me.

'What,' I demand, 'is so funny about you and me having a child together?'

'Oh, you are so brilliant, Stella.' He's still smiling. He hasn't clocked my expression yet. 'You always know how to cheer me up. What?'

Now he's noticed.

'You're not ...' Paul sits up straighter and leans back for a better look. 'You're not serious?'

'Perfectly. And I fail to see why it's so hysterically funny. We're about to get married, we're both in our prime. Why shouldn't we talk about starting a family? It's what couples do.'

'Young couples starting out, maybe. But not us. We don't need to start a family, we already have one. I've got Hannah, and you've got Lipsy, and now you've got Phoenix too. Ah, I see.' He purses his lips into a knowing smile.

'What? What exactly do you see?'

'Phoenix. That's what this is all about, isn't it?'

He walks over to where Phoenix is sleeping in his bassinet. I've yet to introduce them properly, but my grandson, peaceful and angelic on an embroidered white blanket, is perhaps the best ally I could have right now.

With my eyes I tell Paul to go on. I don't trust myself to speak.

'You've spent a week looking after a baby, and now you want one too.' He laughs, and turns back to me. When he speaks again I hear relief in his voice. 'Well, that makes perfect sense. Women are made that way, and Phoenix is your flesh and blood after all. But the thing you have to remember, Stella, is that you're a grandmother now. You've moved up a stage. You don't need to worry about sleepless nights and changing nappies and filling your house with bits of plastic. We're free of all that. You can still enjoy the baby, we can even have him for sleepovers when he's a bit older, and you've already promised Lipsy you'll come back every weekend.' Another laugh makes me wonder if he's taken this weekend plan seriously at all.

'We're about to begin the rest of our lives together,' he says softly. 'God knows we've waited long enough.'

Like a woman drowning, scenes from the last twenty years flash before my eyes: Paul at school, so handsome and cool, walking across the playground with the sun behind him; the day I permed my hair and endured the ridicule of everyone except him, and the gratitude and pure love that flooded my teenage body when he stuck up for me; coming back to Milton Keynes and finding him again, glowering in the corner of a bar, all grown up and serious; his arms around me the day I realised John Dean had gone for good and I was all alone with a baby.

And the day he proposed: Christmas Day. Down on one knee at Willen Lake while I jumped around and blew on my hands to keep warm.

We have history, Paul and I. But in many ways we are still right at the beginning of our story.

'Paul,' I say now, 'are you telling me you definitely, one hundred per cent, do not want to have children with me? Ever?'

His face takes on a pained but kindly expression. 'Are you telling me you want to go through it all again? Really?'

I nod. He shakes his head.

'I don't think it's a good idea, Stella. Our ages, the responsibility ... And what about my new job? You're not thinking about it sensibly, is all. What about all the plans we've made?'

'Are they so important to you?'

What I mean is: Are they more important to you than having a family of our own?

'Are you kidding me?' Paul jumps up and stands with his back to the window. Lit from behind, I can't see his eyes, but there's something in his tone of voice that chills me. 'This move means everything to us, Stella. I'm walking away from the business I started from scratch, you've handed in your notice. Do you have any idea how hard it's been, seeing Smart Homes go under? But I'm letting go, I'm moving on. We both are. This is our adventure. Our chance to be together with no complications. Just the two of us.'

He stresses the last sentence and I wince. My hand slips automatically to my stomach, but Paul doesn't notice. I hear Phoenix stirring in his bassinet. The last thing I need right now is for Paul to experience my grandson's epic wails.

I pull Paul back down onto the sofa and hold his hands lightly, tentatively. 'But can't we make a new start *and* have a baby?'

'No.' This he almost shouts, back on his feet again. Phoenix stirs and mews softly. Now I can hear the low-level snorts and snuffles that precede a good cry. That's the baby, by the way. Not Paul. Or me.

'I just don't think we can, Stella,' Paul says, pacing. 'And, to be honest, I don't see why we would want to. Why would we want to ruin everything that way? What is this obsession with babies, anyway?'

I shush him with my eyes and a strained smile, pointing to the bassinet where Phoenix's hands are starting to emerge above the blanket, reaching and grasping at fresh air.

'Well, you see,' Paul says, triumphant. 'You can't even have a proper conversation when there's a baby around. How do you think you could do up a new house? How could I focus on my new job? Come on, Stella.' He's kneeling now, and reaching for my hand – a scene reminiscent of the one I just replayed in my head. 'Tell me that this is just a silly joke. That part of our lives is over, isn't it? And I, for one, am glad of it. I love Hannah, and I love Lipsy too. But I wouldn't want to go backwards. Life is for moving on.'

'But Paul,' I say, desperately, keeping my voice low, 'you didn't even know Hannah as a baby. Don't you feel you missed out? Wouldn't you love to do it again, properly?'

This has always been a sore point between us, and I'm not surprised when Paul pulls away and hardens his face.

'I'm a good dad to Hannah,' he says stiffly. 'And I would have been more if I'd had the chance. But there's no point trying to rewrite the past, Stella. You more than anyone should know that.'

'But, wouldn't you …' I trail off as, right on cue, Phoenix wakes up fully, realises his tummy is empty and begins to wail. I'm used to it – to my ears it's just, 'Hey, Grandma, where's my bottle?' But to Paul it's like a thousand drills going off in his head while someone scrapes their nails down a chalkboard and plays a piano off key. I can tell by the look on his face – he really doesn't like babies.

'Come on, Phee,' I whisper, picking the baby up and throwing Paul a sheepish smile. 'He's just hungry,' I tell him. 'He hardly ever cries apart from when he's hungry.'

But there's no point arguing with him now. The shutters have come down, and for Paul, the topic is closed. It's not that he's intractable. My lovely, kind, thoughtful Paul is simply scared.

Well, aren't we all?

Besides, the more pressing question is this: How can I marry the man without telling him I'm pregnant? And how on earth can I tell him now?

*

From: paulsmart@smarthomes.net
To: stellahill@wondermail.co.uk
Date: 20 February 2012 21:38

Hi Stella,

Just wanted to say I'm sorry I rushed off earlier. I know we hadn't finished talking properly but you had your hands full (!) and I figured it was best to leave you to it. I hope your last day at work went OK, did they all knit you a bed jacket like you thought? What even is a bed jacket, anyway?

I also wanted to say that I'm the luckiest man in the world, and I can't wait to see you at the altar on Saturday. OK, so it's not an altar, but you know what I mean. (We're still on for lunch Thursday, right?)

This is our time, Stella. In a couple of weeks you'll look back and laugh at all this baby nonsense. Phoenix looks like a right little bruiser – he's certainly got a good pair of lungs on him! I'm sure he and Lipsy and Robert will be more than fine without you.

All my love, Paul x

From: stellahill@wondermail.co.uk
To: paulsmart@smarthomes.net
Date: 20 February 2012 21:52

Dear Paul,

They did knit me a bed jacket and I plan to wear it every night so watch out! I'm clearly very old and past it now, in your eyes anyway, so I'm also going shopping for some incontinence pads and booking in at the dentist's to get a set of false teeth.

This isn't easy to say, but I know you'll be great about it because you care about me and only want what's best for us. I'm having second thoughts about leaving Lipsy and the baby so soon. I know we've been through it a hundred times, but you never really listened when I told you how anxious I was. I don't think it will make much difference if I stay behind for a month or two while you get things going in Derby. We can visit at weekends. You wouldn't mind this too much, would you? (Please say it's OK.) I just want to be here for Lipsy. It's a mum thing.

I can't wait to be Mrs Smart, Paul. You know I've waited so long for this. I've got my dress hanging up right here (wait till you see it), and I can't believe that at 38 I'm finally going to be an 'honest woman'.

Love Stella xxxxxxx

PS: Let's talk about all this on Thursday – now's not the time to make any rash decisions.

From: paulsmart@smarthomes.net
To: stellahill@wondermail.co.uk
Date: 20 February 2012 21:58

Stella, I'm afraid I have to say no way. I just tried to call but you must have your phone on silent – I guess you don't want to wake the baby. (See what I mean?) It's not OK for you to stay behind, this is our fresh start and I don't want to do it without you. I know you are anxious about Lipsy and the baby, I have listened to you go on and on about it for months, but really don't you think you're making too much of it? You do have a tendency to think that no one can manage without you – look at what you were like with your mum last year, paying all her bills and the rest of it. Can't you just look to the future?

I love you. I'm sorry that I don't want to have any more babies, but I don't believe you want that either, Stella. Not really. It's time to know yourself, my love. Stop hiding from the truth and really look at yourself.

Anyway, I'll see you on Thursday. All this is just nerves, isn't it? In a couple of days you'll feel completely different, I promise.

Paul x

Chapter 7

In a couple of days you'll feel completely different, he said. Well, now it's three days on, and I'm afraid I don't.

I sat up late on Monday night and read his last email three times, allowing the words to sink in. Seems my dad isn't the only person who thinks I've got an omnipotence complex.

Know yourself. Stop hiding from the truth. Well, that's all well and good, but if no one's going to listen to you then knowing yourself seems a bit pointless. I've always known what I wanted: Paul, definitely, but here, with my family around us and that sense of continuity that comes from seeing the same landscape day after day, and being surrounded by memories. Maybe losing everything in the fire damaged my ability to start afresh. Or maybe I really am a coward. Whatever the reason, Paul's instruction to be honest with myself has made me face one uncomfortable truth: I do not want to relocate to Derby.

That doesn't mean I won't go. It just means I need him to appreciate that I'm giving up a lot for him. And that maybe he should meet me halfway.

I arrive at Wagamama's ten minutes early, but Paul's already there, craning his neck to look out for me. We're sharing a long table with five other couples: not the ideal setting for an intimate tête-à-tête. I slide my bum along the bench and smile ruefully at my beloved. He grins and stands up to kiss me, but his smile doesn't reach his eyes. He looks anxious. As well he might.

'Hi, guys! What can I getcha?'

Our waitress seems to have American pretentions, but I bet she's as English as I am. I order yakisoba and Paul goes for the chicken ramen. I also ask for a fork – I'm really not a chopsticks kind of gal.

'So,' Paul says, doodling on the placemat with an abandoned crayon.

'So,' I repeat.

He looks up at me. Our eyes meet. For a second or two, our surroundings seem to melt away. There is only Paul and me, joined by a bond that is cemented in our shared history, stronger than perhaps either of us fully appreciate. As he looks into my eyes his expression relaxes, softens. A warmth creeps up through my belly; I have this weird sensation that he would say yes to anything right now. In this single, special moment.

'Kitchen's just told me your food'll be ten minutes, guys. Is that all right for ya?'

The strident voice of the waitress severs our connection, and I slump back, disappointed. Paul mumbles, 'Fine, thanks,' and she gives us a double thumbs up before moving on to the next unfortunate couple.

'Have you had a good week?' Paul says. This banal question is such a comedown after that perfect moment of connectedness I feel as though I've been slapped. All I can do is nod.

'And the packing? Are you all finished? I bet Lipsy can't wait to get Phoenix's nursery sorted out.'

In fact, she's had Robert erecting furniture every evening this week. My bed is the only thing of mine left in the room, and that's set to go into storage in my parents' garage on Sunday.

I say nothing, just listen to him jabber on. Then our food arrives, stalling conversation for a further ten minutes. But my yakisoba goes down in lumps, I'm so anxious, so before Paul has even finished eating I decide to jump right in.

'Look, Paul. I know I said not to make any hasty decisions, but you should know that I've been thinking long and hard about what you said in your email.'

His face lights up. 'Why, Stella, that's great. I knew you'd see sense.'

'Not the kind of sense you were hoping for, I'm afraid. The truth is, I don't really want to move away. That's not to say I won't come with you,' I add as all the colour drains from his face. 'I'm just saying that it isn't what *I* would have chosen to do. If not for your new job and everything, if not for ... Well. I'm just saying, is all.'

He places his chopsticks on the table and looks at them. 'You've picked a great time to come to this realisation.'

'It's not a realisation, Paul. I never *wanted* to move away. I merely agreed to come with you because it was what *you* wanted. Can't you see they are two different things?'

'I can see that one of them makes me feel guilty. As if I twisted your arm, or something.'

Oh, great. Sulky Paul. That's all I need right now.

I reach across the wooden table top and grab both his hands. His knuckles are white.

'I want to be with you. I want to marry you. That means compromise, right? It doesn't hurt to acknowledge it, does it? To be honest with each other.'

Of course, if I was being really honest there is whole other conversation we should be having right now. But until I've got Paul onside with the *idea* of having a baby, I can't dump the reality of it in his lap. Sometimes you have to go about things bit by bit. Sideways. This is one of those times.

'I've been nothing but honest,' he tells me. 'I want to get away from here. I've failed, can't you see that? My business has failed, I feel like a failure. This is more than a new start for me. It's a lifeline.'

'Oh, don't be so bloody melodramatic. You're not a failure, and you know it. Loads of businesses struggle in a recession. Now who's laying on the guilt?'

The couple nearest to us – both blonde and willowy like elfin twins – shift in their seats uncomfortably. I lower my voice, but only a little.

'You were the one who said "know yourself". How about you do a bit of soul-searching too? We're both going off to Derby because of Paul's private affirmation plan, propping up your ego and giving you the opportunity to prove yourself. To yourself, I might add. You don't need to prove yourself to me. You never have.'

Now, where exactly is all this coming from, I'd like to know? But it seems I can't stop myself now I've started.

'There's no reason why you couldn't have just carried on with Smart Homes, just kept plugging away with it until things got better. The lease on the office has another year to run – you're the one who's giving up on it. OK, so you're not making the money you were three years ago – who is? – and I know things were getting really tight. But admit it, Paul, when this offer came from what's his name, Tom, you jumped at it because you saw it as a way out. For you. I'm just coming along for the ride.'

Paul is looking off to the side, refusing to meet my eyes. The waitress comes over to clear, and her cheerful greeting dies on her lips when she sees our faces. The elves slip past us, holding up their arms as if afraid to risk touching any part of our bodies.

'Can we have the bill, please?' I ask quietly.

'Sure thing,' says the waitress. I watch her swing away. She has one of those impossibly pert behinds and a tiny waist. I don't know why the sight of her makes me so sad.

'Well, thanks for the lunch,' Paul says. 'And the heads up. I guess I know where I stand now, don't I?'

'And where is that, exactly?' His sulky expression is wearing my patience thin. When you deal with a stroppy teenager on a daily basis there is no room in your life for placating men. Paul should know this. He's pushing his luck.

'Are you coming to Derby with me or not, is all I want to know?'

As if I haven't told him over and over that I am.

'Don't you care at all about the things that are important to me?' I ask.

'I thought the same things were important to both of us. I thought we were on the same page.'

'We are,' I say softly. 'Except when it comes to having babies.'

A silence stretches out between us. The restaurant is bustling – rising voices and bursts of laughter, shouts from the kitchen and the hum of the heaters – but Paul and I seem to be encased in cotton wool.

'Ah,' he says.

Ah, indeed.

I watch a different waitress walking towards me, holding a tray full of drinks in one hand. On a collision course with her is a child of about five or six, running while looking back over his shoulder, all flailing arms and legs. The waitress sidesteps him neatly and skirts around our table, switching the tray to her other hand. Two tables up, the boy's parents start to scold him.

'Aw, Mum,' he says, drawing out the word into a whine.

I sigh and pull out my purse.

In the end there is no resolution. In real life there rarely is. We have to vacate our seats once the bill's paid; more couples and a party of five are crowding in at the door. The busy shopping centre is no place to carry on a conversation, and before long we are at the car park. I'm parked on the first floor, Paul's car is on the second. He walks me to mine, and then we hug. He laughs, nervously.

'Well, that was intense.'

I nod. It's nothing but the truth.

'See you on Saturday, then.'

More nodding. I cannot think of a single word to say.

'We'll work it out, Stella,' he tells me, whispering the words into my ear as if the closer he gets to my brain the more likely I'll be to believe him. 'You'll see. It will all be fine.'

Like he said, maybe in a few days I'll feel completely different.

Or maybe I won't.

Chapter 8

I smooth my hands down the silky fabric of my dress then pull on my white gloves. Then I take them off again. Feet go into new white shoes – not too much of a heel, we don't want to tower over husband-to-be, do we? Hair is swept into a loose bun and secured with one of my mum's silver barrettes.

Something borrowed.

I'm getting ready in what we might as well just go ahead and call the nursery, peering into the tiny oval mirror which has been hung above the changing table to check my make-up, rocking in Lipsy's brand new nursing chair as I pull on my tights. My family are waiting downstairs. Are they nervous? I know I am. My dad looks dashing in a navy suit with faint pinstripes, a white rose pulled through his left lapel. My mother, beside herself with excitement, is wearing a cream and blue trouser suit that shows off her trim figure and was, she confided in hushed tones, on offer at House of Fraser.

Lipsy and Robert are arguing in the kitchen; I can hear them from up here. I step out on the landing to listen.

'I'm not even ready yet, I've got my hair to do and I've got to get changed. Why can't you do it, that's what I want to know?'

'I am doing it. Look at me. This is me doing it.'

'But you're doing it wrong. You don't hold it that way, no, put it ... Oh, great. Now look what you've done.'

'What I've done? We were getting on fine before you came along and stuck your nose in.'

'He's my baby.'

'He's my baby too.'

I slip back into my room, close the door, and stand with my back pressed up against it. My spine feels straight, empowered. I pull back my shoulders – have I been starting to slouch lately? The skirt of my dress is knee length, gathered, soft over the hips and stomach. Which is just as well, although when I chose it three months ago I had no idea it would be concealing so many secrets.

Here's a secret: I don't want to marry Paul Smart today.

'Mum?' Lipsy bursts into the room, nearly knocking me off my feet. 'What are you doing? It's quarter to twelve. We need to get downstairs and do photos and that.'

'Can I skip the photos, Lipsy? I'm not really in the mood.'

She glares at me. 'Robert has gone to a lot of trouble to borrow that camera and he will be gutted if he doesn't get to play official photographer today. Now come on, get your arse downstairs, will you? Jesus,' she mutters under her breath as she stalks away. 'What bride wants to skip the bloody photos?'

One who isn't sure she wants to be a bride, I could tell her.

'You look nice,' I call out instead.

She turns, smiles. 'You do too, Mum. Really beautiful. Paul's a lucky man.'

Downstairs, my dad presses something into my hands. It's about half the size of my palm and wrapped in white tissue paper.

'It was my grandmother's,' he tells me. 'I've been waiting for ... well, anyway. She would have wanted you to have it.'

Inside the tissue is a silver locket on a fine chain, oval and heavy with delicate roses engraved around the edge. It's empty inside.

'For you to fill with your own memories,' he says, and I look up, surprised. There are tears in his eyes.

'Sorry you had to wait such a long time for my wedding day, Dad.'

He smiles and runs his hand over his shorn head. 'Just grateful I'm not in a wheelchair like one of your old people.'

'My ex old people,' I remind him. 'I can't believe I'll never see them again.'

Although I know I will see them again – I've promised to pop in next weekend. But it won't be the same. Who knew I would end up getting so attached?

'I don't know how you stuck it so long, to be honest. Well, all credit to you. You always were a hard worker.'

'You too, Dad.' I lean in and lower my voice. 'Do you honestly like your new job? Is it not really boring at the DIY centre? You know, having worked in the trade for so many years ...?'

I want him to let me off the hook. Even though it was ostensibly his decision, I still feel responsible that our property business never materialised. Like I built his hopes up, or something.

'It's fine,' he says. 'It's a laugh. A doddle, in fact. Really, Stella. I like it.'

Still, it must be a comedown for him. I'm about to press further when I remember what he said about how I always feel responsible for everyone else's happiness. I clamp my mouth shut and purse my lips.

'How come you two are just standing there yapping?' Lipsy demands. 'There are photos to be taken, balloons to pack into the car, there's a cake sitting in there that's not even boxed up yet. Come on, people!'

Dad follows Lipsy out of the room and I take one more look at the locket before slipping it over my head.

Something old.

I think it is at this point I realise what I'm going to do. The problem is, it's going to take an enormous act of will to see this through. And I just don't know if I'm strong enough.

I take out my phone and re-read Paul's last email. Know yourself. Stop hiding from the truth and really look at yourself.

'Ah, Paul,' I whisper to the clear February sky. 'I wish you hadn't written that.'

Something blue.

*

I have a fluttering in my stomach that is more than nerves. Could it be the baby? Probably not, although as I haven't visited my doctor yet, or thought too much about dates, I guess it's a possibility. I look out of the car window and see a woman pushing a pram that is so old, an antique almost, it makes me smile. I crane my head to get a glimpse of the baby that is carted around so grandly, but then I see that the pram is full of plants.

Disconcerted, I turn away.

My dad drives calmly along the wide dual carriageways, unhurried and unflappable despite Lipsy's panicky comments about how late we are going to be. But Lipsy isn't here with us; she's in the car behind with Robert and Phoenix and my mother. Which means I can talk to my dad again. Openly. I can tell him how I'm feeling and ask for his advice. That's what dads are for, right? And mine has always been brilliant at advice.

What kind of dad will Paul be to our baby, I wonder? Will he regret what he said once he realises the truth. Once I take his advice and stop hiding from the truth.

But when I open my mouth the words refuse to come out. What can I say? I'm not sure I want to get married, Dad. I'm don't think I should go through with it because I'm pregnant and Paul doesn't want children and I'm so confused right now that I can't just go ahead and get married and move away and change everything. I need time. I need space. I need ... I need ...

I need to pee.

'Dad, can you stop somewhere?'

'Stop?' He looks across at me, eyebrows raised.

'I need to use the ladies.'

'Well, we're on the A5, Stella. There aren't any ladies here.' He laughs and rolls his eyes as if I'm about four years old.

'I really, really need to pee,' I tell him gravely, sounding, I'm sure, exactly like a four-year-old.

He pulls off at the next exit, heading for the huge supermarket in a nearby retail park.

As soon as he stops the car I'm out of the door and running for the entrance. People stare at me, and for a minute I'm confused – have I wet myself? Do I have something funny on my head? – but then I realise. Duh! Women in wedding dresses running through Tesco can't be an everyday occurrence.

By the time I'm back in the car we really are in danger of being late. I pull out my phone. There's something I need to do.

'Paul?'

'Stella?'

'How are you?' I say stupidly.

'Well, I'm fine. And you?' His voice is amused – I can read his mind even over the phone. He's thinking: She's probably got lost, or held up for some wacky reason (increased urination due to pregnancy, anyone?), or got a ladder in her tights and wants to go home and change. His thoughts will be benevolent, if a bit miffed.

Or at least, I hope they will.

'Paul, do you remember the conversation we had on Monday? When you came back from your trip?'

He sighs. I can hear voices in the background – is that Lipsy? Are they there already?

'Stella, please can we talk about this later? Like, maybe, after we've got married? You know, that marriage ceremony we're having in about ten minutes' time. And you are where, exactly?'

'But that's just the point, isn't it? This is the kind of conversation a couple should have *before* they get married, not after.' I'm trying to keep my voice low but I can sense my dad's ears twisting my way. We've reached the edge of the car park now and he's indicating to pull out into traffic.

'And we did have this conversation, Stella. We had it on Monday, and I'm pretty sure we had it again on Thursday. Or at least, you did. I haven't changed my mind, and I still think a fresh start is the best way forward for us, and I can't see what else there is to discuss.'

'Look, Paul, the thing is ... I do still want to marry you, OK, you've no idea how much, but there are some things you need to know. Things that will affect everything, and ... well, maybe you won't want to marry me when I tell you.'

My dad looks across at me, then turns back to face the road. His foot presses down on the accelerator. We speed past industrial buildings and take a roundabout practically on two wheels.

Paul is talking again – he hasn't heard a word I've said. 'You're bound to have cold feet, sweetheart. It's totally natural. Why, I've been nervous about it too.' His laugh is confident, assured. It just about breaks my heart to hear it.

I end the call and stow my phone in the little white

bag by my feet. My dad puts his hand on my knee, then takes it away without speaking. We reach the register office in record time; I keep my face averted the whole while.

There is a light drizzle falling when I step out of the car. Well, who plans their wedding for February and expects good weather? We're lucky it's not snowing. There's a man on the roof of the house next door to the register office and he whistles and waves to me. I smile and raise my hand, then dash for the foyer while Dad parks. Once I'm under cover I peer through the double glass doors. My mum and Lipsy are there, but I can't see Robert. I can't see Paul, either. Susan and Joe, former employees of Smart Homes, and two of Paul's friends make up the rest of the wedding party; from Twilight I invited Martha and Jean, and Sally who manages the kitchen, but none of them could get the time off. Velma, of course. Doing her thing again.

I wish Bonnie were here. She'd know exactly what to do. I even wish Billy were here – my brother could at least make up the numbers.

And then Paul appears. I shrink back, out of his direct line of sight. He's wearing the light grey suit we picked out together, with a sharp white shirt and a white rose in his lapel. My heart starts to beat a little faster; Paul in a suit always has this effect on me, but right now it's more than that.

'Stella?'

My dad bursts in, smelling of outdoors and brushing the rain off his arms. He stands next to me with an uncertain smile on his face. 'Shall we go on in?' he says.

'Dad, do you think you could ask Paul to step out here for a minute? There's something I need to ask him.'

'No problem.'

I watch through the glass. Dad approaches Paul, who turns and smiles. Then a frown creases his brow and he looks out to the foyer. Sees me. He pauses, the briefest hesitation, then steps forward. Do I see him square his shoulders as if going into battle, or is that my imagination? My jaw is aching with tension. My palms are sweating.

'Just as well we're not superstitious,' he says, giving me a peck on the cheek.

I laugh, a slightly hysterical sound in the spacious, echoing foyer. 'Isn't it just!' I gush. As if we need any more bad luck.

'You look amazing, Stella. I can't believe this day is finally here, can you? But listen, we'll be going in any minute now. The wedding before ours is running late, thank goodness, but as soon as they come out, we're it.'

I'm nodding but not really hearing his words. Running through my head is: Tell him. Tell him. Tell him right now that you are expecting his baby.

'Will you change your mind, Paul?' I hear myself saying. Out of options, no more oblique routes left open, I have to know. 'Will you change your mind about you and me having a family together?'

Into Paul's silence I could read many things, but for once my mind is blank. He shakes his head; his mouth is set, angry that I've brought it up again, disappointed that I'm ruining yet another perfect moment with all this baby nonsense.

I open my mouth, hoping that the words will come tumbling out of their own accord, for this is the time to tell him, right now, right here. I can't marry a man who doesn't want a family with me, not when I'm carrying the makings of that family in my womb at this very moment. But just then my attention is caught by movement inside the reception area behind Paul's back. The door to the ceremony room opens and out spills a laughing bride and groom, holding hands, eyes locked together. My family are pushed to one side as the wedding party follows; but my eyes are trained solely on the bride's dress. I swallow and rest my hands on my stomach. Paul is talking again but he fades into the background as the bride moves towards me. Her groom holds open the foyer door; she smiles at me as she passes. But I can't take my eyes off the bulge that pushes against the cream satin of her floor-length skirt. It's huge, rounded and proudly displayed. She must be at least seven months gone, if not more. She walks with her back swayed against gravity, the tent of her dress gliding forward as if on sliders.

She looks blissfully and unashamedly happy.

Her new husband, following close behind, catches sight of my horrified expression and glares at me. Protective, as if I were judging her. As if I would. I'm envious, if anything. Something is pressing against my chest and I'm finding it hard to think straight. I force myself to smile at the man, but it's too late. The door to the foyer swings shut behind him.

Paul tuts under his breath, and his disparaging huff brings him back into focus.

'Jesus,' he says. 'No wonder they were running late. Stable door. Horse, bolted.'

I turn away from him, hiding my face. The woman is being helped into a waiting car; her guests are still streaming out of the building. Paul takes my hand and makes to lead me inside.

'I'll follow you in,' I tell him, without looking up. 'Just give me a minute, OK?'

'Right. Well, I'll go in and get things started, shall I?'

I nod furiously and feel the warmth of his hand on my back. 'I love you,' he says, and then he's gone.

My eyes are blurry with tears, but I can make out the silver car outside, and I can see the radiant face of the pregnant bride as she's driven away. I lift up the top layer of my skirt – white silk with tiny sewn-on beads –

and wipe my eyes. When I smooth it down again there are two black smears of mascara just above my knees.

'Stella,' someone calls from inside.

'Stella, it's time.'

'Mum, come on for God's sake. What are you standing out there for?'

'Stella?'

My dad lays his hand on my shoulder. It feels unbearably heavy.

'Dad,' I say, looking straight ahead, surprised at how clear my voice sounds. 'I'm afraid there's been a change of plan.'

There is no way on earth I can march merrily down the aisle knowing that Paul and I have such wildly different ideas of our futures. He'd never forgive me for marrying him without telling him I was pregnant, and it really does seem as though I've stuffed up all my chances of letting him know ahead of time. I'm a coward: a feeble, pathetic coward. I'm the failure, not Paul. But he doesn't deserve to be trapped into a future that he's made it perfectly clear he wants no part of.

'I'm so sorry,' I tell my dad, turning around to give him a pleading look. 'I can't do it. Tell Paul that I ... that I ...'

It's the look on his face that finishes me off. Not disappointment – I could cope with that, I expect that – but pity. And so much love and understanding. He has no idea what's going on, but he's not judging me. He just wants me to be happy.

He nods, just the smallest movement of his head, and turns on his heel. Throws open the double doors and strides away, a man with a purpose. And then, without a single coherent thought in my head, I burst out of the foyer and escape out into the car park.

Traffic is trundling down Aylesbury Street, a constant stream of lorries and cars and buses, and the blare of a horn makes me jump. A whistle pierces the air; the man on the roof is leering down at me, laughing. It's raining now, heavy fat drops of rain, and my hair is soaked in no time. On the pavement, I turn and head for the centre of town, half running, half staggering in my brand new, uncomfortable shoes.

It's only when I reach the crossing at the other end of the street that I realise I'm still clutching my posy of pink and white roses. I stop and stare at it; for some inexplicable reason I hold it up to my nose. There are petals on the floor all around me, and one sharp thorn has embedded itself in the thumb of my left glove.

This is how my dad finds me, who knows how many minutes later. A sodden failure of a woman, standing on a street corner with her silk and satin wedding dress plastered to her trembling body. I throw myself into his car, sobbing and dripping. I'm too cold to speak; but my shivering doesn't stop even when Dad throws a blanket over me and turns up the heating.

On the dual carriageway, I lower my window and hold out the bedraggled posy. I let it go, and in the mirror I watch it fly up into the wind, then land on the road behind us. The green trim flaps hopefully on the tarmac. But even as I watch, a lorry drives over it and the flowers disappear under its gargantuan wheels.

I've just jilted the man I love.

Something new.

Chapter 9

I'm having one of those days when everything touches me too deeply. An old man sitting patiently alone in the back of a car outside the Co-op creates a lump in my throat. He's clutching a small suitcase to his chest, and his watery eyes look full of hope. By the time I've finished my shopping I've convinced myself he's waiting to be taken by his family to an old people's home. It won't be somewhere lovely like Twilight either; it'll be one of those green-corridored institutions with a permanent smell of cabbage and staff who'd rob you as soon as look at you.

I stride out of the store full of determination, fully intending to spring open his car door and rescue him. 'Come with me instead,' I'll say, offering my hand, and he'll look at me gratefully, approvingly.

The lengths I'd go to right now to get some approval.

'I know of a place where they'll take good care of you,' I'll tell the old man, or perhaps, 'Why not come and live with me?'

Mind you, that's not a great idea. There isn't even room for me at home anymore, as Lipsy and Robert keep telling me.

But when I reach the car park, he's gone. Now I'll never know what happened to him, and for a moment I find this unbearably sad.

I am aware all this is crazy. There's just no explaining the way my emotions are messing with my head right now. Take last night, for example: out of the blue came a memory of a book my mother bought for me when I first started university. It was poetry, Emily Dickinson, but I wasn't studying literature. Evidently she figured this was the kind of book a student would need by her side.

I've never read a poem, not from that book or any other. At some point I must have thrown it away, carelessly discarding a precious gift with no knowledge of how I might regret it one day. Last night, when I thought about the book's faded yellow cover and old-fashioned typeface, the memory caused me real physical pain. And it seemed an insult to my mother, the likes of which I could never hope to make amends for.

Of course, she knows nothing about it. She's far too busy being furious with me for ruining her day as mother of the bride to care about some old tome of poetry. In fact, if I did still have it, she'd probably take great pleasure in hitting me over the head with it.

But I know. And, as much as it's possible to miss something you never noticed you had, I wish with all my heart I still owned that book. I might find comfort in a poem or two.

'You took your time,' Lipsy says when I get home. She's turning into a real fishwife – Robert's words, not mine, overheard during yet another row this morning. They argue a lot, and apparently most of it is my fault.

'There's not enough room here, Mum. We can't breathe,' she said when I asked what they were rowing about.

Well, fair enough. I was supposed to be living up in Derby by now, after all. The tearful parting and promises to visit each and every weekend never happened; instead Lipsy and Robert are tearing their hair out wondering what to do with me. The spectre at the feast. An unwanted guest in her own home.

'Could you not find a flat somewhere?' she asked me

over breakfast.

'And pay for it how, exactly? I have no job, no money, no nothing.'

Cue more grumpy behaviour, of course. I've been doing a lot of that lately. Oh, it's not all fantasising about rescuing old men from cars. There's also regret. There's a water-stained, hardly-worn wedding dress hanging on the back of the lounge door that I can't bear to look at or bear to put away. And, of course, I've had the fallout from my long overdue pregnancy confession to deal with.

'You're what?' said my mother.

'You're not!' said Lipsy.

'So, why didn't she marry him, then?' asked Robert.

'Wah, wah,' cried Phoenix.

'Cup of tea?' said my dad.

At least one person didn't want to hit me.

Lipsy took the news fairly well. 'I hate you and I never want to speak to you or even see you ever again,' she said. Well, she would. She's a teenager, after all. But she came round in the end. Lipsy's a pragmatist. Soon she started to see the positive side.

'Now I won't have to find a childminder when I go back to work,' she said, hugging me and drying her eyes. 'You can do it instead. It'll save us a fortune.'

I'm not sure if my mother will ever forgive me, though. Maybe that's where the age-old guilt is coming from. Dad said he'd talk her round, but I won't hold my breath.

'Mum,' Lipsy says, pointing at the Co-op carrier bag in my hand. 'Are you just going to stand there or are you planning on putting that lot in the fridge.'

I have to get out of this house. Having your own daughter treat you like a child is not good for the soul.

'What are you up to this afternoon,' she asks over lunch.

She means: Are you going to look for somewhere else to live today?

I have Phoenix on my knee and I'm trying to eat a sandwich and hold his bottle at the same time.

'You could always move back in with Grandma and Granddad, you know. Oh, she's pissed off with you right now, but she'll come around. You wait, as soon as you start showing she'll be all over you like a rash. You know what she's like about babies.'

Right. Maybe having her not speaking to me might be preferable in the long run. I sigh, and put down the sandwich. 'Actually, this afternoon I was planning to go to Twilight.'

'To visit the oldies or to ask for your job back?'

'The latter.'

'Well, hallelujah! Finally we see some action.'

'But it's not a done deal by any stretch of the imagination,' I tell her. 'Velma hates me, as you know. And they might have filled the job by now. I can't just expect to walk back in and take up where I left off.'

'Oh, come off it,' Lipsy says, her mouth full of bread. 'They'll be over the moon to have you back. Even scabby old Velma. And it's only been a week since you left.'

'Hmm, well. Just don't hold your breath, that's all.'

I don't relish the idea of going back to my old boss and subjugating myself. But the fact is, I don't have many options. If we can't sort something out here, I really will have to find somewhere else to live soon, and for that I'll need money. My future packed up his rented van and drove off up the motorway yesterday right on schedule, as if the wedding-that-wasn't had never happened. It was the oddest thing. I imagine him just carrying on on autopilot, getting in the van, setting the satnav for our new address in Derby, and driving away from Milton Keynes as though I was right there by his side. Maybe he convinced himself I was, that it was all a bad dream. Maybe it wasn't until he approached the services and felt a bit peckish and turned to the passenger seat to say, 'Hey, Stella, fancy some lunch?' that he noticed I wasn't there at all.

Or maybe he figures he's had a lucky escape.

'But why didn't you marry him?' my mother wailed when we were all back at the house again, sitting around staring at the walls, shell-shocked. 'Why, if there's a baby on the way? Didn't you want security this time? Don't you want your next baby to grow up happy?'

'I'm perfectly happy, thank you,' Lipsy piped up. 'Watch what you're saying. Kids can do quite well without their dads, you know. Mums are essential, dads are optional.'

'Oh, well, thanks very much.' This was from Robert, and was followed by stomping into the kitchen and more arguing.

The people in my family always manage to turn the focus onto themselves, no matter what the crisis. Sometimes it's a comforting flaw.

'Will you be OK to look after Phee this afternoon?' I ask Lipsy after lunch, trying to stall the visit with Velma.

'He's my son, of course I'll be OK.'

Never mind the fact that she's barely been alone with him in two and a half weeks. Excuse me for the concern.

'And will you please, please, stop calling him Phee! His name is Phoenix. Phoe-nix. Got it?'

I nod meekly. 'Got it.'

But when I kiss him goodbye, inhaling his smell of milk and talcum powder, I whisper in his tiny, shell-shaped ear, 'Bye, Phee. Love you.'

And somehow this small act of rebellion lifts my mood out of the doldrums for a few glorious minutes.

In the car I turn on the radio to hear Gloria Gaynor singing *I Will Survive*. If this were a Rom Com, I'd sing along now, and an orchestra would start up, and I'd go on to new adventures, which would include meeting a hunky new man who didn't think a single mum with two kids – one a baby, the other a teenager – was a bad risk at all.

But this is my life. So I turn off the radio in disgust, grit my teeth, and drive in the rain to beg for a menial, badly-paid job from a woman who hates me.

I know. It serves me right.

*

'Stella! It's so good to see you.'

'You too, Edie.'

'But what are you doing here? Aren't you supposed to be on your honeymoon?'

Edie is eighty-four and just a tiny bit forgetful, so I'm not surprised she doesn't remember that Paul and I weren't going on honeymoon anyway. I return her hug and allow her to lead me into the communal lounge.

'Look, everyone – it's Stella!'

There are at least fifteen residents in here this afternoon and their faces light up at the sight of me. Well, I won't flatter myself – they don't get much excitement at Twilight. Soon I'm surrounded by familiar faces and I can't stop myself from hugging each of them in turn.

'So, come on then,' says Rosa, the resident octogenarian flirt. 'Where's that handsome husband of yours.' A little flutter of excitement passes through the assembled ladies – the one time Paul visited me here he sure did create a stir.

'And wedding photos,' shouts Violet right in my ear.

'Violet, there's no need to shout at the girl,' Franklin says, rolling his eyes at me. Every female in this place, staff and residents alike, are a little in love with Franklin. Except Velma, perhaps, but that's only because her heart is made of stone. No really, it is. Franklin is the kind of man you dream your own fella will be like when he gets old: dignified and handsome, always well turned out with a nicely pressed shirt and a fresh handkerchief at the ready, and of course he has all his own teeth and a full head of silver-grey hair. But it's his eyes that do it – they are still, at seventy-nine years of age, the brightest, sparkliest blue, and the mischief in them is born out of a desire to make other people happy. I have never known Franklin to cause offence, or to lose his temper or snap or be grumpy. And goodness knows most of them in here have enough to be grumpy about. The incurable, dragging illnesses they suffer; the stacks of tablets to be dished out every day; the children and grandchildren who don't visit but still expect Christmas and birthday presents and prime position in the will. There is a lot of talk about wills, and bowel movements, and food.

It could drag a person down if you let it. But then there's the other side of the coin: the hope in the eyes when the post comes round and there's a letter or a card addressed to them; the laughter and the mischief-making and the bawdy stories they love to share. There are the memories you get to hear about, thick with all of life, of lives well lived. And then, most wonderful of all, are the romances.

I've known for some time that Edie has a thing for Franklin. Not the same kind of benign love we all feel for Franklin; Edie's regard goes far deeper. I watch her now out of the corner of my eye as Franklin teases Violet about her hearing aid. Edie's face lights up when she looks at him – I've seen her giggle like a schoolgirl when he turns his bright light of affection on her, or blush and hide her face, or disappear from the room in confusion. Once I teased her about her toy boy – a whole five years younger than her – but the look on her face told me this was no laughing matter. This was love.

'There are no wedding photos,' I tell Violet and the others, 'because ... there was no wedding.

Violet fiddles with her hearing aid, shouting, 'What? What?' above the clamour of voices and exclamations. It takes me a while to calm them down enough to listen to my explanation, and of course I keep it short, missing out a few essential details.

'You mean you just changed your mind?' says Rosa incredulously. 'But that man of yours, he's gorgeous.'

I nod. There is no denying the truth of this.

'He was a real catch. You've messed up there, girl. There won't be another one like that.'

'Leave her alone, Rosa. Can't you see she's upset?' Edie puts her arm around me and pulls me close. Her hair smells of pears and her cheek is papery and dry next to mine. 'It's all right, Stella dear. You have a good cry.'

How is it that these people who I've known for such a short time can offer more comfort than my own family? Franklin goes to the buffet and gets me a cup of tea – their answer to every problem in here – while Edie strokes my arm and Violet tells everyone, in a voice that's even louder than before, of a man she knew who was also jilted at the altar.

'What happened to him,' I ask, sniffing into Franklin's handkerchief.

'What?'

'What happened to the man?' I shout.

'Oh,' says Violet coyly, 'I married him, is what.'

We all start to laugh at this, and at the look on her face, and for the first time in three days I feel better. I look around at my friends and offer a tentative smile.

'You'll get through this,' Edie whispers, getting to her feet. 'You made the right decision, you know.'

'Did I?' I wipe my nose and look up at her. Between her shoulders is a noticeable hunch – when the hairdresser visits each week Edie has to stand up and bend forward over the sink to have her hair washed. She says she doesn't mind, but I've seen how she gets shampoo in her eyes and the back of her dress always ends up soaked through. She nods her neat little head and smiles.

'How do you know, though? What if I've made the worst mistake of my life? That's what everyone else thinks.'

Edie huffs and gives a brisk shake of her head. 'There's no such thing as a mistake, my dear. There are only paths taken. This was the right decision simply because it was the decision you made. That, my dear,' she adds with a conspiratorial tap of the nose, 'is the secret to living a happy life.'

I watch her shuffle over to the TV and take her place by Franklin's side. He has no idea how she feels about him, but she's content just to be near him. And he's kind to her, as he is to everyone. But is this enough for Edie? I guess it has to be. Her words ring in my ears as I trudge up to Velma's office. Was she right? Did I make the right decision?

Although, when you drill right down to it, I didn't make any decision at all. All I did was ask a question.

Chapter 10

Sort out job: tick. Book doctor's appointment: tick. Throw away wedding dress: tick.

Well, OK, I lied there. I can't bring myself to throw it away, but I've shoved it into a black bin bag and put it in the loft. Where it will no doubt go mouldy because it's still a bit damp, but I just can't bear to look at it anymore.

I've put my ring away in my make-up bag, along with the locket. Paul gave the ring to me for safe keeping, afraid he'd lose it and not willing to trust it to either of his two best men. Typical of Paul that he couldn't choose which of his two best friends to pick and ended up having both of them. He always was a have-your-cake-and-eat-it kind of guy.

Being angry with him helps, but only a little. And when I start to picture Paul having to explain to his friends how there isn't going to be a wedding after all, my mind pulls down the shutters. It's a self-protection thing. My dad wouldn't be drawn on the details. I guess he thought they would be too painful for me to hear about.

The last item on my to-do list is to make a decision about my living arrangements. The way I see it, I have five options. I could carry on living here, in my own home, and force Lipsy and Robert and their three-week-old baby to move out. Unsurprisingly, this is not my preferred option. Or I could carry on living here, in my own home, with them. Ditto above. This tiny house is cramped for two independent adults; it was uncomfortable for three; impossible for three and a baby. It will be beyond impossible for three adults and two babies.

Option three is to move back in with my mum and dad for a while. Well, we might as well just draw a thick black line through that one right off. Option four, a surprise development, is the offer of Jean's spare room. But Jean isn't what you'd call a close friend, and while she might develop into one given time, I wouldn't feel comfortable imposing on her that way ...

OK, the real reason is that I'm planning to keep the baby a secret at work just a little while longer. Which might get tricky if I'm living with a colleague.

Which really leaves only option five: find myself somewhere else to live. Alone. At least for a little while. For the summer, say. When the baby's due – whenever that is – I'll move back home and Lipsy and Robert can be the ones to move out. But at least my conscience will be clear.

Right now, I don't need anything else to weigh heavy on my conscience. If I have to sacrifice some short-term comfort for my daughter's happiness, so be it. At least I'll be making someone happy.

At least I'll have someone's approval.

*

Church Street, Derby
Friday 9th March

Dear Stella,

I've sat down to write this letter at least twenty times but each time I find I don't know where to start. I still can't believe what happened – I can't believe you'd throw away our future just because of a silly misunderstanding. I've wracked my brains to come up with the real reason, and I can only assume that you had cold feet because deep down you just don't want to marry me. Everything else, all your worries – Lipsy and her baby, moving away – we could have sorted out. I know we could. I'd have driven you back there myself every Friday, or at the very least every other weekend. Now what am I supposed to do? Could you tell me that? Am I supposed to just carry on with our plans, our future, all that we'd talked about, on my own? Is that what you really want?

It's not too late, Stella. If you don't want to be married, fine. I wish you'd said something earlier – do you have any idea how embarrassing it was, standing there like a lemon waiting for you to follow me in? And when your dad walked in and said what he said ... I didn't believe him. I thought it was a joke.

Anyway, like I said, it's not too late. We can sort something out, salvage something. Can't we? I mean, it's not like we haven't been through our fair share of troubles. It was hard enough just getting together in the first place! You know how much I love you, you've always known that deep down. Surely you can't just walk away and carry on with your life? I phoned Lipsy this morning and she said you were at work, and when I asked when you'd be home she said you'd moved out! She said you were working back at Twilight – I'm wondering if you ever did really leave at all. And a new place to live? Are you really on your own, I wonder? Is that what this is all about? Please tell me it's not that.

Lipsy said not to phone her again, but I'm not going to apologise for getting angry. It's always the same with you, isn't it, Stella? You just breeze through life doing exactly as you like, being a complete flake and messing things up – the fire last year? Who in their right mind lets their house insurance lapse? – and then for some crazy reason everyone sticks by you, stands up for you, tries to protect you. Well, you don't need protecting from me. Lipsy spoke to me like I was the one in the wrong, like I'd hurt you in some way. Is it because of all that baby business? It was the last thing you said to me, and I've been going over and over it, but it can't be that because you are thirty-eight years old – you are too old to have any more children, Stella. We are too old. It wouldn't be fair on the baby. Tell me how having parents old enough to be grandparents could be good for a baby? And I don't believe you were serious. I truly believe that if you were just honest with yourself for five minutes you'd see that the idea of you having another baby at your age is just another of your wild, crazy ideas.

I won't write to you again, Stella. I'll wait to hear from you, and then we can start to sort this mess out. But I'm not going to have another stupid conversation about babies, OK? If I don't hear from you, then I'll know, won't I?

Never forget how much I love you. But life is for living, Stella, and if you don't want to live your life with me the way we'd planned, then there's nothing more I can do.

Love always, Paul

*

Déjà vu. What does it remind me of, this place? The bedsit I had during my brief time as a student? The grotty studio flat in the YMCA where I lost my virginity in a cider-induced haze? It's not until I wake up on Saturday morning – my second Saturday as a jilter and my second full day in my new home – that it hits me.

This place reminds me of my own house last year. After the fire, but before the vast renovation project I carried out with my own two hands. Don't get me wrong – I'm not living in a burnt-out hovel or anything; 4B Turnmill Street is not as bad as some of the places I might have ended up. But it does have that same air of disrepair and neglect, a kind of shrinking away the moment you put your key in the door, as though the very fabric of the building is ashamed of what it's become.

Which might be why it was the only bedsit available at short notice. The only one within my budget, anyway. I get the feeling it's been empty for some time.

Stephan, who lives downstairs in 4A, calls the building Termite Towers. Really, that should tell you everything you need to know about the place.

But I'm determined to make the best of it. Today is an eight-till-eight shift at Twilight, and I've got a birthday cake in my bag for Rosa, who is eighty-something today. She won't tell anyone her actual age, and frankly I don't blame her. When you reach that stage in life, you have to take your mysteries where you can.

The morning sickness has come back with a vengeance. Since I haven't experienced any nausea since the day after Phoenix was born, I'd figured that was some kind of anomaly and I was going to escape unscathed. Boy, did I ever have that wrong! I think this little guy inside me – or girl, of course – was just holding back until I got the wedding out of the way. Good to know he's so sensitive. But it's vomit city every morning now; this is really not the time in my life to be sharing a bathroom with total strangers.

This morning's vomiting has left me shaken and feeling a little worn around the edges, so when I get to the ground floor and see Stephan's door opening I let out a groan. I really do not want to see anyone right now, least of all an aging hippie with multiple piercings and a permanent aroma of petunia oil.

'Hiya,' he grunts. 'Doing all right or what?'

I tell him I'm fine, but very late, and he shakes his head as if he thinks working at all, let alone on a Saturday, is the devil's doing.

'This you, is it?' He holds out a white envelope. I look at it suspiciously. Then I notice the handwriting on the front. It's as much as I can do not to fall against the grubby walls and sink to the floor.

'Picked it up by mistake, all right?' Stephan says defensively, clearly mistaking my discomfort for annoyance.

'Right. Fine.' I take the letter and offer a weak smile. Satisfied, he slips back inside his own bedsit and closes the door.

The communal hallway in Termite Towers is carpeted in muddy brown hessian; the stairs in an older version of the same. The fibres scratch my hands as I lower myself onto the second stair up. I look at the envelope in my lap.

Why is he writing to me? And here – if he's writing to me here that means he must have spoken to someone in my family and found out where I am. Oh. My. God.

I scramble back up the stairs, half imagining him walking up the short path to the door and banging on it. What if he comes to see me to demand an explanation? God knows, he deserves one.

I do plan to tell him the reason why. It's just a matter of working up to it. I truly hadn't expected him to go away like that. Not so soon. I thought there would be phone calls and conversations, arguments and crisis meetings. Goodness knows I've had enough imaginary conversations with him in my head these last two weeks. But I didn't expect this vacuum, this strange kind of limbo. Lipsy and Robert are playing happy families with Phoenix in my house; my mum and dad are more loved-up than ever; my brother is still travelling, and as far as I know completely oblivious to all the drama he's missing out on. Bonnie is in America planning her own dream wedding, and I haven't plucked up the courage to call her yet and tell her the news. She'll be picturing me setting off into the sunset with the love of my life, and I want to let her think well of me for just a little longer. My life here, and at Twilight, feels unreal. Temporary. Like I'm waiting for my real life to continue. Once I get over this little hump in the road.

Trouble is, I have no idea anymore what my real life is.

And Paul? What is Paul doing? Open the letter, Stella, and find out, says that patient-but-persistent voice in my head. I ignore it, and shove the letter inside my bag instead. I'm already fifteen minutes late for work, and right now work and routine are all I have. Besides, it was that same voice that told me not to marry Paul. I figure it's done enough damage for one lifetime. I may never trust it again.

Chapter 11

'You know, she actually jilted him at the altar.'

'No, really? I heard she just called it off. Cold feet or something.'

'No. He was there waiting for her, the poor chap. All done up in his morning suit, everyone was there, the music was playing, the vicar was ready to start the vows ...'

'I thought it was at the register office, not at church.'

'Well, same difference. And I heard that afterwards, when he tried to call her, she turned off her phone. Can you believe it? The nerve. Just ditch your fiancé at the altar and don't even answer your phone? It's beyond me.'

'Well, yes. And me.'

'And I heard he went on honeymoon alone! Bet he won't be alone for long, good-looking fella like that.'

'No, there wasn't going to be a honeymoon. They were just moving up north somewhere. Leicester, I think.'

'No honeymoon? Well, no wonder it didn't work out. Young people just don't seem to know how to do things properly anymore.'

I take a deep breath, pull back my shoulders, and march out of the supplies cupboard with as much dignity as I can muster. Jean and Velma jump apart; Jean at least has the decency to look embarrassed. Not Velma. She smirks at me and then looks at her watch.

'Martha tells me you didn't come in until half eight

this morning, Stella. You'll have to stay late to make it up.'

'Could I just work through my break?' I ask a little desperately. I'm bone-tired at the moment; the emotional strain coupled with early pregnancy is not conducive to working late.

'You could,' she says as though considering it. 'Or I could look for someone else to do your job, if you like. After all, how committed can you really be? You've already left us once ...'

I sigh and walk away. I've barely reached the end of the corridor before Jean catches me up.

'I'm sorry you overheard that, Stella. Velma, she just started talking about you, and I was trying to put her right, was all.'

'I know.' I give Jean a half-hearted hug. I need all the friends I can get in this place; there's no need to make the woman feel bad about a bit of gossip. I guess I'll have to get used to it – I've already come across at least five of the residents talking about me. Why should the staff be any different?

'By the way,' Jean says, 'Martha didn't tell on you. Velma was watching from the window when you came in. She's just trying to cause trouble.'

I say thank you and allow my shoulders to relax a bit. They're not all out to get me after all. They're not judging me, just gossiping and curious, and I can't blame them for that. But when I stop by for my morning visit with Edie, I can't help but tell her about the conversation I just overheard in the corridor.

'It's to be expected, Stella my dear,' she says. She sits away from me while I strip her sheets, keeping her eyes averted. Some might mistake this for embarrassment – many of the residents here need their sheets changing daily due to incontinence or skin conditions – but in Edie's case I know different. She's acutely aware of the inequity of having someone wait on her, serve her almost, and this is what makes her feel uncomfortable. By not looking at me while I remove her soiled sheets and replace them with fresh ones, or cut her toenails or help her off the toilet, she is sparing me, not herself.

I shake out a sheet, causing a waft of air that knocks two petals off the bunch of lilies by her bed.

'I wish they would just ask me,' I grumble, 'instead of discussing all these rumours.'

'Do you really want them to ask you? Wouldn't that be an imposition?'

'It would be better than making stuff up. I heard Frances on the top floor yesterday saying I'd jilted Paul because I found out he was gay!'

'Stella, why didn't you go through with the wedding?'

I stop and look up. It's disconcerting to see Edie's pale eyes fixed on me. I drop the sheets, walk over to her chair and sit on the footstool, low to the ground.

'Well,' she says, shrugging, 'you wanted someone to ask you.'

I can't stop the tears that come now; they are flowing from some well of emotion I didn't know I had until this moment. I've kept a lid on it, the way I always do: not rationalising my behaviour, more ignoring it. Burying it. It's always worked for me before. But looking into Edie's fading eyes, feeling her warm, dry hand on mine, the emotions finally work their way up to the surface and find a crack.

Eventually, the flood dries up. She calmly hands me a tissue from the covered box on her dresser, and then repeats her question.

'Why didn't you go through with the wedding, Stella?'

'Because,' I say, my voice still shaky, 'because I'm pregnant.'

'Is it Paul's?' Edie asks.

I don't quite fall off my chair, but I am shocked that she feels it necessary to ask.

'Of course it's Paul's. Who else's baby would it be?'

She purses her lips, already treated with the strawberry lip balm she swears by. It occurs to me that I know absolutely nothing about Edie other than her age and that she's lived in the Twilight Retirement Home for five years and has no family. Suddenly this seems unforgivable, and I resolve to do something about it. Right after she's finished her inquisition.

'Does he know? That you're pregnant?'

I shake my head. Edie carries on looking out of the window. I follow her gaze and see a robin sitting on the frost-covered fence outside.

'So, in that case, one of you must be of the opinion that he wouldn't make a very good father. And you worship the ground he walks on, am I right?' She looks at me and I nod, willing the tears away. She purses her lips again and tilts her head to one side. Behind her back, the robin mimics her movements. 'So, in that case, it must be him. He doesn't want a family, and you do. And you've already gone and got yourself in the family way ahead of time, but you're scared to tell him in case he thinks it's a trap.'

I stare at Edie, open-mouthed. She's actually not that far off the truth, but how on earth did she get all that from 'I'm pregnant'? She laughs her dry little laugh when she sees my face.

'Oh, just because I've never been married doesn't mean I don't know about love, young lady. Or how complicated life can be. I've had my fair share of loving, you know. Even if I don't have a lot to show for it.'

The wistful look on her face as she turns away again just tears at my heart. I take her hand. 'Edie, there are loads of people in here who got married, had kids, did the whole family thing, and they have nothing to show for it either. Where are their kids and grandkids now? A visit once a year if they're lucky, for some of them. And you, you're more alive than any of them.'

I've never thought about Edie in this way, but as the words come out of my mouth, I realise that this is nothing less than the truth. She is a wonderful woman, self-contained and kind, feisty and full of life. I hope I'm half as sparky as she is when I'm her age, and I tell her so. She waves my compliments away, but I can see that she's touched.

'Enough changing the subject, my dear. We were just getting down to the nitty-gritty.'

I groan and slouch back on the footstool. How did all this begin, exactly? One minute I was having a moan about gossiping co-workers, the next I'm in the clutches of Bletchley's answer to Miss Marple, having my life dissected.

Where is Velma when you need her? Shouldn't she be checking up that I'm doing my rounds properly? I'm already at least an hour behind.

'Well,' asks Edie, her eyes twinkling mischievously, 'was I right?'

I shrug. 'Half right. Well, maybe more than half. I'm not scared to tell him – I totally planned to tell him before the wedding. But I kind of went about it in a sort of sideways way, asking how he felt about becoming a dad again, sounding him out before I dropped the bombshell.'

'And he baulked?'

'You could say that. Or you could say that he flat-out refused to entertain the idea, laughed at me, got angry with me, and then dismissed the whole thing as the crazy maternal longings of a new grandmother.'

'Hmm. I suppose becoming a grandmother so recently didn't help him see you as a potential new mum.'

'Exactly. He said that I was only feeling this way

because I'd been spending time with Phoenix, and that once we got on with our new life together it would pass. As if wanting a baby is some kind of virus.'

'But, Stella, aren't you missing something? Paul said all those things because he thought it was just an abstract discussion, a what-if scenario. If you'd told him, if he knew you were already pregnant with his child, surely he would have said something completely different.'

I nod slowly. 'And that's the point, isn't it, Edie? If I had just come out and told him straight off, just dumped the news in his lap like a birthday present, I'm sure he'd have pretended to be happy. What choice would he have had? He loves me, we were about to get married. Paul would have stepped up to the challenge. But then, I'd never have known how he really felt. We'd have spent our whole lives living a lie, playing at happy families while all along Paul felt trapped and cheated. Wishing for something else.'

'And once you knew how he felt,' says Edie softly, 'you loved him too much to let that happen.'

I sniff and wipe my eyes with a corner of my pale blue tabard. 'Something like that, I guess. Although it didn't feel so noble at the time.'

'You've sacrificed your own happiness because you didn't want to trap the man you love in a life that wasn't for him. There is something noble about that, don't you think, Stella?' Her face turns to me hopefully, almost pleadingly, and I wonder briefly if we're still talking about me. But I nod my head and smile bravely, and Edie looks away, satisfied.

*

For the rest of the day, I mull over Edie's assessment of the decision I made. I'm not sure how I feel about being painted in such a noble light; however much hindsight is applied after the event, it doesn't change the fact that I jilted Paul and didn't give him a decent explanation, or even an apology. His letter burns a hole in my handbag. What does it say? And how will I feel when I read it?

I'm not sure I can hold it together much longer. There is so much to think about, so many people to consider – not least of all this little life growing inside me – that I feel bowed down under the weight of it. Truthfully, I never expected it to go this far. I thought Paul and I would talk, and then this whole debacle would be cleared up. Somehow. I don't know if I believed we could work it out, but I figured we'd try. And if Paul truly couldn't face the thought of marriage *and* children, at the very least we'd end up friends again.

We've always been friends.

I've lost more than my fiancé and the future I've spent the last few months planning. I've lost my best friend. And I've probably hurt him beyond repair.

At lunchtime I take the envelope out of my bag and place it on the table. The staffroom is empty; there's just me and my thoughts.

Maybe he's decided we *should* talk about the whole baby thing again. Approach it with an open mind. All I need is a nod, a gesture – the possibility of a warm reception to the news I'm holding inside me – and I'll step up with my confession and take the consequences.

Maybe he's regretting the way he hotfooted it out of town; new job or no new job, he could have stayed around for a few days, tried to contact me. Probably he just needed time to think, and now he's calmed down and thought about it, he sees that starting a family together is not such a crazy idea after all.

I put the envelope back in my bag, unopened.

The afternoon passes in a flurry of paperwork, and with Velma off duty at six, I spend the last two hours drinking tea with the residents in the lounge. Edie smiles and pats my arm, but keeps our discussion to herself. At least there's someone I can definitely trust around here.

At the end of my shift I hang around until Martha says, 'Don't you have a home to go to?' to which I respond with a grimace and a pointed, 'No, actually. Not really.'

I make the short journey back to Termite Towers with a heavy heart. When I pull up outside, I check my phone for missed calls or messages. No calls, but there is a text from Lipsy: Hope UR OK. Call me 2nite xx. I sigh, put the phone away, and trudge up the broken concrete path to the place I now call home.

I open Paul's letter the minute I've closed the door to my bedsit.

When I finish reading it, I read it over. And then I read it again. In a minute, when my heart has stopped pounding, I plan to take the sheet of paper – white, A4 business paper, folded carefully into thirds and placed in a business-style envelope – and rip it to pieces. And then I plan to walk calmly down the corridor to the bathroom and flush the pieces down the toilet. And then, most likely, throw up on top of it. But this time it won't be the baby's fault.

Chapter 12

First thing Monday morning I call Bonnie. There's no point putting it off any longer. Telling Edie yesterday broke my silence; if my family aren't judging me – if an eighty-four-year-old woman who barely knows me isn't judging me – then there's no need to keep it to myself anymore.

When she answers the phone, Bonnie sounds far away – which she is, of course, but her voice sounds as though it's been shrunk.

'Bonnie? Is that you?'

'Stella!' she squeaks. 'It's so good to hear your voice.'

'Well, it would be kinda good to hear yours too. What are you doing?'

'Oh, I'm having a peel. I can't put the phone to my ear because my entire face is covered in bandages.'

I look at the phone in bewilderment, then pop it back to my ear. 'You're having a facial peel? You?'

'It's for the wedding,' she explains. As if that, in fact, explains anything.

'So the plans are going well?' I'm shouting now, which is something I don't like doing indoors; the walls in Termite Towers are paper-thin and I'm sure Stephan can hear every word.

'Yes, spiffing.'

Spiffing?

'Excuse me,' I say, smiling in spite of myself, 'can you please put my real friend on the phone? The one you've abducted and replaced with this odd creature who talks like a nineteenth century gent and is having her skin surgically removed.'

God, it feels so good to talk to Bonnie. Crazier than I am, always off on some adventure, keeping it light. If she was here in the room with me right now I might well hug her to death.

'It's so competitive over here, Stella,' she squeaks. 'All the women are TV show perfect. I've got to keep up somehow.'

I shake my head. 'No, sorry, I really want to talk to Bonnie. You don't even sound like her. She's Scottish, you know. Oh,' I slap my head with my palm, 'I get it! You're having a face transplant. It's worse than I thought – give me back my friend!'

Bonnie starts to laugh then lets out a piercing shriek. 'Oh my God, don't do that, Stella. I cannot laugh, it's agony.' At least some of her accent is creeping back in, I'm gratified to hear.

'I'd better go, Stella, they're signalling that it's time to have this rubbed off.'

Ouch!

'I'll call you in half an hour, OK?'

'OK,' I say gloomily, and end the call.

I spend the enforced half an hour sitting on my bed staring at the wall. There is nothing to do in this room. I don't even have a TV. Lipsy said I should take the one out of her and Robert's room, but I declined. Filling this place with home comforts would make it feel too permanent. I really do hope Lipsy and Robert get on their feet soon and decide to rent their own place. Maybe I figure if I slouch around looking pathetic enough, they'll take pity on me and move out. Give me my real life back. But there is a certain poetic justice to this situation: if I needed a way to punish myself for the mess I've made of everything, living in this grotty bedsit certainly fits the bill.

By the time Bonnie calls back I'm glum again, and when I tell her the reason why, she responds with typical Bonnie bluntness.

'Stella, you are a right stupid cow, do you know that?'

Sometimes you need to hear it, sometimes you don't. This is a don't occasion.

'And you're living where? Are you insane?'

I tell Bonnie about the baby, which shuts her up for a few seconds.

'But Stella,' she says, thankfully now talking directly into the phone like a normal person, 'if you'd just come out and told the guy, he would never have said all that horrible stuff.'

Which is almost word for word what Edie said. Maybe Edie could be the new Bonnie in my life. I imagine going clubbing with Edie, her wearing one of Bonnie's sequinned outfits, standing against the bar of Oceana with a cocktail in her hand.

Maybe not.

'That is exactly the point,' I repeat, wearily.

And then Bonnie surprises me. She says, 'It's all that Sharon's fault.'

I sit up, interested.

'Sharon? What's she got to do with it?'

Bonnie's voice from across the Atlantic is clear and authoritative. 'Think about it, Stella. If it hadn't been for Sharon getting pregnant and then Paul and her splitting up over it, you would never have been worried about his reaction to your fantastic news.'

'You really think it's fantastic news?' I ask, touched. So far most people have reacted to the news of the baby as a problem to be overcome, a burden to be endured. Tears spring into my eyes as I think of how joyous the news of a new baby usually is, and how my baby has missed out on all this.

But then, if I'd just come out and told everyone on that very first day, would it have all been so very different? Somehow, I don't think so.

'My best mate's having another baby? Sure it's fantastic news! Can I be godmother, can I, can I?'

I nod, then realise Bonnie can't see me down the phone. Which is just as well – the tears are flowing now, and I'm pretty ugly when I'm crying.

'So,' I say, 'how exactly is it Sharon's fault?'

'Are you crying, Stella Hill?'

'No.'

'Liar. OK, well, maybe not Sharon's fault specifically – she couldn't help getting pregnant, I guess, and she sure couldn't help it that Paul dumped her when she found out she was. But he was pretty much a confirmed bachelor, wasn't he, huh? Until last year, when Sharon comes back into his life and says, "Hey, fella, meet your daughter". Must have been a shock to a guy like him.'

I think about what she's saying. 'When I first found out I was pregnant, I did think about that, you know. I thought about how they split up, and how I hoped it wouldn't happen to us. But I just pushed the thought out of my mind. I'm not Sharon. I mean, Paul and I were meant to be together.'

Silence extends out between us as we both consider my use of the past tense.

'I'm thinking that you didn't push it that far out of your mind at all,' Bonnie says. 'And that maybe you figured you'd jump before you were pushed.'

'What do you mean?'

'How long did you have between finding out you were pregnant and the wedding, Stella?'

I think for a minute. 'Just under two weeks. But I couldn't just announce it, Bonnie. Lipsy had just had her baby. I didn't want to steal her thunder. And then Paul was going on about Hannah and their blasted holiday.

He actually let Sharon go with them, you know. In a caravan. It was weird.'

'It's all getting clearer, don't you think? He was away, leaving you to fret about his reaction, thinking about the whole Sharon thing – will history repeat itself?'

'I wasn't fretting.'

'Oh, I think you were. Subconsciously.'

Bonnie is a committed amateur psychologist. The annoying thing is, she's usually bang on.

'Go on,' I say, reluctantly.

'So, you leave it till the very last minute to tell him, and then you have to sound him out first, and then when that doesn't go as well as you'd hoped, you jump ship.'

I wait, knowing exactly what she's about to say next.

'Because, just maybe, you thought deep down that if you did tell him the truth, it would be him jilting you.'

Sometimes the truth is hard to hear. And sometimes it takes a crazy Scottish lass on the other side of the world to tell it like it is.

'So,' I say, 'is your skin like really sore now?'

Bonnie laughs. 'Fine. Point taken. Counselling session over for today. And yes, it hurts like hell. But I look twenty years younger.'

That would mean she looks about thirteen years old. We laugh together, as if the distance between us is no barrier at all.

'I'll fly over for the birth, Stella,' Bonnie tells me before she hangs up.

'And I'll fly over for the wedding,' I promise. With my three-month-old baby. The thought stops me in my tracks.

'We'll see,' she says. 'We'll see.'

*

'It's due *when*?'

'Mid August is my best guess. Of course, without knowing the exact date of your last period, it is only a guess. They'll be able to give you a more accurate date at your scan.'

Which will also be sooner than I'd thought. According to my doctor, I've missed my twelve week appointment, and the one she's just this moment booking will probably be nearer to the scheduled twenty week scan. By her reckoning, and based on the very embarrassing measurement of my belly a few minutes ago, I'm at least four months' pregnant. Maybe more.

No wonder the morning sickness has been so bad. No wonder I'm putting on so much weight.

Seems I can't get anything right these days.

'But everything's OK, right? With the baby? I mean, missing the scan and not seeing a midwife until now ... It's not a problem, right?'

My GP is a kind and sensitive woman in her late fifties. She doesn't know me very well – I'm rarely ill – but she picks up on the anxiety in my voice.

'You are perfectly healthy, Miss Hill,' she says reassuringly. 'Your blood pressure is fine, the baby's heart rate sounds just right. Do you feel well? Have you had any problems?'

I almost burst out laughing. Any problems? Where should I start?

I tell her about the sickness and the tiredness, which she confirms is completely normal. I'm surprised to hear my blood pressure is normal, though. Who'd have thought I could sail through all this relatively unscathed.

Health-wise, at least.

'Will the father be able to attend the scan with you?' the doctor asks, typing fast into her computer.

Not likely. Unless some miracle occurs in the next seven days ...

I think my miracle days are over.

'He might be able to,' I tell her vaguely. 'Depends on other commitments.'

She prints out the appointment slip and hands it to me, smiling gently but not meeting my eyes. 'I see by your notes you have another child, a teenage daughter?'

I nod. I'm guessing her notes tell her a lot more besides. For instance, that the teenage daughter in question has also just become a new mum herself.

'Well.' She stands and brushes invisible specks off her tweed skirt. 'I wish you the best of luck with everything. And if you need anything else, you know where we are.'

Out in the reception area I'm struck momentarily by a familiar lurching of my stomach. The sickness will pass soon, she said. I'm almost at the end of that phase. Well, I'll believe *that* when I see it. With Lipsy I was sick until the very last month. But I've come prepared: I have mints in my bag and lipstick and blusher to repair the damage to my face and my breath. By the time I emerge from the doctor's surgery, I'm minty-fresh and ready to go.

Which is just as well, because waiting right there on the pavement outside the surgery is my mother.

'I thought we were meeting in town?' I say, after I've given her a hug hello and told her how well she's looking. Which is not a word of a lie. My mother is positively glowing.

'I saw your car parked outside and thought I'd wait for you,' she says.

'But what are you doing here?'

'Just passing by,' she tells me airily.

'But ... now we have two cars,' I point out lamely. I'm thrown, finding her here. Just passing by doesn't cut it, but I'm not sure how far I want to pry.

'It doesn't matter, Stella. We can go in yours and then you drop me back here later.' She tucks her arm through mine and guides me towards my beaten up old wreck of a car.

'Well, OK. If you're sure. Your car's a bit more luxurious, though. Maybe we should take yours. As it's here and all.'

'But I'm rubbish at parking,' she points out, and I laugh, noticing that her late-model Corsa is indeed parked at a very odd angle. I wouldn't like to be parked next to it, that's for sure.

Her invitation to meet for lunch totally caught me off guard. She's hardly spoken to me since the non-wedding; apart from bumping into her when I'm looking after Phoenix she might as well have left the country. I saw the invitation as an olive branch. It might just mean she's forgiven me for ruining her big day as the mother of the bride. Because it was, of course, all about her.

I was tempted to say no. I hardly get any time to myself these days, and I'm completely run off my feet. When I'm not working I'm looking after Phoenix – in effect I have two full-time jobs. Lipsy went back to work earlier than any of us expected, claiming it was her right 'as a woman' to return to her job the way any man would. I can't argue with her logic, but I can – and do – argue with her expectation that I will work as an unpaid childminder for the foreseeable future.

'It's good practice for you, Mum,' she tells me whenever I complain, wafting perfume around her head or plastering on her lipstick. Then, with a kiss for Phoenix and another for me, she skips out of the door, the very epitome of the twenty-first century, have-it-all woman.

As my mother straps herself in and checks her hair in the passenger mirror, I take a deep breath and say, 'So, you were at the doctors too, were you?' and brace myself for the response. I'm not good at personal conversations with my mother. I'm trying to be better, but there's some kind of knowledge barrier going on there. That is, I'd rather not delve too deeply into her problems because they always seem to have a way of turning into my problems. It sounds selfish. It *is* selfish. It's also completely and unfortunately true.

She's been better since Dad came home, though. And the two of them seem happier than ever before, so I can't complain, can I? Even if they are almost too happy, like a pair of lovebirds on heat.

'No,' she says, clearly lying through her teeth. 'I was just passing. Like I said.'

I give her a kiss on the cheek – a reward for having the decency to lie to me and keep me out of whatever it is she's up to. With my mum and dad it's best to operate on a need-to-know basis, and most of the time I really don't need to know.

Lunch is pancakes in John Lewis's cafe, sitting on the glass-fronted balcony watching Milton Keynes' dedicated shoppers file past underneath.

'You want to go easy,' my mother says, watching me pour sugar on top of my pancake. 'All that eating for two stuff isn't true, you know. With your build, not to mention your age, you'll have a hell of a job getting the extra weight off when the baby's born.'

'Let's talk about something else, shall we?' I answer through gritted teeth. 'How are you and Dad getting on?'

'You're really interested?'

'Of course I am!' I'm hurt that she's so surprised. 'Of course I'm interested, Mum. I want you both to be happy. You know that.'

She smiles radiantly and pats my hand. 'Oh, we are. We are. Very happy. You know,' she says, her eyes going all dreamy and unfocused, 'he's a different man since he came out of prison.'

'Shh,' I tell her, looking around the cafe.

'I'm not ashamed of him, Stella, and neither should

you be.'

I glare at her across the table. 'I'm not ashamed. But neither do I want to discuss *prison* in the middle of John Lewis.'

She shrugs, and carries on. 'Well, he's a changed man. More attentive. More loving. And in the bedroom department–'

'So, how's your pancake?' I blurt out. Anything but the bedroom department, please!

'You're such a prude,' she laughs. 'We're not ancient, Stella. We do still have sex, you know.'

'OK, then. This is just getting weird now. I'm not having this conversation, so either change the subject or I'm leaving.'

'Oh, Stella,' my mum sighs, but at least she's stopped talking about sex. Oh no, I spoke too soon.

'Well, if you must know, that was why I was at the doctor's this morning.'

I'm groaning now. A great, long groan, with my legs stretched out under the table and my head thrown back in the uncomfortable chair. Why, oh why do I fall into this situation every time? I try to block out her voice but it isn't easy. Certain words get through. 'Drying up' are two that I can't escape from, and 'lubricant' is another. 'There's lots you can do about it, according to the nurse,' she says defensively, as though I've implied there isn't.

I tuck into my pancake regardless. No point starving myself just because my mother doesn't know suitable lunch topics from Adam. She watches me squirt on extra lemon juice and sprinkle yet more sugar, then she sighs again, shrugs her shoulders, and looks away. I should just leave well alone now. We're out of the danger zone, after all. There's only an afternoon of shopping to get through, and that can't be too bad. Even with my mother.

But that's the other thing about my relationship with

her. I just don't know when to keep my mouth shut.

'It's not surprising he feels the need to keep you happy in the "bedroom department", though, is it?' I say between mouthfuls.

'And why's that?' asks my mum quietly.

'Well, you know. With everything that's gone on.'

The reason I miss the danger signs is, I'm stuffing my face. By the time the frosty atmosphere penetrates my sugar-induced trance, it's too late. My mother's face is white, despite the carefully applied make-up, and her fingers are clenched into fists on the table in front of me.

'You mean,' she says, icily, 'because of the affair.'

'That's not exactly what I meant, no,' I tell her, swallowing quickly. 'I just meant, oh, you know. Stuff.'

'Stuff. Well, that's just typical of you, Stella. Why bother to come up with a proper explanation? Just shut me down and hope I go away. That's what you always do, isn't it? Just like you did to ...'

She clamps her mouth shut suddenly and looks away, but not before I've imagined the words she didn't say.

Just like you did to Paul.

I come out fighting.

'Don't have a go at me,' I snap back, 'just because you made a mistake that Dad had to pay for. What happened between Paul and me has got nothing to do with it. Anyway, all I meant was, it's not surprising that he feels he's got to keep you satisfied now. Wouldn't want the same thing to happen again, is all. There's no need to jump down my throat because of it.'

'For your information, I didn't have an affair with your father's accountant for the sex. It was far more complicated than that.'

She hisses sex so loudly the mother on the next table, feeding her baby some kind of green goo, looks up and glares. I shoot her an apologetic glance.

'Mum, will you keep your voice down, please? Do we

have to do this here? Do we have to do it at all, in fact?'

'You started it,' she says sulkily.

'Yes. I did. And I wish I hadn't opened my mouth now, OK? Anyway, you were the one who brought up your love life, not me. What you and Dad get up to is none of my business. I'm not interested. You did what you did, and Dad went to prison to protect you from the scandal.'

Not for the first time I wonder what on earth attracted my mum to Dad's seriously dodgy accountant. Oh, I've made all the jokes – his eye for figures, checking out the bottom line. They weren't funny then and they're not funny now. I lost my father for eighteen months thanks to my mum's insecurity and his misplaced desire to be the hero.

But at least they are making it work now. I suppose I should be grateful for that. At least one couple have managed to get it right.

'I'm happy that you're happy, Mum,' I tell her, reaching out to touch her hand, an olive branch of my own.

She purses her lips, but then nods and gives a little shrug. For all her faults, she can't hold a grudge for long. Which is just as well, really.

'Changing the subject,' she says, 'I've been meaning to talk to you about Lipsy. I'm a bit worried about her, to be honest.'

'What about my daughter,' I ask, not so subtly reminding her of the hierarchy. Lipsy is *my* daughter, and it's up to me to worry about her.

She slowly pours out a cup of tea, then sips it, looking out over the balcony to the shoppers below. This is my mother's domain, this state of the art shopping centre with its glass walls and marble seating, high-tech lighting and row upon row of retail outlets offering escape and excitement. This lunch was supposed to be a quick refuelling exercise before hitting the stores to buy yet more stuff for Phoenix. Now I fear it's heading in a completely different direction.

'It's not right that Lipsy's gone back to work so soon,' she says, putting down her cup carefully. 'Surely you agree?'

I shrug. 'I've noticed that I'm babysitting Phoenix so often I might as well offer to adopt him,' I say, faking a laugh.

Ha, ha. Funny joke. I'll be laughing on the other side of my face in a few months, right?

My mother gives me a look that's hard to read. 'You were the same, you know. When you had Lipsy. Your dad and I, we ended up doing the lion's share of it.'

'That's not true,' I say, stung. 'I did everything – I don't know how you can say that. Dad was at work all the time, and you were ... well, you were brilliant, of course, but I wasn't going out all the time, going to work and then popping off here, there and everywhere like Lipsy is. Besides,' I add, trying to keep the bitterness out of my voice, 'she has Robert. I had no one.'

'I'm worried about her. And I'm worried about you,' she adds. I look up in surprise.

'Me?'

'You're pregnant. You've just lost your fiancé, your plans have gone haywire, and you've had to move out of the house you love. And you're working those long shifts, and looking after Phoenix. You look dreadful, Stella. Have you even brushed your hair today?'

I haven't, as it goes. But that's not so unusual. With long hair you can usually get away with it. Tousled, is what people think. It's trendy.

Or so I thought.

'Hey,' I joke, 'keep talking, why don't you? You're making me feel really good about myself.'

She says nothing for a while. Just when I'm breathing

a sigh of relief, she stands and picks up her bag, throwing it dramatically over her shoulder.

'I just can't talk to you when you're like this,' she says, making me feel about thirteen all over again. 'Sometimes I feel like I hardly know you at all.'

And with that, she stalks out of the cafe, leaving me staring after her like a total idiot.

And leaving me with the bill, of course. But no change there.

'What was all that about?' I say to the woman opposite with a rueful shrug. She looks away and wipes her baby's mouth with a flannel.

I watch my mother walk across the square below. From up here I can see that her roots need doing, and that she's put on weight across her hips. That's where I get it from – something else to blame her for. A tall man carrying a big square package in front of his face looks like he's about to bump into her as she reaches the shops on the other side. I jump up protectively, raising my arm and opening my mouth to shout out a warning, but what can I do from up here?

She dodges him nimbly, like a woman half her age, and I sit back down again, feeling foolish. I think about how I should have stuck to my original plan – avoid all conversational topics except the most shallow. It's the only way to stay safe, especially with my mother. Give her an inch – just the tiniest opening – and out it all pours.

But then, as she disappears into the crowd, I find that I miss her terribly, and I wish I was down there by her side, shopping and chatting, leaving all our problems behind for just a few innocent hours. And I'm unaccountably annoyed at myself for messing it up once again.

Chapter 13

'Again?'

'Yes. If it's not too much trouble.'

'Well, of course it isn't too much trouble. But ... Lipsy, it's my afternoon off. I had some stuff to do.'

'But I've got to get ready for the party. I can't do that with Phoenix under my feet all the time.'

'I'll have to look after him there. There's hardly room to swing a cat in this bedsit.'

'Well, duh! I wasn't planning on bringing him all the way over there. Besides, I thought you could help Grandma with the food.'

'What food? Hang on a minute, what party?'

'Oh, Mum. You're so funny. It's not a surprise anymore so don't worry. Robert let it slip last week – he's rubbish at keeping secrets.'

'I'm not being funny, Lipsy. Seriously – what party?'

'Bye, Mum. See you in half an hour, OK?'

I end the call and look at the phone as if the answers might suddenly appear on its black screen. Nothing. So I dial my dad's mobile.

'What's this about a party?' I ask as soon as he picks up.

'Lipsy's party?' he says. I can tell by his voice that he's smiling.

'I don't know, Dad. That's why I'm calling. She wants me to babysit so she can get ready, but I'm not to worry as it's not a surprise anymore. Although it is, isn't it? To me.'

'Good joke, Stella,' he says, laughing. 'See you about six, OK?'

'I wish people would stop telling me how funny I am and just tell me what the hell is going on!' I scream into the phone.

After a shocked silence, my dad explains. I apologise and hang up, glad I'm in my room alone and no one can see my red face.

Is being four months pregnant and recently estranged from your fiancé a good enough reason to forget your own daughter's birthday?

I thought not.

But I'm sure I knew nothing about the party.

'Your mum was going to remind you when you met for lunch the other day,' my dad explained. 'We figured you might have forgotten with everything else you'd had going on.'

I shut up when I heard this, still feeling vaguely guilty for pissing her off, although still without much of a clue how I'd managed it. Just by being myself, I guess. Seems I can't help it.

When I arrive at Lipsy's – or should I say when I arrive home, this technically still being my house, after all – I hold out my arms for the baby, not trusting myself to say another word, birthday or no birthday. This is the fourth day in a row I've looked after Phoenix, and the excuses are getting flimsier by the hour. She only works part-time, but then there was the shopping trip with Rosie – Phoenix would be so much better off at home than being dragged around the shops, she pleaded. Don't go then, I countered, but Lipsy's face told me what she thought of that idea – and the day before that it was an appointment with the hairdresser. On Wednesday, my late shift, it was lunch with Rob in the staff canteen – no babies allowed.

'Surely Rob would love to show Phee off to his

colleagues?' I reasoned.

Lipsy fixed me with a steely glare. 'His job is hanging by a thread, Mum. Do you really think bringing a screaming baby into the office says "Look at me, I'm a professional"?'

She had a point, but I still thought it was a shame.

'And will you please stop calling him Phee? You know it winds me up, why do you do it? He's my baby, mine and Rob's, and we've named him Phoenix. Deal with it.'

There is this strange role reversal going on at the moment. Lipsy is the mother, not only of Phoenix, but also of me. I daren't do anything that might upset her. It's like walking a tightrope – who knows what might upset her at any given moment? I think it's the stress of going back to work so soon, but there's no way on earth I'm going to be the one to tell her that.

Which is why I acquiesce now and take Phee – I mean, Phoenix – without further argument. She's doing her best, I know that. I do remember what it's like being a new mum. And it was worse for me – I didn't have a Robert to help out and change nappies and bring home the pennies and keep me warm at night.

I pointed this out to Lipsy once and once only. I won't dare mention it again.

'Thanks, Mum,' she says now, planting a kiss on my cheek. 'There's a stack of bread to be buttered if you get chance, and some of those pineapple and cheese things to make too. Grandma will be here soon, so you'll have a bit of help.'

'Great,' I tell her. 'That's just ...'

But she's already disappeared up the stairs.

*

Lipsy's party looks to be a sorry affair, what with Billy

travelling and most of Lipsy's friends at work or away at college. For my part, I'm still stunned that I managed to forget my own daughter's seventeenth birthday. I even offer to do an extra feed and stay the night, so both Lipsy and Robert can have a drink and a lie-in tomorrow.

In my defence, in years gone by it's never been necessary to remember Lipsy's birthday all on my own. Usually there is a weekly, and then daily, countdown to the big day, accompanied by a list of required presents, and often a demand for some kind of ridiculous themed party. Last year she had a horse riding party over in Brickhill woods – a disaster on four legs. The year before that it was a pink Cadillac and driving around Milton Keynes with six of her friends, sipping alcohol-free champagne (that's what she told me it was, anyway) and hanging out of the windows looking cool. Right. And wasn't the year before that the year of the make-over party when Rosie's mum phoned to accuse me of dressing her daughter up like a 'ho'? Lipsy had to explain that one to me, I have to confess.

But never, ever have I been allowed to forget the day before.

'Surprise!' calls my mother as she opens the door. My dad is behind her, smiling a private kind of a smile. Something about my mother's glittery tone sets my teeth on edge, and I have to make an extra effort to relax my shoulders.

'Oh,' Lipsy says, coming down the stairs, miraculously transformed into something ethereally beautiful. 'What a lovely surprise.'

I glare at her, and then at my mother. 'I thought it wasn't a surprise anymore?'

They ignore me and trot off to the kitchen, arm in arm.

After a minute or two I follow them. Better that than

let them talk about me behind my back.

The kitchen is, of course, a complete disaster area. I've spent the last half an hour ransacking the airing cupboard for something nice to wear. I was sure I'd left some clothes in there when I got kicked out. Not for the first time, I lament the loss of my old wardrobe full of smocks and tunic tops and baggy leggings that have stood the test of time and many expansions of my waistline. My current uniform of baggy combat trousers with a loose T-shirt hanging over them is hardly great party gear, but I guess it will have to do.

Note to self: time to go shopping for maternity clothes. I can't put it off forever.

'Mum,' Lipsy hisses behind me. 'Where are the sandwiches? What have you been doing?'

I ignore her and start to pile peanuts into little dishes.

'What's that smell?'

We all look at my father, whose nose is wrinkled up in disgust.

'I think it's the nappy bin,' I tell him. 'Lipsy, you have been emptying it, haven't you?'

'That's Rob's job, not mine,' she snaps.

'Where is Robert, anyway?' asks my mother.

Lipsy tells her he's on his way home from work early, and I bite my lip. His job can't be that much in jeopardy if he's finishing early for a party, can it? I peer in the bin and shake my head.

'Nope, it's not this that smells.'

Lipsy puts her nose to Phoenix's bottom, then looks at me with her eyebrows raised. 'I think it's a fresh one,' she says.

Ordinarily I'd have told her to do it herself, but I see my chance to escape for a while, and besides, I'm too tired to resist.

By the time I've got Phoenix into clean clothes – the nappy leaked, don't ask – the party is in full swing.

Robert is home, and two of Lipsy's old school friends are drinking cider in the kitchen. Rosie and Lipsy are sitting on the sofa with their heads together, and Mum and Dad are cuddling up to each other in the corner. Ugh. Is there anything worse than parents who are intent on showing the world how much they love each other? In your own lounge, in your favourite armchair, leaving their mark like two oversexed alley cats?

'Oh, there's the baby,' someone cries, and before long I'm surrounded by cooing girls and poor Phoenix is being patted and stroked like a piece of dough. Lipsy won't like this, I think, and sure enough she appears at my side to extract him from my grip as though I was about to offer him up for general consumption. Any minute now she'll be saying 'He's a baby, not a toy,' and the atmosphere of joyful praising of a cute new baby will be lost.

While no one is looking, I slip over to the presents that are laid out on the coffee table. With my back to the room, I deftly remove every last tag and pocket them. Now Lipsy won't know who bought her what, and my failure to buy her a present will go unnoticed.

But when I look up I see my dad watching me. Whoops. Not unnoticed after all. He extricates himself from my mother's grip and slides over to my side.

'How are you bearing up, sweetheart?'

And just like that he's reminded me that I'm here alone at my daughter's party when I should, in an ideal world, have a husband at my side. I should have travelled down this morning, finding time to stop on the way to pick up something thoughtful and clever from the motorway services, and then wafted in, resplendently beautiful in my brand new designer maternity dress. While Paul looked on proudly and told everyone how well the new job was going, how deliriously happy we were, how glad he was about the baby ...

Meanwhile, back in the real world, my feet are swollen and aching from all the hours I'm spending on them, I forgot my own daughter's birthday, and I'll be lucky to have a single item of clothing left soon if I continue to expand at this rate. I sigh and reach for the offered glass of Buck's Fizz.

'Dad,' I say, 'I honestly don't know where to begin.'

He smiles and gives me a hug. My mother glares at me over his shoulder, pointing to the glass in my hand and making cut-throat signs across her neck.

'Doesn't she drive you insane?' I ask my dad when he releases me and steps back.

'Who?'

'Your wife, of course. My mother. Come on, tell the truth – wasn't it just a tiny bit of a relief to be away from her for a while?'

He catches my expression and starts to laugh. 'No, actually. I missed her like crazy. You know, you two are so similar. I think that's the problem. That's why you clash all the time.'

Don't you just hate it when people say that? I had a boyfriend once whose best friend hated me. No, he really hated me. Took every opportunity to put me down. And whenever I tackled the boyfriend about it he'd whimper and say, 'Oh, you two are so alike. That's why you don't get on. It's such a shame.'

Yeah, a shame you just likened me to a complete git.

I shake my head at my dad and sip the Buck's Fizz. Yummy. Surely the tiny amount of alcohol in here will be offset by the super-healthy orange juice. Think of all that lovely vitamin C.

'You should take some time off, Stella,' my dad says. His tone is light but his expression is deadly serious. 'We're all really worried about you.'

I sigh. Not this again. 'I can't,' I tell him. 'I need the money.'

'We can lend you some money.'

'No, you can't. I know you two are struggling to get back on your feet as well. We all are. Besides, I need the job, Dad. I enjoy it. More than I realised. I'm glad I didn't give it up, actually. If anything good has come out of this sorry mess it's that I'm still there with those lovely people. You should come over and meet them one day, they hardly get any visitors, you know. There's this one old lady, Edie, she's just brilliant, she–'

'Yes, but you need friends your own age as well, Stella.' He pulls me into another hug, one arm wrapped around my shoulder. 'You need some outside interests, give you a sense of perspective. You need to find time for yourself. Look at your mum and me,' he adds, and I instinctively pull away. My mum and dad's relationship? No thank you. But Dad has other ideas and huddles me closer. 'Even after all we've been through, we still recognise that we need lives outside our marriage. Your mum's got her job now, and her baking and her sewing, and I've got my new job and my cycling. With Bonnie in America, and Paul ... Well, you really need to think about opening up your social circle some.'

He's right, but I'm not about to admit it. Besides, where the hell would I start? I could join the bridge club at Twilight, but that's about it. Instead I decide to tease him about his cycling. Because he hates it. Oh, I'm still a child at heart, and teasing my dad is still just about the most fun to be had without alcohol.

'You know what they call men like you, Dad? MAMILs.'

'Mammals?'

'No, M-A-M-I-L. It stands for middle-aged men in Lycra.'

'Oh, very funny.' He smiles uncertainly while I crease up. 'Your mum happens to think I look very sexy in my Lycra tights.'

Well, that sucks all the joy out of the moment. Yuk! There's an image you don't want in your mind on a Friday afternoon. On any afternoon.

'What?' he says, poking me in the ribs. 'You don't like me in tights or you don't like the thought of your mum *really liking* me in tights?'

'Both, actually. I'm a normal person. That kind of stuff disgusts me.'

'She really digs me in my padded cycling shorts too. She loves to run her hands up and down my–'

'Stop!' I shriek, prising him off me and running for cover.

He struts towards me, puffing out his chest. 'I'll give you MAMIL, young lady.'

This is what I love about my dad. Despite the fact that he's clearly mad – and likes to wear Lycra – he's so much fun.

I notice Lipsy smiling at me and shaking her head, and I raise my glass in a toast. She raises hers and then turns away. I wheel around, laughing, but my dad's not by my side anymore. He's crossed the room and taken up his former position, wedged against my mother, their hands entwined. I try to ignore the lump in my throat, and tell the room in general that I'm just popping upstairs for something.

No one hears me.

*

When I've pulled myself together enough to come back down, I find my dad holding court and tapping on his glass with a spoon. He clears his throat.

'If I could just have everyone's attention for a moment,' he says, smiling broadly, 'I'd like to say a few words.'

He has his arm around my mother, and Robert has

his arm around Lipsy, and one of Lipsy's school friends has an arm around Rosie. Her other friend is holding Phoenix, looking proud and terrified at the same time. I, however, have no one. This is, of course, all my own fault.

Dad starts talking about Lipsy and how proud he is of her now she's a mum, and I try to catch my mother's eye. She looks worried, a look I got so used to seeing last year I became immune to it, but one that's been mercifully absent since Dad came home. But now her eyes are tipping down at the edges, and her fingers are twirling furiously at her hair. Is it my imagination or is she deliberately avoiding looking at me? We haven't talked since she stormed out on lunch, which is clearly why I knew nothing about this party. Or maybe she did tell me and I just plain forgot. It's not like I haven't got a lot on my mind.

I'm about to wave my hand to get her attention when my dad clears his throat again and the room falls silent.

'Maggie,' he says to my mum, and then to my astonishment he falls down on one knee, grabs her hand, and holds it up to his cheek. 'Maggie, I love you. Thank you for being mine, for everything you've put up with over the years. Will you marry me, Maggie, all over again?'

'Yes,' she whispers, and she leans down and kisses him full on the lips.

'Get a room,' shouts one of Lipsy's friends. My dad smiles and stands up, and everyone starts to clap.

Everyone except me, that is.

'You're married already,' I tell them, stepping forward. I'm pointing out the obvious, seeing as everyone else in the room seems to have gone a bit crazy.

Dad pulls my mum in a little closer. You couldn't fit a razor blade between them. 'It's called renewing your vows, Stella. It's a gesture, to show the world that we're putting the past behind us, moving on.'

'Well, why don't you just go on a cruise, like normal people?' I say sourly.

'Not a romantic bone in her body, is there?' Lipsy says behind me. I swing round to look at her.

'That's not fair. I can be romantic. But I don't get this, is all. It's just drawing attention to it all over again. Can't we for once just put the past behind us? Why keep dragging it up like this?'

'No one's dragging anything up, Stella,' says my mum. 'Except you.'

'What do you mean?' But I know what she means, and I hate to admit she's right. Is this what she was looking so worried about? My reaction? I'm sick of being the baddie in this family.

I decide to have one last attempt at sanity. 'Look, I get it that you want to renew your vows, it's lovely, really. But isn't it better to do it quietly? Privately? Do you really want everyone looking at you, Mum? Thinking about what you did?'

'Stella.'

'No, Dad. It needs to be said. Why do you think Billy's gone away again? Why do you think he's so loath to come back? None of us thought it would be easy when you came home, but the last thing we expected was to keep having our noses rubbed in it like this.'

'Keep your voice down,' Lipsy hisses, and I look around to see multiple pairs of eyes staring at me. I take a deep breath and will myself to calm down. Getting worked up is not good for the baby.

My mum sips her wine and places it carefully on the window sill. 'Howard' she says, addressing my dad and ignoring the rest of us, 'I'm not surprised Stella isn't happy about it. After all, weddings aren't going to be her favourite topic right now, are they? Not after the mess she made of her own.'

Chapter 14

From: lipsyhill@mad4mail.com
To: paulsmart@smarthomes.net
Date: 16 March 2012 23:45

Dear Paul,

I know when you phoned me a few weeks ago I asked you not to call again, and I'm sorry if I was rude. Thank you for the birthday card and the money you sent. That was very thoughtful.

I hope things are going well for you in Derby with the new job etc. I'm emailing because I thought you might want to know how my mum is. The thing is, she's not too good. That job of hers is hard work, and she's very tired and very sad. It was my birthday party today and I think she was missing you a lot. She got snappy with my granddad and grandma, who have just announced they are renewing their vows at the end of June. I think it's because she was reminded of the wedding and feels bad that she called it off.

I feel bad that she's had to move out of the house, and I wondered if you are planning to stay up there permanently or are thinking of coming back anytime soon. Robert and I have been talking and we feel that if the two of you were to just sit down together and talk you could work things out. You always have before.

There are things you don't know, Paul. But it's not for me to tell you. I just wondered if you might be coming back to Milton Keynes, or if you have gone for good.

Lipsy

From: paulsmart@smarthomes.net
To: lipsyhill@mad4mail.com
Date: 17 March 2012 00:16

Dear Lipsy,

Thanks for your email. It was a surprise to hear from you, but I'm glad you got the card and the money. How is your baby? I hope you're not finding it all too much, and are getting plenty of sleep. Please say hello to Robert from me. It's something I regret very much that I didn't get to say goodbye to you all properly.

I'd very much like to know what you are talking about when you say: "There are things you don't know". What things? Is it to do with the real reason your mum called off the wedding? I really think I should know, don't you? It doesn't seem fair to keep me in the dark. Does she have someone else? That's the only thing I can think of. I did write to her at the address you gave me but I didn't get a reply. Perhaps you could send me the address again, just in case I got it down wrong. In fact, I think I must have written it down wrong, because that part of Bletchley is a bit rough, actually. But if she got the letter and chose not to answer, that says it all, really, don't you think?

I'd prefer it if you kept this to yourself, Lipsy – can I trust you to do that? – but things aren't going too well here. This job isn't exactly what I thought it would be – I think Tom might have overestimated the need for rental housing in Derby. Really, it's quite depressing, and I can't seem to set my mind to it. It must be easier for your mum, being around her family and everything familiar, but for me coming here – where I should have been coming with my wife – it's been very, very hard. I'm stunned that I haven't heard from her, to be honest. At least a phone call or even a text to explain, never mind answering my letter.

Which only leads me to believe, despite what you said in your email, that she is perfectly happy with her decision and has no intention of changing her mind. Or even talking to me about it. If I hear from her, I might reconsider. But until I do, I don't feel I can contact her again. And I think that's what you were asking, wasn't it?

It's really up to her, Lipsy, not me. If she wants to get in touch she knows where I am. I'm sorry that she seems unwell and is working too hard. But it is, after all, only her choice.

Best wishes, Paul

*

'Hold on, Stella. Just stay there and I'll get help.'

'No. No, don't go anywhere. Could you just ... could you just hold back my hair for me? That would be a real help. If you don't mind terribly.'

Edie obliges, and I lean back over the sink with a groan. So much for the morning sickness ending soon. It seems to be getting worse if anything. And now I'm subjecting an old lady to my vomiting – in her own bathroom, for goodness sake. Please tell me it doesn't get any more humiliating than this.

'Hello? Anyone home?'

'In here, Franklin. Come on in.'

Oh, Jesus. You couldn't make this up.

'Stella? Is that Stella under there, Edie? What on earth is wrong with the girl?'

'She's being sick, Franklin, dear. Could you be a pet and pass me some of those baby wipes by the bed. I think I've got some on my slippers.'

I'm about to apologise when another wave hits me, and I'm doubled up and retching by the time Franklin retrieves the wipes. Wordlessly, he hands me one and I dab at my mouth and chin.

'Glass of water?' Edie asks. I nod, weakly.

Franklin helps me over to a chair, then stands back with his hands on his hips, a puzzled frown between his bright blue eyes.

'Is she ill?' he says to Edie.

'Sort of,' she replies. They look at each other. It's like I'm not even in the room. Franklin nods and taps his nose.

'Got it. Right, I'm off. Hope you're feeling better soon, Stella, my dear.' At the door he turns and gives me one of his mischievous twinkles. 'In about six months or so, eh?'

Edie laughs, and I turn to her, incredulous. 'What, are you two psychic or something? Do you talk with your minds?'

'Oh, don't be silly. It's obvious, isn't it?'

'I hope not,' I groan, wiping the sweat off my forehead with the hem of my tabard. 'I can't cope with Velma finding out.'

'Why?' asks Edie. 'She can't sack you, can she? I thought there were laws against that sort of thing these days.'

'She won't sack me, no. But she'll make my life a misery. She'll give me all the shitty jobs to do, the worst shifts and the heavy lifting. And you just know she'll put me on bed pan duty for a month if she hears about the morning sickness. It would be her idea of fun.'

Edie tuts and returns to her slippers. There are little white marks on the navy velour where she's rubbed at them with the wipes.

'I'm sorry about the splashing, Edie. I'll buy you some new slippers.'

'You know what, Stella? I didn't like them anyway. I'm going to upgrade to some of those slouchy knitted ones that are all the rage these days. I could do with something a bit trendier. Could you pick me some up next time you're at the shops? You're not to pay for them, mind. I'll give you the money. No arguments.'

I nod, smiling. The thought of Edie in "trendy" slippers cheers me up no end. 'Well, all right. But next time you just stand well back, OK?'

Edie agrees and tops up my water glass.

'I'd better be getting back to work,' I tell her, trying to stand. My legs are like jelly and I feel lightheaded. I wobble and then flop back into her easy chair.

'Don't worry. Franklin's gone to create a diversion so you can have a rest.'

I look at her in amazement. 'How do you know that? Did he tell you all that with just one look? You two are so ...'

I trail off. What I was going to say might come across as inappropriate. I was going to say they are so sweet together. But if my suspicions about Edie's true feelings for Franklin are correct, she might not appreciate my noticing.

'Have you heard from Paul?' Edie asks. She's sitting on the edge of her bed with her hands tucked in under her legs. Her feet don't even reach the floor. I shake my head.

'Just that one letter.'

'And you still haven't answered it?'

'What can I say? Besides, I can't believe he practically accused me of seeing someone else. And told me I was old. Too old to have any more children, anyway.' Edie and I both look down at my stomach. The tabard hides it well, as do the baggy clothes, but under all this I'm definitely starting to show.

'You can hardly blame him for clutching at straws, Stella,' Edie points out reasonably. 'You didn't give him much to go on.'

Our ears perk up at a noise in the corridor. Footsteps, lots of them, running past, and shouting.

'That'll be Franklin hard at work,' she says with a grin. I laugh and roll my eyes. Goodness knows what he's up to.

'You'll have to tell him one day, Stella,' Edie says when the noise dies away. I let the silence drift. I really don't know how to answer.

Franklin bursts into the room, saving me from further interrogation, his eyes bright and full of life.

'Oh, that was hysterical,' he announces, flopping into the chair opposite mine. Edie watches him with open admiration. I wonder how he can fail to notice.

'What did you do?' I ask, tentatively trying to stand again.

He looks around at Edie and grins widely. 'I didn't do anything. But poor old Violet has lost her false teeth again, and she swears that Bernie's taken them as a practical joke. She's had the whole staff out searching for them. Said she'd call the newspapers if they weren't found in the next hour.'

'Franklin!' I'm shocked. 'You didn't steal Violet's teeth? That's taking it a bit far, isn't it?'

'Don't worry, Stella,' Edie says, laughing. 'I'm sure Violet knows exactly where they are. She's probably hidden them under her pillow. Not sure Bernie will be too pleased, though.'

'He can handle it,' Franklin says. 'He plays enough practical jokes around here. About time he learned his lesson.'

'Two birds, one stone.'

'Exactly.'

I watch the two of them, amazed. 'You even got Violet in on it?' I say to Franklin. 'I just can't believe it. Why?'

Now it's their turn to look amazed. 'I can't believe you have to ask, Stella dear. You are the best thing to happen to this place in a decade, and we were all so happy when you came back to us. We couldn't bear to lose you again, so we need to look after you. Especially now. In your ... condition.'

Edie looks meaningfully at Franklin, then raises her eyebrows at me. I sigh and then nod.

'Feel free to tell him, Edie. And Violet and the others. But please ask them to keep it to themselves. I really don't want Velma to find out, so it's probably best if none of the staff know yet either. Let me keep this quiet as long as I can, OK?'

She nods. 'It'll make it easier to cover for you, if the others know too.'

'I know.' I give her a quick hug. Her bones feel fragile and far too small. I turn to Franklin and tell him thanks. He shrugs as if it was nothing, but his face beams up at me all the same.

When I leave the room, they are looking at each other but not talking. I wonder if they communicate like that all the time, if it's easier than words in a place like this. And I wonder if Paul and I would have ended up like that given time; in tune, calm and comfortable, rubbing along day by day.

As I walk down the corridor towards the staffroom, I think about Edie and how much she's helped me already, and I think about how I can return the favour. Maybe it's not too late for her to find love. Maybe I could lend a helping hand.

Or maybe not. My track record in the romance department is not exactly flawless. Probably I should leave well alone.

Shame, though. They really do make the perfect couple.

*

I get through my shift with no more mishaps, and at five past five I'm ready to head for home. I stop by the library on my way through town and borrow two thrillers. This is not the time for fiction of the romantic variety. Home Bargains is open, so I pop in and buy a bright blue lamp, a red knitted throw for my bed, and a fluffy green cushion in the shape of a pair of arms. It's one way to get a hug, I suppose. As I approach the checkouts, I throw a writing pad and envelopes into my basket. Just in case. And then I head for Marks and Spencer. All this hard work and throwing up makes a girl hungry.

The new stuff brightens up my bedsit no end, and I waste no time in nuking the ready meal in my mini microwave, sitting down on my bed to eat it, a book propped up on my knees. As I tuck in to the sausage and mash with gravy I feel an odd sensation in my stomach. It's like a bubbly feeling, champagne bubbles rising to the surface, but tickly too. It stops, and then starts again. I put down my tray, pull up my top, and take a look at my belly.

It's looking pretty rounded, more so than yesterday I'm sure, but there's nothing on my skin. Nothing itchy or tickly or …

Oh my God. Of course! In a flash I realise what this feeling is. It's the baby. Kicking – or what passes for kicking at four months or so. Fluttering, really. Tiny little fluttery movements, invisible to the eye.

'Hello,' I whisper.

Funny if the baby said hello back.

But maybe in a way it is saying hello. Hello, I'm here, and I'm growing. Look at me.

Tears spring to my eyes. I stroke my stomach and whisper hello again. There's a baby in there, a real little person. Funny how easy it is to be pregnant, to be sick and feeling really ill, watching yourself thicken around the middle, but to somehow forget that there is an actual baby inside you.

I look at the writing paper and envelopes still lying by the kettle where I dropped them earlier. Paul, you should be here to feel this, to experience this with me. I should have pushed through your fears, tried harder to tell you the truth. Or just told you, and lived with the consequences.

I'm living with them now, anyway.

The bubbles start up again, and suddenly I'm laughing. From tears to laughter, as if it really were champagne, as if there was nothing but me and my baby: no problems, no trauma, just a happy future stretching out ahead of us. Why, I can't imagine how I've felt so lonely for the last few weeks. I wasn't alone at all. In fact, I'll never be alone again. Not for at least sixteen years.

I lie back on the bed and place my hands gently across my stomach, fingers entwined. And in my mind, I begin to compose my letter to Paul. It's time to answer him, I think. It's time to let him know.

Chapter 15

I'm still in the throes of my epiphany when I arrive at the hospital on Monday morning for my scan. Today I should get a real actual due date, and from that I'll be able to start planning. I feel like planning. I feel like my future is kind of exciting.

Which is why I don't feel completely depressed to be the only woman without an eager man in tow. I take a seat next to a tall couple wearing matching sweaters. They turn and give me identical bright smiles.

Then I think about the mileage Paul and I would have got out of those two and my mood dips just a little.

I remind myself that I'm not alone because I have Bump with me. And I remind myself that he or she will always be with me now, no matter what. Until he or she is about sixteen, of course, and decides I'm embarrassing and useless and fit only for scorn.

Which leaves me with sixteen years of pure, unadulterated neediness. And this time, I'm going to love it. That's the thing about becoming a mum the second time around: you know how quickly all the good bits pass. Lipsy's baby years seemed to pass in a flash, and before I knew it she was an inquisitive toddler, then a loud and confident schoolgirl, and then ... well, then it gets kind of messy. One minute my daughter is kind and helpful, into ponies and following the rules and making sure her homework is done on time, the next she's replaced by a sullen teenager who barely tolerates me and is only interested in boys and how many new spots she's got this week. Then, in the blink of an eye, this Lipsy is replaced by mum-to-be Lipsy, wholesome and thoughtful and grateful for the smallest gift. How I wish I'd paid more attention to those lovely afternoons we spent painting her bedroom side by side, sharing jokes and silences, and Lipsy grabbing my hand to rest it on her tummy when her baby kicked.

Now she's been replaced again, of course, by grumpy, workaholic Lipsy, constantly complaining and often too tired to raise a smile, let alone a laugh.

'Oh, *when* will he be able to sit up on his *own*?' she wailed down the phone last night. 'My arms are dropping off with holding him.'

Soon enough, I thought. Too soon. Because isn't that the cruel joke about having a child? What is sheer torture to go through at the time becomes a wonderful experience you missed out on looking back. Hindsight is most painful of all with children. Every stage of their life looks golden over your shoulder, impossible up close.

But this time I'm going to get it right. I'll savour every single second. Sleepless nights? Bring them on. Toddler tantrums? What fun! No moaning from me.

'Stella Hill?'

I'm it. I push myself up from the plastic chair, smile at Mr and Mrs Matching Sweaters, and follow the nurse down a short corridor. She smiles at me and says, 'No daddy today, then? At work is he?' For a minute I think she's talking about my dad, and I wonder if I was supposed to bring him with me, and why.

But then I realise my mistake and feel like an idiot.

Then I feel pissed off. What if there wasn't a daddy? What if he was sick, or dead, or had left me to go and live on a commune in Australia? What if I'd got pregnant by a one-night stand and had no clue who the daddy even was?

Or what if I'd ditched the poor daddy at the altar because he insisted he didn't want any more children?

I bite my lip and follow her instructions to climb up onto the bed, raise my top up to my chest, and relax.

Relaxing ... how do you do that again? Isn't it what comes after a chilled bottle of dry white wine and a massage? Not what happens while you're having some kind of clear jelly rubbed onto your tummy while lying on a padded table about as wide as a scaffolding plank.

'This might feel a bit cold,' she says cheerfully as she applies the instrument she's clearly just pulled out of the fridge to my slippery stomach and begins to move it up and down.

I watch the black screen on the wall anxiously. There's nothing on it that resembles a baby, but ... wait! What was that?

'Ah, there we are,' says the nurse. She pokes the instrument hard into my tummy and points out a head and a foot, and shows me the heartbeat – which is terrifyingly fast and makes my own heart pound in sympathy.

'Do we want to know the sex of the baby?' she asks, writing some notes on my file. I get the impression it's nothing to her either way. I think about Paul, and wonder what he would say if he was here right now.

He should be here. I have no right to keep this from him. Whatever my reasons, I know deep down there will be a time when I'll have to account for this, for denying him this, and the thought makes my insides squirm.

'No,' I tell her. 'No, I don't.'

At least that way we'll both be in the dark. Sort of.

It's over far too quickly – I could happily have watched that screen all day. Soon she's handing me a scratchy paper towel to wipe the jelly from my stomach and turning off the machine.

'Here's something to show to your family.'

I look at the blurry photo the nurse hands me. My baby. A new life. Photographic evidence.

Maybe I should send Paul a copy with his letter.

'Miss Hill?' says the nurse, and then she smiles and reaches out to grab a tissue from her desk. 'Here, take this. You'll be all right. It's an emotional experience, seeing your baby for the first time. Wait until you meet him or her for real!'

I blow my nose into the tissue and manage a feeble grin. I don't tell her I've been through all this before, or that little more than a month ago I watched my own daughter give birth to my grandson. Instead I climb down from the bed carefully and pull up my jeans. The requirement for a full bladder means I'm now bursting for a pee, and I hop from foot to foot while the nurse consults her chart.

When she tells me the baby's due on or around the thirteenth of August I give her a wry smile. Like Paul said, lucky I'm not superstitious.

'Good luck,' calls the nurse as I hurry from the room.

'Thanks,' I say. I sure am going to need it.

Chapter 16

I've just stepped out of the shower when the doorbell rings. Lipsy and Rob are at work and I'm babysitting Phoenix on my day off. As usual. The shower in the shared bathroom at the bedsit is worse than useless so I tend to make the most of the facilities whenever I'm back home. I think of it as payment for my child minding services. And after all, it is my shower.

I quickly throw on my vest top and knickers, then wrap myself in Lipsy's dressing gown and skip downstairs to answer.

The last person I expect to see when I open the door is Sharon.

She looks like she's just stepped off a film set, all glowing skin and freshly brushed hair, skin-tight jeans and an artfully distressed brown leather jacket. Do all tall, well-built women feel this way when they see a skinny, beautiful, well put together siren, or is it just me? I'd quite like to strangle her.

'Sharon,' I gush, 'what a lovely surprise. Come on in.'

'Stella?' She seems put off her stride by the sight of me, but it's so fleeting I think I probably imagined it. 'I'm so sorry to call by unannounced,' she says, stepping into the hallway and taking up as much room as a peanut, 'but I was wondering if we could have a quick chat. Is that OK?'

'Yes, of course it is,' I say warmly. 'Come on through to the kitchen.'

The kitchen is in turmoil as usual, but I bite my

tongue to stop myself apologising for it. 'Tea?' I ask pleasantly. 'Coffee?'

'Just a glass of water for me,' she says. 'Spring, if possible,' she adds as I reach for the tap.

I ignore her and fill a dusty glass from the cold tap, putting on my best fake smile as I hand it to her. Then I sit, trying to cover up my enormous legs with the dressing gown, and at the same time trying desperately to hold in my stomach.

'I've tried you on your home number,' she says, staring at me with a strange look in her eyes. 'There never seems to be any answer.'

'Lipsy and Robert work very hard. And in the evenings they tend to turn the phone off so it doesn't wake Phoenix up.'

'Ah, yes of course. Where is he? Can I see him?'

'He's asleep,' I tell her. I don't say if she can see him or not.

There's a short, uncomfortable silence, and then she says, 'It's so good to see you, Stella. I'm sure I heard that you weren't living here anymore, but I must have got that wrong ...'

'No. You got it right. I'm babysitting.'

'Ah.'

I narrow my eyes. Seems like I didn't imagine her surprise after all. 'So, if you didn't expect to find me here, why did you come round to have a word with me?'

'Actually,' she says with a disarming laugh, 'I was hoping to talk to Lipsy.'

'About?'

The word comes out harsher than I'd planned, and she jumps a little, then laughs again.

'Oh, just stuff. But it can wait.'

I don't think so. There can't be many topics she has in common with Lipsy, and try as I might I can only think of one.

Paul Smart.

'If it's about Paul, I'd rather you talk to me,' I tell her stiffly. 'Lipsy has a lot on her plate right now and I don't want her to be dragged into this.'

She looks off for a moment, as if finding it hard to think of the right words. I'm not fooled. She knows exactly what she wants to say, and I'm not looking forward to hearing it.

'Yes,' she says, sweetly, 'you're probably right. It is you I should be talking to.' She takes a little sip of water, wrinkling up her pert nose as if it's polluted.

I don't respond. Let her sweat. Sporty girl like her, she should be used to it.

'Paul's asked me and Hannah to visit,' she says eventually. 'Hannah is really missing him, and I thought it might be good for her to spend Easter there. But it's a long way for her to go on her own.'

I work it out in my head. 'Hasn't he been seeing her on his weekends?'

Sharon shakes her head. 'He's been too busy getting settled in. But he's really keen to have her visit. And me too, of course ...'

She tails off, but I can fill in the blanks. I think back to half-term and the way Sharon foisted herself on Paul and Hannah, and I wonder if she's doing it again now.

Or maybe it's Paul who's instigating it.

The thought makes me feel completely sick.

I take a deep breath, then bend over quickly, worried she'll see my stomach. Sharon must not find out about the baby. When Paul finally hears about it, it has to come from me.

'Well, I hope you have a nice time, Sharon, but I really can't imagine what business it is of mine. Or Lipsy's, for that matter.'

'No,' she says vaguely, 'it's just that ...'

And as she tails off again, looking out of the window

with her perfect hair catching the light, I suddenly realise what's going on here.

God, I am such an idiot sometimes.

'You've come to make sure the coast is clear. You've come to find out if it's really over between Paul and me so you can have a stab at him. I'm right, aren't I? That's what this is all about.'

She flinches, but soon recovers. Waving her hands as if to waft away her own crassness, she says, 'I wouldn't have put it quite like that, Stella. But it would help me to know why you broke up with him. It might make it easier for him to move on, too. If he knew.'

Is that what he wants, I wonder? To move on? Not to reconcile or sort things out. I figured he'd still be waiting for me to respond to his letter – it's taken me this long to get past the stuff he wrote in it, for one thing – but it's only been a month.

I think about my own letter, half-finished in my bag. It's what you'd call a work in progress – so far I've managed five words, and two of them are Dear Paul. The other three? I miss you. I guess it's as good a way as any to begin.

But if he's moving on, maybe I'm wasting my time. And if he's moving on in the direction of Sharon, I'm definitely wasting my time.

'Did he specifically ask you to go and visit him with Hannah?' I have to know. I think back to how easily I accepted Sharon going along with them last time. Maybe I was wrong to be so trusting. Could it be that she's always wanted him? It was Paul who ended it, after all, but she still chose to go on and have his baby. Without him.

Something the women in Paul's life seem to do a lot.

And then getting back in touch with him after all those years. Always round his flat, popping in with a form to sign for Hannah's school or an invitation to a parents' evening or to drop off some photos. Always wearing something skin-tight or super-short, hair and make-up just so, that brittle smile of hers fixed to her face like a mask.

Sharon smiles disarmingly and pats my hand. 'You mustn't get worked up about it, Stella. After all, you've had your shot at him. If he needs a bit of comforting ... Well, let's just say that even if he didn't ask me outright, he sounded relieved when I offered to come up with Hannah. We're staying for the whole of Easter. I didn't have to twist his arm.'

I snatch my hand away and jump up. Kettle. Fill it. Give me something to do, time to think.

How can she sit there and look so smug?

'Don't you think it's a bit soon?' I ask without turning around. 'It's only been a month or so.'

'Are you saying you think you two might get back together?' Her voice has hardened. I stare down at my hands for a moment. Nails bitten down to stumps, fingers white with tension. Then I turn and look at her, my hands on my hips, my expression tight.

'He never talks about you, you know,' she sneers. 'I've asked him about what happened, but he just says it's over. He says it was your decision and that's that. In fact, I hope you won't think I'm speaking out of turn here, but ...'

For a moment I wonder why she's stopped talking. She's staring at something; her mouth is opening and closing but no words are coming out.

Which is a relief, frankly.

Until I realise what she's staring at.

Ah.

'Stella?' She's staring at my stomach. My beautiful bonny round bump, displayed to its full advantage and peeping out between the top of my knickers and the bottom of my vest top. I pull the dressing gown back over it and tie the belt more tightly. It is, of course, too late.

'Are you ...? Are you ...?'

I'm tempted to make a joke of it. 'I've been comforting myself with pies,' I could say. Or, 'It's just really bad wind.' But I don't think she'd believe me. Annoyingly, I can feel my eyes tearing up again – what is it with these bloody hormones? I turn back to the kettle, and the noise as it comes to the boil drowns out whatever she says next.

'Stella?'

I jump – she's standing right behind me. She takes my hand and leads me back to the kitchen table. I don't pull away this time.

'Does he know?' she asks. Her voice is barely a whisper. I shake my head. She nods, and an expression passes over her face that's hard to read.

She makes the tea in silence, and I watch her skinny back and try not to think about how perfect she is for Paul. They both love the outdoors: running, skiing, mountain biking. They have Hannah, of course, which is a bond I've never seriously considered before. What if they do get back together? I'll only have myself to blame, but when the baby comes, what then? Then I'll be in Sharon's place, and she'll be with Paul. In my place.

It's all just too confusing.

What if I tell Paul about the baby now, today, and ask him if we can give it another go? What if I just ring him right now and ask him? For the sake of the baby. And what if he says yes? I need Paul to be with me because he *wants* to be, not because he has to be, or even because he should be. Which has always been the problem. If I tell him now, how will I ever know for sure?

And if I don't tell him? Well, that's not an option anymore, is it? Sharon will tell him as soon as she leaves this house. Or maybe she'll wait until she gets to Derby and break it to him gently. After all, she knows how hard it was for him to find out about Hannah after eight years of secrecy. She won't want to risk him going through that again. If Sharon's set her sights on Paul, there'll be no more secrets. She's far too wily for that.

We sip our tea in silence. I have no idea what to say to her now, and she seems lost in thought. I'm starting to wonder if either of us will ever speak again when I hear Phoenix stirring upstairs. I send a message up to the ceiling: *Thank you.*

'I'd better go and see to him,' I tell her. My voice is croaky. I clear my throat.

'Right.' She nods. Without the false smile fixed to her face, Sharon is actually very pretty. It stabs at my heart to think about it, but I'm fairly sure she and Paul will be happy together. And maybe having her around will help him get over me. I shouldn't begrudge him that, should I?

Sharon puts one foot outside the front door, then stops and turns around.

'Stella, before I go, there's something I want to say.'

'What?' I'm so tired now I just want to get rid of her and go and lie down in the nursery with Phoenix. There's this overarching sense of anticlimax.

'I don't blame you.'

'Right. What?'

'I don't blame you, for not telling him.'

'What do you mean?'

'Nothing. I understand, is all. And I just wanted ... it doesn't matter.' She turns away with an infuriating little shake of her head and heads for her car.

'Wait,' I call. 'Sharon, wait. What do you understand?'

With nothing on my feet and most of my body on show I am not going to run after her. Nor am I going to stand on my doorstep shrieking. I call her name once more, and she stops and turns to look at me. Her eyes are full of a sympathy I don't want to see.

'I'm sorry,' she says. 'Really, really sorry.'

Then she jumps in her car and drives away.

Chapter 17

Phoenix is the reason I finally close the door. Phoenix is the reason I manage to pull on proper clothes and clear my head and get on with the rest of my day. Phoenix, and the baby inside me, who is suddenly active, bouncing and bubbling away in there as if it can sense that something just turned its world upside down.

By the time Lipsy arrives home I'm calm and together.

'Jesus, Mum, what the hell happened to you? You look terrible.'

Or so I thought.

I tell her about Sharon's visit. Holding Phoenix on my lap, making a game out of bouncing him from one knee to the other, helps to keep me calm.

'That's just horrible.' My daughter's expression is almost as shaken as my own. I get to my feet and give her a hug.

'It's OK, sweetie. It doesn't matter. If they are getting back together, I guess it just means I did the right thing after all. I mean, maybe I had a sixth sense or something.'

Or maybe Paul's downright refusal to start a family with me was because of Sharon. Who knows what happened between them while they were stuck in a caravan together night after night. Come to think of it, all my problems started around about the same time …

'No, Mum,' Lipsy says. She looks like she's about to cry. 'It is not OK. It's not OK at all.'

I'm comforted, if a little surprised, by her distress. While we get Phoenix ready for his bath I feel closer to her than I have for a long time. 'I love you,' I tell her when she comes into the bathroom carrying fresh towels.

'I love you too,' she says. Her face is drawn; the skin under her eyes is purple. She's working too hard. Well, aren't we all? But I'm not going to spoil the equilibrium by telling her.

We kneel on the bathroom floor side by side, throwing water over Phoenix, who giggles delightedly. Seeing him in his funny little bath chair makes me realise how much he's grown.

'He's so long,' I say to Lipsy. 'Look – his head barely reached the top of that a couple of weeks ago. He won't fit in it soon.'

She smiles. 'I'll put it to one side for you, shall I? For the baby.'

I give her a sideways hug. 'You'll always be my baby, you know that, don't you?'

'I know. It's all right, Mum. I know.'

I hope she does know. Sometimes it's easy to get a little lost, to forget what's really important and to lose sight of the people who care about you. Something I know all about. But as I sit back on my heels and watch her wash her baby's hair, shielding his eyes with an upturned hand, I realise that Lipsy is nothing like me. She's capable and strong. She knows what she wants and she always gets it. And she's not a baby anymore, either. She's a woman, a mother, and a damned good one too.

*

As soon as Robert walks in the door, Lipsy issues him with a list of instructions and drags me to the pub. I try to protest – I've got an early start tomorrow – but Lipsy's having none of it. We order non-alcoholic spritzers and I settle into a booth opposite the bar, shuffling my bottom along the seat until I'm facing straight out. Lipsy slides in beside me and slaps two packets of crisps on the table.

'Dinner,' she says, laughing. She picks up her glass and holds it out to be chinked. 'Cheers! Here's to having a wonderful man who's quite happy to put the baby to bed while his girlfriend lives it up at the pub.'

I stare at her, my own glass frozen mid-air.

'Oops,' she says, wrinkling up her nose. 'Guess that was a bit insensitive.'

I give her a wan smile. My non-alcoholic spritzer is a pale imitation of the real thing.

'I'm glad you still think Robert is a wonderful man, though. Sometimes lately, with you two rowing a lot, I've been worried that things aren't right between you. You know, with the age difference and all ...'

Lipsy laughs and shakes her head. 'Oh, Mum. You are so old-fashioned. All couples argue, it's healthy. And Rob is perfect for me. He keeps me grounded. Really, you have nothing to worry about. We really are blissfully happy.'

Oh, well. At least someone is. Maybe that was the problem with Paul and me: we didn't argue enough.

Lipsy puts down her drink and sighs. 'But, happy as we are, I guess we can't go on like this forever, can we?'

'Like what?'

'With us living in the house and you in a bedsit. I mean, I can see it's not fair, you know. I'm not a monster.'

'Who said you were a monster?'

'Grandma. Well, not a monster exactly. But she said I shouldn't be letting you live in "that place" in "your condition". I'm sorry, Mum. I guess I've been really selfish.'

'It's not that bad,' I lie. 'Once you get used to it and

all.'

'Don't get mad with her, OK, but Grandma said she drove past your place last week and there were drug dealers hanging around outside.'

'Oh, that would have been Stig and Barry. They're all right once you get to know them.'

'Mum! You're on first name terms with the resident druggies?' She drops her head into her hands and groans. 'It's worse than I thought.'

'Well, they aren't druggies, Lipsy. Dealers never take their own drugs. They're far too sensible.'

'Listen to yourself, Mum. What's happened to you? One minute you're the bride to be, the next minute you're pregnant, single, and living in squalor. I blame myself entirely – Rob and I should never have made you move out.' She bashes her fist on the wooden table and I wince. 'I honestly expected you would get back with Paul in no time. We both did. We all did. That's why I gave him your address when he phoned, that's why I even …'

'What?'

'Nothing,' she says morosely. 'It doesn't matter. But listen, are you sure about him and Sharon? I just can't see him going back with her. He loves you so much, Mum.'

'Loved me. Past tense. No matter what the rights or the wrongs of what I did, Lipsy, he's never going to forgive me for walking out on our own wedding. And I don't blame him.'

'But it was only because of what he said to you. Because you were confused about the baby, about the future. If you could just tell him that, just explain …'

'I didn't expect him to disappear so quickly afterwards, that's for sure. I kind of thought he might stick around and sort it out. But when you think about it, Paul's always been a bachelor at heart. That's what kept us apart so long, and it was only when he found out about Hannah he began to think differently. I guess asking him to start a family with me was pushing it too far.'

'But if you'd just told him the truth?' Lipsy's eyes are wide and innocent. Uncomprehending. How can I expect her to understand? I barely understand myself.

'We've been through this, Lipsy. Once I knew how he felt, it was too late. Don't you see? I couldn't trap him. I loved him too much.'

'Loved. Past tense?' she says, eyebrows raised.

I shrug. 'What difference does it make? He's made it perfectly clear how he feels about having a family, and even if I did tell him about the baby – even if I told him right now and begged him to reconsider – there's no guarantee he'd come back to me. But even if he did, I'd never know if it was for the right reasons. No, Lipsy. I just need to focus on what's important and leave Paul and Sharon to it.'

'Isn't Paul important to you anymore?'

'Of course he is.' I can't keep the sadness out of my voice. Attempting to keep positive is wearing me down. 'But right now there are more important things to worry about. You and Phee, for example, and the baby of course. And figuring out where we're all going to be living in about four months' time.'

For once she doesn't berate me for calling him Phee, but I don't know whether this is a good sign or not. A group of young lads wearing fake stag antlers push through the door and herd around the bar. The noise level increases and someone turns up the music to compensate. I look at my phone to check the time.

'But he wouldn't really go back to her, would he?' Lipsy says. I have to strain to hear her; she seems to be talking mainly to herself.

'I think if he does it will be because of Hannah. When

you have a child with someone you're linked forever. I guess you'll always feel something for that person.'

As I say the words I wonder about Paul and his sense of duty. And I wonder what his sense of duty will demand when Sharon tells him about my baby.

How long will it take for him to get in touch?

And what will I do if he doesn't?

'Sounds like a trap,' Lipsy says, wrinkling her nose. 'If Robert did the dirty on me I'd never get back with him, child or no child. I'd rather be on my own.'

She means it as well. I sip my spritzer and make a silent wish that Robert never falls foul of Lipsy. He won't know what's hit him.

'Come here,' I say, pulling her in for another cuddle. But the guys at the bar are giving Lipsy the once over, and she pushes me away, embarrassed.

It's still light when Lipsy and I head back to the car, and I drive the short distance to drop her off. The clocks went forward last weekend, giving us an extra hour of daylight, and only now is the sky starting to turn that dusky purple that makes everything look fuzzy. Before long it will be summer, and I'll be wafting around in cotton dresses, showing off my bump to the world, making the most of the sunshine. A feeling washes over me, and it takes a couple of minutes to place it.

Happiness. Just a tiny sliver of happiness, bubbling up in my chest. Or maybe it's excitement. Same thing. As I pull up outside number three Chaplin Grove I'm suddenly convinced that everything is going to work out fine. How, I've no idea. But I'm having a baby, I have a family who loves me and a job I think might be my true vocation – maybe these things are all that matter.

I lean over and give Lipsy a sloppy kiss on the cheek, and laugh when she wipes her face with her sleeve.

'Mum?' she says as she gets out of the car. Her eyes look enormous.

‘Yes,’ I answer with a smile.

‘Don’t give up on Paul just yet, OK? You never know what might be around the corner. He might surprise you. He might change his mind.’

I smile again and shrug, and watch her safely into the house. Then I turn the car around and head for home.

My daughter has hope and blind faith, which can’t be a bad thing. But all mine has been used up, I’m afraid. From now on, me and Bump are on our own.

*

From: lipsyhill@mad4mail.com
To: paulsmart@smarthomes.net
Date: 3 April 2012 20:06

Dear Paul,

How are you? I hope things are going OK. The reason I’m emailing is, I’ve heard that Sharon and Hannah are coming to stay with you for Easter, and I think you should know that my mum thinks you and Sharon are about to get back together. Is this true? I can’t believe you would do that to my mum, no matter what’s happened between you. I know that my mum still loves you, and we are all surprised you haven’t sorted it out by now, to be honest. Are you sure you won’t just come and visit her? I’m sure you’d be glad if you did. You might get the answers to all your questions.

It might also be best if you came to see her before Sharon’s visit. Will you come?

Lipsy

From: paulsmart@smarthomes.net
To: lipsyhill@mad4mail.com
Date: 3 April 2012 22:31

Dear Lipsy,

Hannah is due for a visit at Easter, but there's been no mention of her mum coming too. I've just rung her but she was very strange on the phone and I'm not sure what's going on there.

Rest assured I am not going to "get back together" with Hannah's mum. Why would Stella even think that? I just can't understand what's going on in her head. But I'm not going to visit your mum, Lipsy, for the reasons I stated in my last email. If your mum wants to talk then I need to hear it from her, not you. I just can't risk it. I'm sorry. What happened was too painful and I can't risk getting hurt again.

You asked how things are going – they aren't too good, actually. It seems I don't have the "killer instinct" to succeed in the rental market (Tom's words, not mine). He thinks my "personal problems" might be getting in the way. I'm not sure how much longer I can stick it up here, to be honest. But please keep this to yourself.

I miss your mum so much. I think about her all the time. Could you tell her that? That I think about her every second and I wish I could go back and do it all again. This time I'd figure out what was wrong and put it right, I know I would. But I still don't know why she called off the wedding, and that just tears me apart. Can you imagine how that feels? Do you know why? Can you tell me?

Paul x

From: lipsyhill@mad4mail.com
To: paulsmart@smarthomes.net
Date: 3 April 2012 22:40

Dear Paul,

I can't tell you, Paul, but I do know why. And I really think that if you came back here and met up with her it would all become clear to you. I can't force you. Just think about it, OK?

Lipsy

Chapter 18

At the end of April I finally go shopping for proper maternity clothes, something I've been dreading. But once I've tried on my first pair of jeans I realise it's not so bad after all. In the changing room at Mothercare they have strap on bumps so you can tell how the clothes will fit at different stages of the pregnancy. Right now I have a pretty big round bump that pushes proudly over the top of the elasticated blue jeans, but in a few months, according to the label on the bump-strap, I'll be sticking out so far I won't be able to see my feet.

I buy the jeans, along with some smart grey leggings and two tunic tops in blue and beige. Ordinarily I wouldn't be seen dead in beige, but it's either that or shocking pink, and I draw the line at looking like an extra from CBeebies. Into my basket I pop some roomy tights and a maternity bra, and I'm done.

On my way back to the car I pass Cafe Crème. Last year I had a part-time job in my favourite coffee shop, but I've hardly been in there since I handed in my notice. Should I pop in now, treat myself to a mocha frappuccino? I'm just about to decide against it when I spot my mum and dad sitting at what was, in happier times, mine and Paul's favourite table. They have their heads together and appear to be reading something on my dad's phone.

Before I can talk myself out of it, I take a deep breath and walk right on in.

'Stella!' Dad spots me first and jumps up, taking my

bags out of my hand and pulling over an extra chair. 'It's so good to see you,' he says, beaming.

He's glad to see me, but my mother is harder to read. 'Mum,' I say with a nod. She smiles, but her lips are thin. Dad asks what I want to drink, then speeds up to the counter, leaving my mother and me sitting in an uneasy silence.

'How are you?' I ask, at the exact same moment she says, 'We were talking about Billy.'

'Oh, right. Billy.' The golden boy. 'Is he going to make it back for the blessing?'

The blessing that I've managed to push out of my mind completely, but it's only a couple of months away. Not long until the day I'll have to sit in church and listen to my mum and dad eulogise about each other. Yuk. It would be great if my brother could be there to suffer along with me.

She mumbles something about the cost of air travel and I lose interest. If Billy wants to come back he'll be there; if he doesn't, he won't. Billy always does whatever he likes, no responsibilities, not a care in the world.

I'm not jealous. Much.

Dad returns with my coffee and a pile of chocolate muffins, which lifts the atmosphere somewhat.

'What did Billy's text say?' I ask him through a mouthful of muffin.

Dad looks at me blankly.

'You were just talking about him with Mum. And I saw you looking at your phone. What did he say?'

My parents look at each other and something unspoken passes between them. They remind me of Edie and Franklin, but with fewer wrinkles. Funny how it's sweet in a pair of octogenarians, but in one's own parents it's really irritating.

'What?' I say, putting down my cup. 'What's going on?'

Mum is the first to jump in with an answer. 'Nothing,' she laughs, reaching out to pat my arm. 'You're in a funny old mood today, Stella.' But her tone is too upbeat, considering how annoyed she's been with me lately, and her other hand is twirling furiously at her hair. She'd be a rubbish poker player. My father is looking pointedly out of the window, humming.

What are they up to? Whatever it is, it doesn't look like I'm going to get it out of them without the thumbscrews, so I give up and return to the muffins. I'm just tucking in to my third when my dad, who obviously thinks the coast is now clear, speaks up.

'Actually, Stella, there is something we wanted to talk to you about.'

I nod and raise my eyebrows. Can't talk. Eating.

'Your mother and I, we were wondering about what's going to happen when the baby comes along.' They look at my bump as if half expecting to see the baby's little head poking out. I give my stomach a reassuring pat and smile radiantly.

'Well, I think what usually happens is, the mother goes into labour, and the baby makes its way down the birth canal, finally exiting via an opening which is located between her–'

'See,' says my mother, interrupting with a sour look on her face. 'I told you she couldn't have a serious conversation about it.'

'Oh, I'm sorry. Did I offend your sensibilities?' I grin at my dad. 'Bet I didn't offend yours.'

He shakes his head, not rising to it. If we were alone now he'd be laughing his stripy socks off.

'What we meant was,' my dad says, ploughing on regardless, 'where you will live when the baby comes along. You and the baby can't live in that bedsit, and you can't very well share your house with Lipsy and Robert and their baby too. And you won't be able to work, will you? So, your mum and I, we've come up with a plan.'

I sit back and absorb this. Really, I should tell them to butt out. It's my business, after all. But I figure I might as well hear them out.

'Go on then,' I say. 'What's your plan?'

'Well, we figured that the best way forward is for us to convert our garage and family room into a self-contained flat for you and the baby. I've drawn up some plans, look.' He pulls a sheet of paper from his pocket, unfolds it and slides it across the table. 'We'd use the existing utility for the kitchen – your mum doesn't mind at all, do you, Maggie?' He looks up at her and she smiles. Reluctantly benign. 'And here is where I'd put in a little bathroom – proper full size bath for the baby – and you'd be able to fit two small bedrooms in here and a living room. Also,' he adds, his voice rising with excitement, 'we would partition off part of the garden here, so you'd even have your own outside space. Really, you'll be completely self-contained. Don't you think it's a great idea?'

I love my dad. I really do. So I keep my feelings to myself for a moment and smile encouragingly.

'Wow, Dad. You've gone to a lot of trouble drawing all this up. You should have been an architect, never mind a builder. It looks amazing.' This is true. If I were seventeen, and if I could bear to live within a mile of my parents, this would be the perfect pad. But I'm not, am I?

'What do you think of it, Mum?' I keep my voice light. She shrugs, and I see my dad's expression tighten.

'She thinks it's a great idea too, Stella. But she also thinks you won't go for it.' He looks at her, a little nervously in my opinion, as if unsure of how much to share. 'I think it would be good for us,' he adds. 'As a family.'

The bonding effect of close proximity in extended

family relationships, as written by my dad, Howard Hill. Marks out of ten: two and a half for effort.

'It'd cost a fortune, though,' I offer.

'We could borrow on the house. Interest rates are low, we still have a lot of equity, and this will only add value. Granny annexes are all the rage right now. Just think, in years to come, we could move in there ourselves and you could have the main house.'

I nod my head slowly. I'm trying to imagine that scenario without breaking out into a cold sweat.

'At least,' he says, jumping in before I can speak, 'at least say you'll think about it. OK? Just think about it. Please?'

'OK,' I tell him, avoiding my mother's eyes. 'I'll think about it. And thank you. Really. It's a lovely idea, and very, very generous. It really is.'

He rewards me with a wide grin and an awkward hug. As he reaches for me his hand brushes his phone and the screen lights up. Over his shoulder I can see his text messages, and my eyes scan for Billy's name. Nothing. But right at the top and highlighted is a text from my daughter. I'm pretty sure this was the message they were reading when I walked in. But why lie about it? I crane my neck to try and read some of the message, but my mother follows my gaze and snatches the phone off the table. She throws it into her handbag, then her hand emerges holding a white and gold card. She scoots the card across the table, an unreadable look in her eye.

'Stella,' she says, 'could you just sign this birthday card for Sarah?'

'Sarah?' I rack my brain but come up empty. Dad moves away and clears his throat.

'You know!' She wafts at the air impatiently. 'Your great aunt Alice's daughter's cousin. It's her fiftieth birthday next week and we're all signing her card.'

I shrug and reach for the pen. Mum's hand obscures

most of the writing, but I can make out a tacky gold embossed script. I write *Love from Stella* and add a couple of kisses for good measure. Mum pulls the card away and slips it back into her bag.

Is it my imagination or is her smile just a tiny bit triumphant?

Chapter 19

Three weeks later a new resident moves into Twilight. Her name is Maude, and she is the very epitome of graceful old age. White hair coiled up into a bun with a few wisps curling around her neck; clothes courtesy of Country Casuals: tweed and expensive wool with just the right amount of silk and lace to keep her looking feminine. The staff gathers together in reception whenever we get a newbie, and none of us can take our eyes off her as she strolls in ahead of her possessions, followed by a hint of Chanel No.5 and three young men carrying designer suitcases. In her arms she carries a furry handbag, and I wonder what make it is. Something expensive, no doubt. While the others whisper and stare, I find myself feeling sorry for Maude. She's clearly used to better things. While there's nothing intrinsically wrong with the Twilight Residential Home – we care for our residents incredibly well, in my opinion – it isn't what you'd call five star luxury. If Maude is used to lunching at Woburn Sands or staying overnight at the Dorchester, she'll be sorely disappointed with Twilight's offerings.

Still, best to make her feel welcome from the outset, soften the blow a little.

'Hi, I'm Stella. You must be Mrs Beresford. Pleased to meet you.'

She smiles warmly and holds out one hand. 'Call me Maude,' she says. Her voice is cultured and soft; her hand is encased in a long grey glove despite the bright

May sunshine. The furry bag tucked under her other arm suddenly begins to move. I step back in alarm as the bag unfurls itself and jumps to the floor.

It's not a bag. It's a cat.

'And that,' says Maude, not missing a beat, 'is Jackson.' She turns to her entourage and begins to issue directions. The one nearest me, a blonde guy in his early thirties with wide shoulders and a cheeky smile, pulls a face behind her back. I grin. Then I see Velma eyeballing me, so I hotfoot it back behind the reception desk.

'Stella,' Velma hisses, 'that women had a cat.'

'Mmm. She did.'

'How did that happen?' she demands, glaring at me, then at Jean, then Martha, then back to me again.

'I guess someone forgot to explain the no pets policy to her,' I say innocently. Velma is the only person allowed to induct new residents; she would have been the first point of contact with Maude Beresford. Therefore it's her fault entirely, and I enjoy watching her squirm.

Oh, how we pay for the smallest moments of fun in our working lives.

'Stella,' she snaps, 'perhaps you'd like to go and inform Mrs Beresford that she must dispose of her pet this instant. And while you're at it, I need you to do a full fire safety check. Log each room for extinguishers and fire blankets, then report back to me by lunchtime.'

She knows this is impossible. There's no way I can check every room in three hours and carry out all my regular duties. The residents come first with me – and she knows it – so she's set me up to fail. Again. Never mind giving me the onerous task of upsetting Maude on her first day.

Velma smiles victoriously; Jean and Martha look on in sympathy. I head off towards the stairs. Might as well get on with it. Besides, I might get another look at the cute guy if I head up to Maude's room right now. My hormones are all over the place, and I'd quite like to indulge in a bit of harmless flirting with a good-looking guy.

'Stella,' Velma calls out just as I reach the bottom step. I stop and turn around. She's leaning on the reception desk with an evil glint in her eye. What now?

'We need to have a meeting later about your appearance,' she practically shouts across the wide open space of the reception area. 'You are looking decidedly scruffy lately, and if you don't mind me saying so, very out of shape. I've seen you huffing and puffing all the time. If you're too unfit to do your job we need to have a chat about it, OK?' She finishes with a sickly smile and a rueful nod at someone standing behind me. I swing around and come face to face with the cute guy. Great. Time for a cutting comment, something to show her she can't mess with me, win back a shred of my dignity.

Time for something clever to pop into my mind ... Something ... Anything ...

Velma smiles again and disappears into her office. The guy with the shoulders gives me a troubled glance, then edges around me as though I'm contagious and heads for the exit. My shoulders sink and all the fight ebbs from my body. There was a time when I would have wiped the floor with the Velmas of this world. I think back to Loretta, my arch rival at Smart Homes, and the numerous times we crossed swords. I was a force to be reckoned with back then, with Paul behind me every step of the way.

Not anymore.

Seems like I've lost more than the love of my life. I've lost my ability to stand up for myself too. No more feisty Stella, no more wisecracks. Whenever I crack a joke these days, or try to be clever, I just end up offending someone. There was a time when people thought I was great; a bit flaky maybe, but generally a good person. Now, I'm not so sure. My mum and dad are keeping secrets from me, Lipsy is guarded about something too, and Bonnie and Billy are too far away to really care. And Paul? What does he think of me?

I'd honestly expected to hear from him by now. Has Sharon told him about the baby? I'd expected a phone call, or at least another angry letter. The Paul I know wouldn't sit back and do nothing. He'd demand answers, an explanation. He'd want to sort things out. Even if what he wanted to sort out didn't include getting back together – how could it, after all? – it would be important to him that he made arrangements for the baby's future. Especially after missing out on Hannah all those years ...

Maybe that's it. Maybe he is so angry with me for not telling him myself that he can't bring himself to get in touch.

I reach the top of the stairs and lean my hand on the rail to catch my breath. Velma's right about me being out of shape, even if she doesn't realise the real reason for it. Underneath this extra large tabard my tummy is getting pretty big, and I'm struggling to keep up with the work here. Looking after Phoenix between shifts isn't getting any easier either, but I've put off telling Lipsy she'll need to find a proper childminder soon. Whenever I hint that I'm finding it a struggle she just laughs and says it's good practice for me. Which is true, I guess. It's also true that I may be so worn out by the time my own baby comes along I'll have to hire in help myself.

As if in response to this sacrilegious thought, Bump gives me a hefty kick, and I can't help but smile and place my other hand on my stomach. But then I snatch it away and look around warily. No one in sight. Edie and Franklin seem to think I can keep it to myself for ages yet, but I'm not so sure. And right now, I do not think I could face Velma's reaction to the news that I'm pregnant. I don't think I could face it at all.

Nor can I face telling an old lady who has just moved into her final dwelling place that she must 'dispose' of her beloved cat. It was Velma's mistake, so Velma will just have to deal with it. Besides, if I can't stand up to the woman face to face, the least I can do is cause a bit of trouble behind her back. I give Bump a surreptitious pat and try to suppress a grin. Then I head off in the direction of the kitchen for a saucer of milk and a tin of tuna.

This must be Jackson's lucky day.

*

Jackson, it turned out, was perfectly happy to curl up in Maude's wardrobe on top of a rolled up blanket and spend most of his time in hiding. Sally, who manages the kitchens, agreed to supply Maude with cat food and a litter tray, eager to be part of my plan to hoodwink Velma. Seems I'm not the only member of staff with a low opinion of our esteemed boss.

After I'd explained Twilight's no pets rule to Maude, along with my cunning plan to circumvent it, I brought Franklin and Edie in on the secret.

I could tell instantly that I'd made a mistake. Maude had Franklin under her spell in no time, and Edie was left out in the cold.

'It's just Franklin's way,' I tell Edie as we sit in the TV lounge watching Maude gush to a crowd of admirers. Franklin is acting as introducer and all-round charmer. He hasn't so much as looked at Edie since we entered the room.

My shift ended an hour ago, but I decided to stay on a while. After all, what do I have to go home to? Better to stay here amongst friends, cadge a free dinner from

Sally, and try to prop up Edie's rapidly deteriorating facade of unconcern.

'Oh, I'm not bothered about all that,' she says bravely. 'Why, Franklin and I are just friends, after all. And Maude seems simply lovely.'

And therein lies the problem. Maude is lovely in every way. Kind, generous, cultured without being condescending. She's already tamed Violet, and that was no mean feat. Even Bernie has given up his favourite chair for Maude.

'You know, Edie,' I say, searching for a topic that will draw her attention away, 'even though I've been working here for almost a year, I don't know very much about you at all. Is it true you worked at Bletchley Park during the war?'

The old manor house that had been converted into a code breakers' haven during the Second World War was just down the road, and many of Bletchley's older residents had worked there years ago, quietly and secretly plugging away to crack the Enigma code. It was Jean who told me about Edie's past; she also said the older woman refused to talk about it to anyone. I'm curious to see if that reticence extends to me. Edie and I have become quite close, after all. She is like an honorary grandmother to me, and I've told her so more than once.

A ghost of a smile crosses Edie's face. She takes her time in answering. 'You know, Stella, I've known couples who were married for over thirty years and didn't know that they both worked at Bletchley Park during the war. It wasn't until the government declassified wartime information in the seventies that people would talk about it at all. Even then, we still felt bound to the secrets we'd promised to keep.'

I watch Edie watching Franklin and think about secrets. A secret baby, and now a secret cat. Not really on a par with the importance of Edie's former career.

'What did you do there, Edie? Can you tell me about it?'

She shakes her head. 'Not really. The thing is, Stella, you keep a secret for too long, it becomes part of yourself. Part of your identity. For years I had no one to tell, no one would have been interested anyway. And now ...' She tails off and looks down at her hands. They are twisted up with arthritis, her knuckles all lumpy and bulbous. I think about Maude's graceful, bejewelled hands and feel a little hitch in my heart.

'And now?' I prompt.

'Well, what's the point in going over it all?' she says gaily, the twinkle suddenly back in her eye. 'It's all water under the bridge, as my mother used to say. I was useful, that's all that matters. I made a difference. How many people can say that at my age, Stella? It's important, don't you think?'

We move our heads simultaneously to look at Maude again. Franklin is laughing at something she's just said, and Rosa is holding out a box of chocolates, offering up more than just a hazelnut whirl. No one is watching the TV, and for the first time in the history of Twilight the volume is turned down so low it can barely be heard.

I reach out and take Edie's hand in mine. 'It's the most important thing in the world, Edie. More important than anything.'

I can feel my eyes tearing up again, and I blink furiously to stop the flow. But just then something happens to restore my faith in the world. Franklin looks across to where we are sitting and his eyes meet Edie's. Even from here they are bright blue and piercing, and I'm startled by the intensity of his gaze. And even though there is no discernible expression on his face, other than his usual good humour, by my side Edie visibly relaxes. When Franklin finally looks away, I turn to face her.

'Edie, were you and Franklin at Bletchley Park at the same time? Did he work there too?'

She smiles just a little and nods. A tiny movement, more of a jerk really, but it gives me the confidence to risk one more question.

'And did you know him back then? Were you ... friends?'

She doesn't nod this time, but a tear forms in the corner of her eye and then trails slowly down her face. Only I can see it, sitting so close, but I pretend I haven't noticed. I pat her hand and heave myself out of my chair. 'Cup of tea?' I ask, but I don't wait for her to answer before walking quietly away.

Chapter 20

From: paulsmart@smarthomes.net
To: lipsyhill@mad4mail.com
Date: 9 June 2012 08:46

Dear Lipsy,

I got two invitations to your granddad and grandma's blessing this morning – one from them and one from your mum! Did you know about this? Are you sure she wants me to come? I don't know what to think. Nothing for months, and now this. I'm happy for them, Lipsy, and I appreciate the invitation, but I'm not sure if I should come. Has she said anything to you about it?

Paul x

From: lipsyhill@mad4mail.com
To: paulsmart@smarthomes.net
Date: 9 June 2012 10:13

Dear Paul,

That's fantastic news! I'm so excited! Yes, she did tell me that she was thinking about asking you along. I think it's her idea of an olive branch or something. Maybe she thought it would be easier for you to just turn up on neutral territory. We're all going out to dinner afterwards, and you're welcome to come of course, but you and Mum might want to go off somewhere and talk. Please say you'll come, Paul. You can't very well say no now she's invited you herself, can you? That would be the end of it for sure, don't you think?

By the way, I walked past your old office the other day and there were decorators in there. Have you decided to rent it out? The old Smart Homes sign is still up.

Please say you'll come to the blessing. I just know everything will be fine as soon as you see her.

Lipsy

PS: Did Sharon ever tell you about visiting Mum?

From: paulsmart@smarthomes.net
To: lipsyhill@mad4mail.com
Date: 9 June 2012 12:52

Dear Lipsy,

I'm still thinking about it, but I guess you're right. If she really wants to see me ... and she did go to the trouble of sending me a card herself. OK, I'll come. Actually, I'll be back in Milton Keynes by then. The decorators you saw are getting the office ready for me. I'm reopening Smart Homes! It'll be just me to start off with, and I'm going to take the business in a different direction. All this cut-throat stuff isn't for me, and I've been thinking about doing something a bit more meaningful with the business. But anyway, at least I'll be around to sort things out once and for all. Or not, as the case may be.

Sharon comes up every fortnight and drops Hannah

off but she doesn't stay. She's different with me these days, actually. I have no idea why. And no, she's never mentioned going to see Stella. Why are you so interested? Actually, that's another reason why I'm coming back. It's not fair on Hannah for me to be so far away. Really, looking back, I can't imagine it would have worked out for Stella and me here. She was right, you know. She didn't want to move away, and I should have listened to her. There are lots of things I wish I'd listened to her about. I just hope it's not too late now.

Well, see you in a couple of weeks then.

Thanks, Lipsy. For everything.

Paul x

*

'Scrub or peel?'

The beautician standing above me is frighteningly beautiful. If the products she sells are even halfway responsible for that clear, glowing skin and firm jaw line, I'm buying a bucket full.

'I don't know,' I tell her, star-struck. 'Which do you think?'

She pulls an enormous magnifying glass down from the stand behind her and peers at my skin. 'Hmm,' she says. It's the sound of despair.

'How about both?' I offer helpfully.

She shakes her dainty head and purses her lips. She taps her perfectly manicured fingernails on the tray by my head. In the background, tinkling music trips around the room. Lipsy is on the bed next to mine having her back massaged by a woman who could be my beautician's twin. There are about twenty candles strewn around the room and the walls are painted chocolate brown. It screams calm. So why am I so tense?

For one thing, I'm not entirely sure what I'm doing here. When Lipsy announced that she'd booked us in for a spa day, I was so shocked I dropped the phone.

'Are you sure you want to take *me*?' I asked when I'd retrieved it from the bedding. I was in bed because there's not much else to do at nine o'clock on a week night in bedsit land, and Bump and I were exhausted.

'Of course I do,' she laughed. 'Who else would I take?'

Rosie. Or my mother. Or even, at a push, Robert. 'You have tons of friends, Lipsy. You must be able to think of someone more fun to take than your mum.'

She sighed. Not a good sign. 'Don't start feeling sorry for yourself, OK? You're coming and that's that. I've checked with work about your shifts so you can't wriggle out of it, and I've got the whole weekend off and Rob's looking after Phoenix. It'll be great. Bonding and all that.'

Bonding? She must have been reading Robert's parenting books.

'Will Robert be able to cope on his own, though?' I ask, stalling. 'He's usually so busy at work ... Doesn't he have overtime or something?'

'Mum! You sound like you don't want to come with me. Anyway, Rob's job is fine now. The crisis is over.'

'Really? You didn't say anything.'

'Well, I'm saying now, aren't I? They made a couple of people redundant, but it was more early retirement or something, so he's safe. In fact ... Well, I wasn't going to tell you this yet, we were going to announce it after Granddad and Grandma's blessing, but the thing is, he's had a promotion.'

'Wow. That's great news, Lipsy. So, you'll be better off then?'

I was mentally packing my bags and moving back in

to my lovely little house. If Robert could just earn enough to move them all into a flat of their own ...

'He's not going to get paid any extra, but it's not all about money, is it? It's about responsibility and showing how indispensable you are.'

With my bubble burst, I sat back and let her prattle on. Allowed myself to be persuaded that spending a small fortune on a spa day was in fact a good idea, not a complete waste of resources and time. And now here we are, being pampered by two aliens masquerading as perfect humans.

My alien decides a facial scrub is the best option, and proceeds to apply a paste to my face that smells suspiciously like Weetabix. With gravel mixed into it. I lie back and think about Bonnie and her facial peel, glad I've escaped that dubious pleasure.

After three hours of scrubbing and pummelling, Lipsy and I are released into the swimming pool for more relaxation. Lipsy is svelte and gorgeous in her two piece bikini; I am a beached whale in my maternity tankini.

'Mum,' she says when I emerge from the changing rooms, 'you are enormous! When's it due again?'

'August,' I snap. 'Early August.'

'But that's still ages away.' She laughs and splashes me as I lower myself onto the side of the pool.

'We can't all be skinny mummies,' I tell her, dipping in one big toe, then the other. The water is lovely and warm. As grumpy as I sound, I'm actually looking forward to a nice swim.

'If you lie on your back you'll float,' she says when I'm fully immersed.

'Right. That's it.'

I'm bigger than her, so I can create even bigger splashes, and soon she's completely drenched.

'Stop! You'll wash all the essential oils off my face.'

'Your face doesn't need essential oils, Lipsy. You're

seventeen, for God's sake.'

We swim along side by side, until Lipsy gets bored and takes off in an elegant crawl. I plunder on with my lopsided breast stroke, enjoying the weightless sensation of being in the water. After twenty minutes we clamber out, wrap ourselves in white fluffy dressing gowns, and lie on wooden steamer chairs sipping mineral water.

'This is the life,' Lipsy says.

'Sure is. Shame we have to work at all, really. Be nice to do this every day. Minus the scrub,' I add, gingerly touching my face. 'That was a bit brutal.'

'Ah, but you look amazing, Mum. Ten years younger. Just think how gorgeous you'll look for the blessing next week.'

I shrug. 'Suppose so. It's not a big deal though, is it? Just a couple of hours in church.'

I feel Lipsy tense by my side. 'Come on, Mum,' she says, her voice falsely casual, 'you're going to make a bit of an effort, aren't you?'

'Effort? How do you mean?'

'Well, you're going to dress up, right?'

I hadn't planned to. I make a noncommittal noise, and Lipsy carries on.

'I think that tube dress you've got is perfect, you know. That biscuit-coloured one from Tiffany Rose? You absolutely must wear that.'

'You really think so?'

'I insist on it.'

'Well, OK then. Whatever.'

I can't get all excited about my mum and dad's blessing, I just can't. Everyone's going on about it like it's a real-life wedding, and while I know it's sweet and all, I just can't get behind it the way Lipsy is. Maybe it's because my mum's been so weird with me lately. One minute she's berating me and storming off across the city centre, the next she's asking me to sign birthday cards

elsewhere.

Lipsy, Robert and Phoenix arrive, and I slip into the pew beside them. A distant relative of my dad pushes us all along from the other end until I'm crammed up against the aisle. I turn to check if everyone's here, and that's when I see him.

Paul.

Lit from behind like an angel, he's standing in the arched doorway looking drop-dead gorgeous and completely bewildered.

Paul? Here? I rub my eyes and look again. He's still there. He steps inside the church and looks around. Runs his hand through his hair. Then he turns and slides into a pew near the back.

Oh. My. God.

My head snaps back as though it's on elastic. Did he see me? I don't think so. He looked uncertain, but not angry. Anxious. Intense.

He looked amazing.

The music starts up – the wedding march, for goodness sake, which seems particularly inappropriate right now – and I try to calm my breathing.

'Lipsy,' I hiss.

'What?'

My mother steps up to the front of the church where my dad is waiting. He's wearing a dark grey suit with the faintest pinstripe and looks dignified and handsome. He turns to face her and beams. The sound of chatter that has filled the church dies down and there is an expectant pause.

'Paul's here,' I whisper. Lipsy pulls a face, mouths, 'What?'

I lean over and whisper into her ear. 'Oh,' she says, smiling widely and nodding. 'That's great, Mum.'

'No,' I tell her, 'it is not great. It's a bloody nightmare. What is he doing here, anyway?'

'Shh,' says someone behind me. I don't bother to turn around, for obvious reasons.

Someone must have invited him. How would he even know about it otherwise? Someone who has a vested interest in getting us back together, perhaps. Someone who likes to meddle.

'Is this your doing?' I say to Lipsy.

She gives me a wide-eyed look, innocence personified, then gestures to the lectern. The vicar is stepping up, smoothing down his black robes and smiling benevolently at the congregation. He starts to talk. His voice is high-pitched and artificially loud. I lean over again, and tell my daughter, 'If it was, I'll never forgive you.'

Lipsy shakes her head and looks away, but I'm sure I can detect the trace of a nervous frown across her forehead. I turn back to face the lectern. The vicar's words are a blur to me, just a buzz of noise. Dad starts to speak, reading from a crumpled piece of paper.

Surely Lipsy wouldn't do that to me? Surely my little girl wouldn't go behind my back and invite Paul without telling me anything about it? Maybe it was my mother. Maybe she invited him just to spite me.

But why on earth would he accept?

I don't dare risk turning around to see if he's still there. Maybe it wasn't him after all. Maybe I was hallucinating. I mean, he can't be here, can he? That would be crazy. Unless ...

Unless he's come to confront me about the baby. Of course. That's it! Sharon's only just told him and he's furious. Or she told him a while ago and he's been brewing, waiting for the right opportunity to humiliate me. What could be a better venue for my humiliation than my mum and dad's blessing? It's kind of poetic.

I thought he hated confrontation. I underestimated him.

My stomach gurgles with anxiety. I'm trapped here now, until the service is over, but as soon as possible I'll find a way to get out of here before Paul sees me. I try to focus on the ceremony; my mother is talking now, her voice low and indistinct. But my reaction to seeing Paul is messing with my head. The first thing I felt? Total and utter joy.

Followed by complete panic, of course. But there's no denying that lifting of my heart when I saw him. His face, so dear to me for so many years; that walk of his with his shoulders held wide and strong; his curly blonde hair glinting in the sunlight. My Paul. My nearly-husband. Why, oh why, just as I'm starting to get over it and find the silver lining, why does he have to turn up now?

I risk a quick glance around the church, searching for an alternative exit. There is a door to the left of the lectern. As soon as the service is over, I'll jump up and make a run for it. Let Lipsy deal with Paul. I'm not a coward, far from it. I'm perfectly ready to face him and face the consequences. But not like this. Not with my beautiful bump poking out like an accusation and sixty pairs of eyes upon us. We'd be a spectacle. And if Paul has come to confront me, it will happen in a place of my choosing, not his.

And it will happen with me wearing something more demure than a Tiffany Rose tube dress and high heels.

The ceremony wears on; my mind is blurry with half-formed thoughts and imagined conversations. But most of all I'm thinking: How has it come to this? How did Paul and I end up this way, estranged, poles apart, with our values and our goals so misaligned? I should have seen it coming. I should have been more careful.

Bump gives me a sharp kick, and I blink away sudden tears. Not that kind of careful, I say to my baby. Not so you wouldn't be here. But maybe if I'd done things in a different order, maybe it would have worked out better.

Or maybe it would have just been much, much worse.

Before I've had time to properly prepare myself, the service is over and my mum and dad are turning to face the expectant eyes of the congregation. I look around wildly. Any minute now they will walk past me and I'll have to stand and follow them out of the church. Right past Paul's seat. My heart hammers and my palms begin to sweat.

It's Phoenix who saves me.

The baby is sitting on Robert's lap, and Robert has been struggling to keep him quiet throughout the entire ceremony, jiggling his knees and bouncing Phoenix up and down and saying, 'Shush now, shush now,' under his breath like a meditation. But all this has done is work Phoenix up into a frenzy of frustration, and now he's kicking up a storm. Robert passes him to Lipsy, who passes him back to Robert so she can take a photo of her granddad and grandma as they prepare to leave the church. We all stand as they walk past, and I suddenly see my opportunity.

'Here, give him to me,' I cry, holding out my arms.

'No, it's OK.' Lipsy looks confused, scanning the pews behind us. Everyone is standing now, and the organ has started up again. The noise level is rising, and so are Phoenix's cries.

'Give him to me,' I tell Robert, who gladly obliges. 'You go on ahead,' I say encouragingly. 'You and Lipsy.'

With Robert's arm at her back, Lipsy has no choice but to move forward with the crowd, leaving me behind. I bury my face in Phoenix's neck and breathe a silent thank you. He smells of talcum powder and vomit. The two best smells in the world right now.

I sit down to wait it out. My eyes are closed and I listen to the chattering and the congratulations die away as everyone leaves the church. Phoenix is calm now. I have that effect on babies. I'm good with babies. This thought cheers me, and pushes some of the anxiety away.

Then I hear his voice behind me.

'Stella?'

I take a deep, shaky breath, and stand up. Shift Phoenix to my right hip and turn, slowly, to face him.

Chapter 22

At first, his face is open and happy. Not angry. That's a good start. But before I've had time to process this fully, his eyes slide down to my stomach.

'Stella? What the ...? Jesus Christ.'

He sits down heavily on the pew behind him, now at eye level with my huge, magnificent bump, and proceeds to stare at it wordlessly.

For once, words fail me too. I jiggle Phoenix on my hip, the silence in the church impossibly loud and invasive.

Paul says, 'Is this some kind of a joke?'

I laugh; I can't help it. It's a sharp, unexpected sound, and Phoenix gurgles in response. Does Paul think I've shoved a pillow up my dress? Am I the kind of person who would do that at her parents' blessing? I know he thinks I'm flaky, but honestly. That's just ridiculous.

I see by Paul's expression that laughter was not the correct response. I take another deep breath. The intensity of his stare makes talking difficult, but I have to find out what he knows.

'Obviously it's not a joke. I thought you knew. Didn't you know?'

'How the hell would I know?' He looks up at me incredulously. 'You're pregnant?'

'Sharon,' I say, struggling to make sense of the shock on his face. 'Sharon told you. Didn't she?'

'Sharon?' Paul says, standing. Clearly being at eye level with my stomach is not where he's most comfortable right now. 'Why the hell would Sharon tell me? Are you saying she knows about this?'

'Of course she does. She came to see me – didn't she tell you?'

He shakes his head slowly, his expression clouded and confused.

I can't process this. She didn't tell him. But why? It doesn't make sense.

Unless ...

Oh, I've been very stupid. Even more stupid than usual. It was such an easy conclusion to jump to: Sharon and Paul; her scheming to get him back; me the injured party. I thought the worst of her. But it seems I got her very wrong indeed.

She didn't tell him because it wasn't her secret to tell. And right now I'd put money on the fact that Paul hasn't seen hide nor hair of her since she found out I was expecting. I guess it brought it all back, reminded Sharon of her own pregnancy, of her own rejection. That's what she was trying to tell me as she left; I was too stupid to pick up on it.

But here I've been, thinking he knew and was choosing to do nothing about it, when all along he still had no idea.

'You're pregnant?' he says again. I nod, then look down at my bump and stick it out a bit further. A tiny shrug, more of a twitch really, lifts my shoulders. It's the body language equivalent of, 'Well, duh!' and it's a huge mistake. Paul's expression hardens.

'I see,' he says. Something like a shudder goes through his body and the colour drains from his face.

'Paul,' I say, reaching out my hand automatically, 'I didn't mean for you to find out like this. It's just, well, you see, I was waiting for–'

If my hand was a poisonous snake he couldn't have thrown it off any faster. I take a step back, concerned about the anger in his eyes.

A movement at the rear of the church catches my attention, and I turn to spot Robert hovering there, looking decidedly uncomfortable. Beyond him I can see out into the sunshine, pockets of people milling around, unaware of the drama they're missing out on. Once the photos are over they'll pile into cars and head for the pub where my mum and dad are treating us to lunch. Really, it is just like a proper wedding. It's a much better attempt at a wedding than mine was, at any rate.

'Shall I take Phee?' Robert calls when he realises I've seen him. I nod and he walks forward tentatively. Lifts the baby from my arms, says hello to Paul, then hotfoots it from the scene. I don't blame him. Right now I wish I could go with him. And I miss the feel of Phoenix on my hip. I had a feeling Paul might hold back in front of Phee. Now there's nothing to hold him back.

'So,' Paul says, 'this is the big secret, is it?'

He's leaning against the high wooden back of the pew, feigning a relaxed posture the way men do when they are trying to intimidate. 'This,' he waves his hand at my bump, 'is what it was all about, is it?'

No point denying it now.

'Yes,' I tell him, keeping my voice soft. 'This is why I couldn't marry you.'

He nods slowly. I can almost hear the cogs shifting, processing. Will it all fall into place for him now? Will he remember the conversations we had?

'Paul?' I say tentatively. I reach out for his hand but don't touch him yet. I visualise the next few minutes, how it's all going to come together. I'll rest his hand on my stomach, and then he'll look at me with tears in his eyes and say, 'We're having a baby?' And then I'll nod and kiss him and all will be well.

There'll be a lot of crying. And a hell of a lot of explaining. But at the very least, Paul and I can get on with being parents-to-be. I know he'll want to be involved. We can go back to being friends again. It will be better than nothing, better than not having him in my life at all. And I'll do my best to make it up to him. No matter what he said, no matter how he wants to live his life, it was wrong of me to keep it from him for so long. Wrong to break up with him without telling him the real reason.

However confused I was, however hormonal, it was still wrong.

I reach out a little further and touch his fingers.

He snatches his hand away and takes a step back. 'You're pregnant,' he says, spitting the words out like an accusation.

'We're pregnant,' I correct him with a gentle smile. 'I'm having our baby. I've been wanting to tell–'

'And this is why you called off the wedding?' he shouts, not listening. 'You must have been pregnant already, then. And what, you were just going to keep it to yourself forever? Leave me always wondering why?' His expression is starting to cause me pain: he looks stricken, desperate. This is not the reaction I was hoping for.

'I was going to tell you, Paul,' I say with a nervous laugh, suddenly aware of how lame it sounds. 'The week before the wedding I tried and tried. Don't you remember? When I asked you how you'd feel about starting a family? But it didn't ... I didn't ... I *was* going to tell you about the baby. Honestly. But–'

'Honestly?' Paul's voice is hoarse with emotion. 'Honestly? You wouldn't know honest if it jumped up and smacked you in the face. You are a disgrace. I'm disgusted with you. And as for that,' he points at my bump, 'I feel sorry for it.'

My cheeks burn with shame. Paul's words are like arrows in my heart, but worse is the look on his face.

His expression is one I have never seen before, and hope I never see again. He is looking at me like I'm scum, shit on his shoe, like I'm the absolute worst person in the world.

'Come on, now. There's no need for that.'

We both whirl around. My dad is standing at the back of the church. The double doors are closed behind him, and in the gloom his face is unreadable. He starts to walk around the perimeter, not looking in our direction, a silent guardian. I want to run to him, but I'm rooted to the spot.

Paul turns back to me. He's not finished with me yet. 'So this is why you invited me here today.' His voice is low, urgent. 'So you could humiliate me again. Isn't it enough that you broke my heart, destroyed my future, took away everything I believed in? What the hell did I do to deserve this, Stella? Just tell me that. Tell me what I did that was so terrible you had to let me find out like this?'

I can't speak. He's almost crying. There are no words to explain how painful it is to see my wonderful Paul reduced to tears. I want to hold him, to try and explain. It's not all bad news, is it? Yes, we want different things out of life, and my falling pregnant meant that we couldn't carry on with the future we'd planned. But he's talking like I've done something terrible, like I'm a truly horrible person. All I did was fall pregnant by the man I love. The man I thought, wrongly, would be happy to start a family with me. And what does he mean, I invited him? He seems to be talking in riddles.

My dad is standing somewhere behind me now. I can sense him. Not too close, but close enough.

'We're having a baby,' I whisper so only Paul can hear me.

'And I'm very happy for you,' he says through gritted teeth. 'I hope you and the father, whoever he is, will be very happy together.'

Shock makes me slow. That and the sinking in my stomach as the full impact of his words hits me. I stumble forward, reaching out blindly for support. The polished wood of the pew is warm to my touch from where Paul was leaning against it only moments ago. But even as I grip it, it starts to cool. My hands are like ice. My teeth begin to chatter.

A pair of arms around me. Strong, capable, but not the arms I want. Dad presses me to his chest, and I rest my cheek against his white carnation and let the tears come.

'Don't worry, Stella,' he says softly. 'He'll come round.'

But he doesn't know Paul like I do. No one knows Paul like I do. He is stubborn, and once he gets an idea in his head it's almost impossible to remove it. And right now, Paul Smart thinks I'm carrying another man's child. Which is not very smart at all. In fact, it's downright the most stupid thing I've ever heard.

*

Next time I look up they're all here. My mum, Lipsy, Robert and Phoenix, all crowded round me in a great big extended hug. Lipsy looks terrified; Robert is gazing off to the side, embarrassed, with Phoenix asleep in his arms. My mother is the only one whose expression offers me any comfort. She's smiling, a warm, forgiving smile, and when I meet her eyes she takes my face in her hands.

'Come on,' she says, 'let's go and eat. I don't know about you, but I'm starving.'

I could cry all over again, but I've cried all my tears. I'm desiccated from crying – there is not a single millilitre of moisture left in the whole of my body. Also, I'm so hungry I could faint. When you're pregnant, your bodily functions don't stop just because your heart is breaking. When you're pregnant, you just have to carry on.

'I know a hotel up the road where they're having a wedding breakfast right now,' I say with a sniff, wiping my eyes on my mum's sleeve and then taking her hand firmly in mine, 'and we're all invited.'

And like that, we exit the church. Connected by a hand or an arm or at the very least the brush of a coat, we walk out into the sunshine. My family and me. Five adults and two babies, ready to face the world.

Chapter 23

From: paulsmart@smarthomes.net
To: lipsyhill@mad4mail.com
Date: 30 June 2012 15:31

Lipsy,

I cannot imagine what you think you're playing at, but thanks to what I can only assume are your efforts, at least now I know the real reason your mum dumped me. All that "you should come see my mum, then you'll get all the answers" stuff – well, at least now I know what it was all about.

I thought I deserved better, after being a friend to your mum and your family for all these years. Never mind what she's done, I expected more of you. Someone should have told me. Well, I hope she's happy with her new man and their baby. It all makes sense now. Tell your mum that even though I'm back in MK I'll keep out of her way. I'd prefer it if you didn't contact me again either.

Paul

*

Food. The great comforter. I've ingested an entire roast chicken, five potatoes and a pile of vegetables the size of my head before I start to feel even marginally calmer.

The wedding breakfast – I keep calling it a wedding breakfast because every time I do my mum's face breaks into a gigantic smile – is just for family and close friends, and the friends have been shoved to the other end of the table. We have a function room to ourselves, and the twee decor, with curtain swags and a fake candelabrum on each wall, is surprisingly soothing. I'm surrounded by the people who love me, and like this, I might just get through it.

Paul thinks I'm pregnant by someone else. That's a truth I can't shy away from. Of all the stupid, ridiculous ... Well, what did I expect? Paul's a gold medallist in jumping to the wrong conclusions. Look at what he was like about Joshua. And John Dean. But this? This takes the biscuit.

OK, I called off the wedding and never quite got around to telling him exactly why. But, hey – figure it out, genius. You don't want to start a family, I'm in the family way. Recipe for a happy life? No, not really. I set him free. You'd think he'd be grateful, once the shock had worn off. But no, Paul has to go on a typical Paul Smart not-very-smart flight of fancy that has me running off and getting knocked up by another guy.

'Are you OK, love?' my mum asks, leaning over.

'Was I muttering to myself again?' I say, embarrassed. She nods. Ah, great. I smile and wave to my mum's friend Anne and her daughter, then I turn my chair so their view of me is blocked.

'What I don't understand is, how on earth he thinks I had the opportunity to meet someone else. We spent every second together, apart from when we were working, for goodness sake. And, tell me this – shouldn't someone who is so dead set against having a baby be a bit more concerned about contraception? Huh?'

My mum nods and pats my hand. She's heard this twice already, but has the grace not to look bored. Dad leans in and goes to top up my glass, but I put my hand across it. I'm allowing myself a tipple today, but not more than one. The last thing I need is a hangover and another shedload of guilt to add to my already unmanageable load.

'He's an arse,' my dad says definitively.

'Yes,' Mum agrees. 'He is. An arse.'

The way she says 'arse' is so funny, I crease up laughing despite myself. Lipsy looks up.

'What's the joke?' she says. Her face is a picture of anxiety. She knows she's in for it later, but I'm not laying into her here. I've made enough of a spectacle of myself for one day.

I'm about to say something cutting, when her phone beeps and she fishes it from her bag. I glare at her: this is a family meal, not to mention a chance to comfort me, not an opportunity to check her messages. I try to catch her eye, forbidding stare at the ready, but as she reads her face grows even paler than usual and tears well up in her eyes. She slams the phone down violently and takes a deep, shuddering breath. Robert reaches for her hand.

'What's up?' he says. He's feeding Phoenix, holding him awkwardly with one arm while trying to balance the bottle with the same hand. Phoenix doesn't seem to mind, though. At least there's someone in our family who doesn't have a care in the world.

'Nothing.' Lipsy shakes her head and shoots Robert a warning glance. My antennae are up and receiving immediately.

'Who was the text from, Lipsy?'

'No one,' she says. 'And it wasn't a text. It was an email.'

I can see that she regrets this addition as soon as it's out of her mouth.

'Who emails you?' I say with a laugh. 'I thought you lot were all Facebook and Twitter now. Or texting. And no one spells properly anymore,' I add, turning to my dad. 'It's all "great" spelt with a G and a number eight, and "R U OK". No wonder the education system in this country is going down the pan.'

I think I might be a little bit drunk. I haven't had alcohol for months, and this one glass of wine seems to have gone straight to my head. I hope Bump isn't getting any. Must shovel in some more food to soak it up.

I might not have given the email another thought if not for what happens next. Out of the corner of my eye I see Lipsy slip her phone under the table to my mother. Then I watch, pretending to be absorbed in my chocolate cake and fresh whipped cream, while my mother reads something on the screen, steals a quick glance at me, then hands it back to Lipsy.

I throw down my spoon and shove my hand across the table, palm up.

'Give me that phone right now.'

Lipsy jumps and nearly drops the phone into her pudding. 'What?' she says, clearly stalling for time. Trying to think of a reason to say no.

'Don't play the innocent with me,' I tell her. 'Today has been weird enough without you sharing secret messages with your grandma. Just hand over the phone, Lipsy. You're in enough trouble as it is. Don't make it any worse for yourself.'

Reluctantly, with a lot of grumbling and muttering, she hands me the phone. Then she lifts Phoenix from Robert's arms and takes over feeding. Obviously assuming I won't be too hard on her if she's holding my grandson.

This must be bad.

I give everyone a warning glare, then drop my head to read the email showing on the screen.

Funny how it isn't even a shock to see that the message is from Paul. I guess I must have figured out that they'd been in touch. The shock is the realisation that my mother was involved in all this somehow. And then, when I look up and see my dad's guilty face, the shock multiplies.

'You too?' I say to him, astonished.

He nods and lowers his head in shame.

'Oh. My. God. My whole family have been conspiring against me? It was you lot who invited Paul to the blessing?'

I'll be damned if I'm going to call it a wedding breakfast now.

'Well,' I say, indignation making my voice a little pompous, 'even though the man has just practically called me a whore and accused me of carrying another man's child, I have to say I agree with him, Lipsy. He's right to be angry with you, and you really shouldn't contact him again. In fact, I absolutely forbid it.'

Chapter 24

'Two sets of five, and everything to play for.'

I'm sitting in the residents' lounge while Edie plays double rummy with Franklin, Violet and Rosa, and listens to my account of the weekend's events. She's good at multitasking. With her pedigree it's not surprising.

Franklin shuffles the pack one more time then deals ten cards each, deftly turning over the last one and laying it down with a flourish. He loves cards. They all do. But double rummy is a complex affair involving two packs and six separate games. Rosa is supposed to be keeping score, a running total of the losing hands, but I don't trust her one bit. I've a feeling Franklin is keeping an eye on her, but you'd never know it from his devil-may-care expression.

'Your turn, Edie,' he says. She picks up her cards and swiftly moves them around in her hand, splaying them out in a fan shape when she's satisfied. She picks up a card from the top of the pack, regards it carefully for a full minute, then sighs and lays it down. Turns back to me.

'What I don't understand,' she says, holding her cards to her narrow chest, 'is how they pulled it off. I can see why they did it, but how did they get Paul to think you'd invited him?'

I pull my chair in a little closer. 'You'll never believe it. They conned me into signing the invitation. Said it was a birthday card for some distant relative.'

Edie snorts with laughter and I give a little huff. 'It's

not funny. I feel really, really stupid. Not to mention completely humiliated.'

Rosa is staring hard at her cards while the others look on impatiently. The impatience of the older generation was a surprise to me when I first started working here. You'd think they had all the time in the world to play cards, say, or read a book or finish a project. But no – there's a sense of urgency about the folks here that is hard to explain. It's not just the sense that time may be about to run out. It's more of an itchy restlessness. Maybe after a life of rushing from one task to the next it's impossible to slow down. Even when you can. Even the residents who are forced, by illness or incapacity, to do little more than sit and watch TV all day do so with an inherent urgency, gobbling up the images on the screen, impatient for the next programme to begin. They make me tired just watching them.

'I'll buy that,' shouts Violet the minute Rosa throws down a card. She duly parts with two pence – this card playing is a serious business, carried out with prize money at stake – and then seizes her new card with relish.

'Much good it'll do her,' Edie whispers to me. 'She's collecting aces. No one ever gives away aces when it's two sets of five.'

'But Rosa just did,' I point out.

'She's playing with Violet's head. Mind games. Trying to psych her out.'

I suppress a giggle and shake my head at Edie.

'Can you really understand why they did it?' I ask. She raises her eyebrows questioningly. 'You said just now that you could see why they did it but not how. Can you really?'

And if you can, could you please explain it to me?

'They want you to be happy, Stella. And they probably thought that getting the two of you in the same place at the same time would enable you both to finally sort things out.'

'That's pretty much what they said,' I agree. 'But it kind of didn't work out that way, did it?'

She shakes her head. Picks up a card, swaps it for one in her hand, then throws the spare away. 'You can't blame them for trying. They're your family. They just want what's best for you.'

Which is what, exactly? Now that Paul thinks the worst of me, should I run to him and try and explain? Or leave things the way they are? I'd love to ask Edie for advice. She has an aura of competence about her, of contentment and wisdom, the quiet peace of someone who's seen it all. But it would be crossing a line, and I'm not sure she'd feel comfortable with the question. Anyway, it's not her mess to sort out. It's mine. And sitting here discussing it with Edie is not going to progress me any further along that road.

I stand up and stretch out my legs.

'Whoa!' says Franklin. 'Someone's forgotten their tabard.'

I look down at my bump and smile. 'Not forgotten, Franklin. Deliberately discarded.'

Four pairs of eyes regard me warily.

'Stella,' Edie says, 'are you sure you're ready to do this?'

'Not really. But I'm sick of hiding it, Edie. I'm sick of feeling guilty about this baby. Now Paul knows, it seems crazy to try and keep it from Velma and the others. Besides, I've completely run out of clothes baggy enough to hide it anymore.'

'It is a very large bump,' says Rosa, her lips pursed in concern.

'And that bloody tabard is so uncomfortable now.' Although strangely practical. I kind of miss it. When the baby comes I might even buy one to wear at home.

This is just one of the reasons why I will no doubt be on my own forever.

'But what about Velma?' Edie asks. 'What will she say?'

'She can say whatever the hell she likes,' I tell them bravely. 'This is two thousand and twelve. There are all sorts of employment laws to protect mums-to-be. She'll just have to deal with it, won't she?'

Rosa claps her hands delightedly, and Violet and Franklin join in.

'You go for it, Stella,' says Franklin.

Edie stands up and lays down her cards.

'I'll come with you,' she says. 'Just in case.'

I start to protest – I'm pretty sure Edie was only one card away from two sets of five – but then I notice where her eyes are trained. Making her way across the TV lounge, stopping to give each resident she passes a pat on the arm or a brief hug, is Maude. And she's heading straight for the card table.

'Come on, then.' I grab Edie by the hand and we race for the opposite exit. Race is perhaps overstating it somewhat. An arthritic old lady and a pregnant care worker – we must make an odd sight as we burst out into the corridor and collapse, giggling, against the wall.

Edie follows me as far as the staffroom, then says she feels quite tired and might just go for a little lie down.

'You'll be fine on your own, Stella,' she says, still keeping up the charade that this was why she left the game of cards.

But as she turns to walk away, I just can't help myself. It's the sadness in her eyes that does it. Life was perfect for Edie before Maude came. And even though Twilight's newest resident is sweetness and light personified, I can only imagine how hard it must be for Edie to see herself replaced as Franklin's favourite.

'It'll wear off soon, you know,' I say.

She looks around, surprised. Raises a drawn-on eyebrow.

'What will, dear?'

I swallow. Too late to back out now. Stepping closer, I smile and say, 'You know what Franklin's like. It's just the novelty – a new face, someone to charm. But you and him, you've always been so ...'

How to put it? I've seen the way he looks at her, how protective he is of her. And I'm sure Edie's feelings for him go way beyond close friendship. But what do I know of love in your twilight years? I can't even figure out love in your thirties.

Edie smiles and shakes her head. 'Oh, Stella, you are funny. I'm fine, really I am. You mustn't worry about me. You've got enough on your plate. Now, run along and face the music. I can't wait to hear all about it later.'

But Edie can't hide the way her smile slides off her face as she turns away to open her door.

*

'Martha, where's Velma?'

Figuring it will be best to just get it over and done with, I've decided to seek out my boss and confront her with the news as soon as possible. Martha's face is a picture of confusion, astonishment, and finally delight, as she takes in my bump.

'Oh, Stella,' she says, leaping off her chair and running around the reception desk to hug me. 'You never said! How on earth did you manage to keep this to yourself?'

'A combination of baggy clothes and subterfuge. And the help of a few of our lovely residents,' I tell her with a smile.

'Ah, well. It all makes sense now. All those times Velma couldn't find you and Edie said you'd been helping her in the garden. I thought, gardening? That's not in Stella's job description.'

'Edie's been a star.'

'And that time Bernie stole Violet's false teeth – was that you too?'

'A diversion. I was throwing up all over Edie's slippers at the time.'

Martha shakes her head in amazement. 'Wow. You're a sly one, aren't you? So, how far gone are you? Looks like you're about to drop.'

'It's all the cakes I've been eating. Actually I've got over a month to go yet.'

'Jesus! You're enormous for eight months. My Dora was half your size right up until the end. It really is incredible you've been able to keep it hidden. Mind you, I did say to Jean the other day that I thought you'd been comfort eating after your break up with ... Oh, my. What about Paul? Is this why you broke up? Didn't he want a baby? Or ...' Her eyes go wide with alarm. 'Isn't it his?'

Et tu, Brute.

'Contrary to popular opinion,' I say huffily, 'I am not carrying another man's child. Now, if you could just tell me where Velma is, I'll get out of your hair.'

Martha gives me a look that says she thinks I protest too much, and that I've just confirmed her suspicions, then tells me that Velma has been called out to meet with the board of directors.

'Really? What for?'

'I don't know. It was all very mysterious. The secretary phoned this morning and said Velma had to go to head office at twelve o'clock sharp.'

'Interesting.' I look at my watch: it's half past one. I can't help but hope that Velma is right now being given a severe bollocking. Goodness knows I could think of enough reasons for her to be in trouble with the board.

She's evil to her staff, indifferent to the residents' needs, and so power-crazed she has a photo of herself above the reception desk. I look up at it now and smile.

'She won't be back before the end of my shift, then,' I say with a fake sigh. 'What a shame.'

'Wait till Jean hears about the baby,' Martha calls as I head off to finish my rounds. I lift a hand to wave but don't turn around. Let her be the one to spread the word amongst the rest of the staff. Saves me a job.

I finish up in double-quick time, and head into the lounge to say goodbye to Edie. Mid afternoon on a Sunday everyone gathers in here for family visits. Of course, hardly any families actually visit, but the ones who do are shared out amongst the residents like chocolates. Today there's an adorable little girl with a red flower headband standing in the middle of the room reciting Humpty Dumpty to an audience with hushed, delighted faces. A woman who must be her mother holds a baby to her shoulders and bounces up and down on her toes. I smile and wave to Sally from the kitchen, who looks down at my stomach and gives me a thumbs up. Sally has three children, all of them under four, and often says she doesn't know why she works at all with the cost of childcare what it is.

Which starts me thinking again about how I'll manage when Bump comes along.

I love my job, and even though the money isn't wonderful, it's enough to live on. I need to look into my rights pretty damn quick, and work out just how long I can afford to stay home with the baby before I'm forced to start thinking about childminders. And speaking of childminders, Lipsy had better sort herself out with one soon. I'm not going to be able to keep up with one job for much longer, let alone two.

These days, that dodgy friend of hers isn't looking like such a terrible prospect.

And it's right then, as I'm leaning against the flock wallpaper at the edge of the TV lounge, that the thought pops into my head. It's just the tiniest grain of an idea, a seed that plants itself in the front of my brain and begins to grow. I watch the little girl singing; I take in Sally's encouraging smile. I consider all the hopeful expressions of joy on the faces in front of me.

I need a pen and paper. Right now.

Chapter 25

By the next morning I'm buzzing with excitement and I know exactly what I'm going to do. A quick phone call to Twilight's board of directors gets the wheels in motion, and if the secretary is surprised at my suggestion she doesn't show it. I don't mention Velma. It's none of my business. I've got three days off work now and I'm going to use them to move forward with my life. Suddenly my priorities are clearer than they've been for years. My new baby needs me, that's number one. He or she needs a home and a loving, calm, happy mother. I'm going to work hard on that. Lipsy and Phoenix are priority number two. I've been woefully negligent of my daughter – as evidenced by her frantic, and disastrous, efforts to bring Paul and me together. If she'd felt able to talk to me properly maybe none of that would have happened. Oh, I blame myself for a lot of things. It's time for me to make it right, and the first thing I'm going to do is take Lipsy to see my mother. I have a plan that I think might solve all our problems. Well, maybe not all of them. But hopefully quite a few.

The third priority is Paul. I have to disabuse him of the idea that I'm having someone else's baby. To do this I'll need to talk to him. I've dialled his number five times already but hung up before it began to ring. I need more time. I need to think it through. So for now I'm going to pop it in the part of my mind called Ignore, and get on with everything else. I have to, for sanity's sake.

Paul and I – maybe we'll never manage to sort it out. I

have to consider that possibility. Maybe we've had our chance. Maybe we've had too many chances. And each of us, in our own crazy ways, has messed it up again and again. When I saw him on Saturday I knew that there will never be anyone else for me. He's the love of my life, and there was a time when I would have done anything for him. Before I found out about the baby. Before I found out how diametrically opposed our views about family life are. And it tears me apart to have lost him. Seeing him in the church, feeling how he lifted every cell in my body, made me vibrate with love and desire ... Even now, I can't believe we won't get back together. Life without Paul seems unimaginable. But I'm not sure if we even deserve to be together anymore. I just don't know. So right now I'm focusing on priorities one and two, and Paul will just have to wait a little longer.

'Grandma's?' complains Lipsy when I tell her where we're headed. She wanted me to babysit today but I flat-out refused. Since the Paul debacle she's not pushing me so hard. But I doubt the moaning will ever stop, no matter how bad she feels.

'Great, Mum,' she whines as I strap Phoenix into his car seat. 'My first day off in ages, and you're taking me to Grandma's. I really wanted to go shopping.'

'What do you need to buy?' I ask.

'Nothing,' she says. 'Just, you know, shopping.'

'So you desperately needed me to babysit for you so you could go shopping for nothing?'

She nods and shrugs her skinny shoulders.

See what I'm up against here?

When we arrive at my mother's, I let us in and call out a cheery hello. She appears from the general direction of the kitchen wearing a comedy apron and covered in flour.

'Hey, Mum, nice underwear,' I say, adding a wolf whistle for good measure. The apron has a woman's curvy figure, neck to thighs, clad in a black basque. 'No wonder Dad can't keep his hands off you,' I tease, grinning.

Since the blessing, things have been easier between us. I don't know exactly why, but I'm glad of it. I need all the help I can get right now, and smooth family relations are a great way to start.

'Very funny, Stella,' she says. And then she notices Lipsy and Phoenix standing behind me. 'Phee!' she cries, making a lunge for him. 'Sorry, I mean Phoenix. Oh, how lovely to see my little boy.'

Lipsy gives me a look over her grandma's shoulder, but I put on my most innocent face. It's not my fault people want to shorten Phoenix's name, is it? If Lipsy doesn't like it, she should have picked a different name.

'Hi, Grandma,' she says wearily. 'What are you up to?'

'Aha. You'll have to come and see.'

In the kitchen a flour bomb has gone off, and there is barely a surface which isn't littered with bits of cake or icing sugar or some kind of cooking detritus.

'Doing a spot of baking, Mum?' I ask nonchalantly.

'Funny, Stella,' she says again. 'I'm trying to make the perfect Victoria sponge,' she explains to Lipsy. 'Fancy giving me a hand?'

Lipsy shrugs and allows an apron – not of the saucy variety, thank goodness – to be tied around her waist. My mother's excitement is palpable. She's never managed to get me involved in mum and daughter baking, but I think having Lipsy around might be perfect for her. I smile to myself and pull a chair up to my mum's huge kitchen table.

'So, to what do I owe this pleasure?' says my mother, beaming. 'I don't usually get to see my two girls and my great grandson on a Monday morning.'

She's still feeling bad, that's partly why she's being so

nice to me. But I've forgiven them all for their subterfuge. They had the best of intentions. Never mind that the road to hell is paved with good intentions – I've made enough mistakes of my own in the name of trying to do the right thing to be in any position to judge others.

Still, it's nice to have a surprise up my sleeve. A way for her and dad, not to mention Lipsy and Robert, to make it up to me big time.

I accept her offer of a cup of tea, and once she and Lipsy are elbow-deep in flour and cake mix, I drop my bombshell. Casually at first, then with the killer blow.

'So, Mum, I've been thinking about that offer you and Dad made.'

'What offer was that?' chirps in Lipsy.

'Your grandma and granddad offered to convert the garage for me and the baby to live in.'

'Wow! Really? That's so cool.'

My mother beams at her some more. This is all going perfectly to plan.

'Isn't it?' I enthuse. 'And it would be so perfect, having someone on hand to babysit whenever I wanted to go out. And anytime I didn't feel like cooking I could just come in here and join in with Mum and Dad. That garage is actually really big, you know. There's easily room for two bedrooms and a lounge.'

'So cool,' says Lipsy again. 'And it'll all be brand new? You'll be able to choose the fit out and everything?'

'Yup. And guess what? They're going to partition off a part of the garden for us too. Our own outdoor space to boot.'

Lipsy tuts and mutters how jammy I am. I'm having a hard time keeping a straight face.

'Have you decided to take us up on the offer?' asks my mother. I can't tell from her expression whether she's truly behind the idea or not. Probably it was my dad's brainchild. A chance for him to get back into renovating again, add a bit of value to the house and solve a few housing problems along the way.

Lipsy looks across at me expectantly, but I shake my head. 'No. It's such a lovely offer, but it's just not right for me. Not at my stage of life. And the thing is, I already have a house all of my own. It would be wrong of me to take you up on it, Mum. Selfish and wrong.'

I wait. Lipsy spoons some of the cake mix into a round tin, then stiffens and swirls around to face me.

'Oh my God! I've just had the most amazing idea! How about if we move in instead?'

'Who?' I say, feigning confusion.

'Me, Rob and Phoenix, of course. Grandma, don't you think it's the perfect solution? We can move into the new flat and mum can have her house back. Oh, it'll be wonderful. Our own place, with a garden for Phoenix to run around in. Mum, you don't mind, do you? You did just say it wasn't right for you.'

I heave myself up and hold out my arms. Lipsy runs across the kitchen and gives me a floury hug.

'I think it's a brilliant idea, Lipsy. I don't know why on earth I didn't think of it myself.'

'No,' says my mother, wryly. 'I don't know why you didn't, either.'

I smile at her over Lipsy's head and she grins back. 'You'll be able to see your great grandson every day,' I tell her. 'And you can teach Lipsy here how to cook.'

'And you can bring the baby over for play dates with Phoenix when it's older. Oh, I'm so excited.' Lipsy turns to my mum and claps her hands. I honestly haven't seen her this animated since her eighth birthday and we hired a magician with real white rabbits. 'Don't you think it will be perfect, Grandma?'

My mother lifts Phoenix out of his bouncer and holds

him high in the air. 'Perfect. And what do you think, little man? Could you live in Great Grandma's garage, do you think?'

'Will Granddad mind?' asks Lipsy, looking worried all of a sudden.

'Mind what?'

His timing is uncanny. I give him a kiss on the cheek as I walk past, and leave Lipsy to explain. On the way out I catch sight of myself in the over-sized hall mirror. 'My work here is done,' I say to my reflection in a mock superhero tone.

Now there's just the rest of my life to sort out.

*

I figure things on the home front will change pretty quickly now – Lipsy will be chomping at the bit to get my dad started on the conversion – so as soon as I get back to my bedsit I phone the landlord and give notice. Then I take a cup of tea downstairs and knock on Stephan's door. Apart from his habit of picking up my mail, Stephan has proved to be the perfect neighbour. He never bothers me; I never bother him. Occasionally we meet in the hall, and once or twice I've sat on the stairs with him chatting about nothing at all. He's quiet, self-contained, and if he has any friends I've never seen or heard them. Like I said, the perfect neighbour.

Soon I'll be back living next door to Joshua's goth tenants. I think I'd swap them for Stephan any day.

Unfortunately Stephan's out – or more likely refusing to answer because he thinks it's the bailiffs – so I trudge back up the stairs. Just in time to hear my phone ringing. I slop the cup of tea down on the sideboard and launch myself across the room: it might be Paul.

I look at the screen.

It's not Paul.

'Hi, Dad,' I gasp, totally out of breath.

'Are you OK?'

'Fine. Just ... been ... running ...'

'You shouldn't be out running in your condition,' he says, clearly outraged.

'Up the stairs,' I finish.

He laughs. 'Oh, right. Listen, you sped off so fast earlier I didn't have time to talk to you. There's something you need to know.'

'Is it OK?' I ask, alarmed. Dad putting the kybosh on my perfect plan is not in the script.

'What?'

'Lipsy and the whole converted garage thing. Did they tell you? Are you OK with it?'

'Oh, sure. Yeah, great idea. Don't know why you didn't suggest it yourself, to be honest. You're not as sharp as you used to be.' He laughs again and I pull a face at the phone. The problem with being a master manipulator from behind the scenes is you can't take any credit.

'So what did you need to talk to me about?'

'It's about Paul.'

Suddenly the atmosphere in here has become decidedly frosty. I said I'd forgiven my family for getting involved. That doesn't mean I've invited them to carry on with it.

'Now, before I start I want you to know that he came to me. He phoned and asked if I'd meet with him. I thought about saying no, but he was pretty insistent, and I couldn't help myself, Stella. I was still angry with him for all the stuff he said to you. I wanted to put him right.'

I flop down on the bed. The unmade bed, with the unwashed sheets and the bunched up duvet. I've let myself go lately, I admit it. Maybe it's not such a bad thing that my family want to take over running my life.

'Go on,' I say tiredly.

'I met him at the office. Smart Homes' old office? He's moving back in there, did you know about that? Relaunching on his own, doing some kind of property renovation-stroke-rental business for housing associations and charities. I wasn't really listening, to be honest. I just wanted to throttle him.'

He pauses for a reaction but I wait him out. Eventually he carries on. 'Anyway, to cut a long story short, I just thought you should know that I put him straight.'

'About the baby?'

'About everything. I told him I was with you the day you called off the wedding, and how torn up you were after what he said about not wanting to start a family with you. He cottoned on fairly quickly, give him his due, said that as you already knew you were carrying his baby that must have been quite a blow.'

'And then some!'

I realise I've not taken a breath since my dad started talking. My head is spinning, and it's not just the usual hunger taking over. 'So? What did he say then?'

I can almost hear my dad shrugging. 'That was it, really. I told him and then I left. I know you didn't want us getting involved, but I figured we'd already done so much damage by forcing the two of you together like that, the least I could do was try to sort out the misunderstanding. You two, you've always been so …'

He tails off, but I can imagine what he was about to say. 'Go on, Dad. Always been so what?'

'The misunderstandings. The jumping to conclusions. Ever since the fire last year, ever since you two realised you meant more to each other than just friends, it's been one thing after another. Your mother and I, we've wanted to bang your heads together this last six months, to be honest. What we did we did out of frustration. I'm sorry, Stella. It sounds harsh. But I know all about mistakes. I've suffered because of my own, and I've made those I love suffer too. And I know more about false pride than you or Paul ever could. So I did what I did, and I said what I said, and if you're angry with me I'm sorry. But there it is.'

The room swims and comes back into focus. My eyes are brimming with tears and I blink furiously to make them go back in. I'm not angry. Far from it. I only wish my dad was sitting on the bed next to me and not just a voice on the phone.

'I love you,' I tell him, my voice little more than a squeak. 'And I'm really, really grateful.'

'I love you too, Stella. And I've always been proud of you. You'll sort this out, I know you will. Only, no more misunderstandings, OK?'

'OK,' I whisper. I stare at the phone for a long time after he's hung up.

I guess my problem is, I don't know how to choose my battles. There was a battle I should have fought, but instead I just walked away. But maybe there comes a time when you're too tired for fighting. And maybe that's the day when you risk losing more than the love of your life. Maybe that's the day you risk losing a little piece of yourself.

Chapter 26

When I go back to work on Thursday I'm buoyed up by the knowledge of what I've agreed with Twilight's board of directors. This very morning I got a letter from them confirming everything. As I stow my bag in a locker, I wonder if Velma's heard about the pregnancy yet.

I'm only five minutes into my shift when I find out the answer to my question.

She finds me in the TV lounge. I'm on the late shift today, which means I'm helping to clear up after lunch, and I've got three residents to get ready for their physiotherapy sessions. Edie is one of them, and I'm looking forward to getting her on her own later. I've got something planned for her too. I'm ready to take on the world at the moment.

Except for the little corner of the world called Paul Smart, that is.

I'm trying to convince Violet that it's not time for *EastEnders* yet when I become aware that the room has gone quiet. Violet stops struggling for the remote control and looks over my shoulder. Then she turns her eyes to me and makes a cut-throat gesture across her neck. I stand slowly, smooth my maternity dress over my bump, and turn to face my boss.

'Ah, Stella,' she says, all business. 'There you are. In my office, please. Right away.'

I take a step forward, but Franklin blocks my way. Edie steps up beside him, followed by Rosa and Violet and the five other residents who can stand on their own.

Even Bernie shuffles forward on his Zimmer frame. I see Sally step out of the kitchen and position herself by the far wall. Maude, our newest resident, looks on from the sidelines, clearly amused.

The residents position themselves in a semicircle with me in the middle. Velma steps forward, her face set in hard lines.

'Don't go anywhere with her,' Franklin whispers. 'Make her talk to you right here.'

'Stella,' she says warningly. 'My office. Right now.' She can't take her eyes off my bump. Probably asking herself how she missed it all this time; kicking herself for missing the opportunity to make my working life as difficult as possible during those tiring, sickness-imbued second trimester months.

I clear my throat. Franklin nudges me in the side. 'Erm, I think I'd prefer it if we talked here. If that's OK?'

You show 'em, Stella. Sounding like a real force to be reckoned with. Not.

'It is not OK. I have some things to say to you and I would rather do it in private.' Her face is turning red now, which is not a pleasant colour on someone with steely grey hair and jowls. I take a step forward, but a small hand on my arm holds me back.

'Anything you have to say to Stella about the baby you can say right here in front of all of us.'

I flash Edie a grateful smile, but my eyes are trying to warn her off. Velma can't do anything to me now – nothing serious, anyway. These lovely people have seen me through the difficult months, but it's less than two weeks until my maternity leave begins, and that's all been squared with the powers that be, entirely over Velma's head. As much as I'm loving this impromptu showdown, I can't let these guys make an enemy of Velma for my sake. She'll still be here long after I'm gone, and she has a myriad of ways to make those who cross her pay.

'Thanks, everyone,' I say, trying to keep it light. 'Thanks for all the support you've shown me since you found out about the baby.' Might as well let Velma think she wasn't the only one in the dark. 'But it's fine, honestly. Velma only wants to have a little chat about when I'm starting my leave. Isn't that right?' I turn to her and she forces a quick nod of her head.

I follow her out of the lounge, down the corridor, past reception – where Martha and Jean are huddled with their heads together, whispering – and through into Velma's office.

There are no family photographs in here, because Velma doesn't have a family. She's a career woman, she told me once, and there was no room on her agenda for kids. Or a husband. I hope for her sake it's been worth it. Being the manager of a retirement home is a pretty important job, and incredibly rewarding too, but somehow I get the feeling her heart's not really in it.

'Sit,' she tells me, so I do.

She perches on her desk and sneers down at me, openly staring at my belly. 'They all believed the lies you told about calling off the wedding, but it seems to me like the truth is right here in front of us.'

I'm not going to rise to it. I'm not.

'Way I figure it, either you got knocked up by someone else and your fella found out just in time, or he got cold feet and dumped you at the altar. Not the other way around.'

Everybody's got a theory. And some are surprisingly creative.

'Is there a work-related reason you needed to talk to me, Velma? Only, I've got to get Edie and Mr Price ready for their physio sessions, and you know how they don't like to have their routines disrupted.'

She grimaces and picks up a yellow manila file from

her desk. 'It's a shame you didn't feel you could confide in me,' she says, as if this was even possible. 'I had to hear about it from head office. They've sent your maternity leave forms for you to fill in.'

'Great,' is all I answer, and I hold out my hand. She doesn't hand over the file, though. It seems she has more to say.

'Word will be out there by this afternoon, no doubt,' she says with a dismissive wave of her hand, 'but I wanted to be the one to tell you my news. In person,' she adds pointedly.

I shift in my seat. Lately it's getting harder and harder to get comfortable in any position. My back aches, my stomach feels like it's going to drop off it's so heavy, and my bladder is constantly squeezed to dribbling point. But I make myself look interested. The sooner she gets this over with, the sooner I can get out of here and give my back a good rub.

'I'm leaving.'

I tip my head to the side. Did I hear right?

'You're leaving?' I say incredulously. 'Why?'

'On to bigger and better things,' she says with a tinkling laugh that is entirely false. I laugh along with her, also falsely, and heave myself out of my chair.

'Well,' I say, holding out my hand for the file, 'I wish you every success in the future. And thanks so much for telling me. In person. Now, if you don't mind, I've got to get on.'

When I exit her office, yellow file in hand, Martha and Jean jump back. They've obviously been listening at the keyhole.

'Well, go on, then,' I tell them once the office door is firmly closed behind me. 'What are you waiting for? You'd better go and spread the good news.'

But as I walk away, rubbing my aching back with my free hand, I can't help but feel sad for Velma. The sudden meeting with the board of directors? The even more sudden resignation from a job that defined her? I'm not stupid. She jumped before she was pushed.

Which is, when you think about it, exactly what I did with Paul.

By the time I make it upstairs, Edie's physiotherapy session is already under way, so I get on with my other afternoon jobs and keep an eye on the time. It's essential I talk to Edie today. But my plan will need a bit of help from the catering section, so once I've tidied up the laundry room and sorted out the evening's meds, I wander down to have a word with Sally.

'Have you heard?' she says the minute I poke my head around the kitchen door. She's standing at one of the huge industrial sinks, washing a gigantic copper saucepan. 'Velma's gone.'

'Gone? What, like totally gone? Already?'

'Yup. She was told to clear her office, apparently. Put out on garden leave for her notice period.'

'Poor thing.'

Sally does a double take. 'Poor thing? You couldn't stand the woman.'

'I know, but it doesn't mean I wanted to see her chucked out of her job.'

I lean against the reflective metal worktop, taking my weight on my elbow.

'From what I hear,' Sally says with a shrug, 'she's been on a warning for ages. Something about fiddling the budgets. Siphoning cash.'

'Who did you hear that from?'

'Martha. Who else?'

Who else indeed.

'Do you think it's true?' I ask.

She shrugs again. 'Probably. Most of the stock we get in here now is cut-price rubbish, but apparently the board has been upping the budget for months. Anyway, we're well shot of her.'

I imagine Velma paying for this year's exotic holiday with money she's taken out of Twilight's shallow pockets. The thought doesn't make me angry, it just makes me sad.

'Yes, well. Maybe we are. Except …'

'What?'

'Better the devil you know and all that. The new manager might be even worse.'

Sally snorts. 'Worse? I can't imagine how. You know, Stella, you should apply for it.'

'Me?' Now it's my turn to snort derisively. 'Very funny.'

'No, really.' She dries her hands and gives me a thoughtful look. 'You'd be a brilliant manager. You care about the oldies more than anyone I've ever met.'

'They don't really like being called oldies, Sally,' I say, wincing.

'See! You even know all the politically correct terminology.'

'But …' There's so much wrong with her suggestion I don't know where to start. 'I've only been in the job a year. I've got no qualifications, no experience of managing anything, and in case it's escaped your notice, I'm just about to go off on maternity leave. Even if I was a suitable candidate, the board would never give *me* the job.'

'I might apply for it,' she says quietly, pleating the tea towel in her hands.

'Sally! You should. That's a great idea. You've been here forever, and the "oldies" just love you so much. And you manage your own budget for the kitchen now, so you've got experience of that. Go for it, girl.'

She shakes her head dismissively. 'I can't, Stella. It's the childcare. It would cripple me. With shifts I can just about manage but if I was here nine to five I'd never be able to afford it. Even with the increase in salary.'

'But wouldn't you like to work nine to five? See more of the kids?'

'Of course I would. But it just wouldn't work.' She throws the tea towel into the empty sink and brushes off her hands. 'Anyway, doesn't hurt to dream. So, did you want anything in particular or did you just want a gossip?'

I tell her about my plan for Edie, and she agrees to help me out. Before I go I give her a quick hug. I'm not quite ready to announce it publicly yet, but I've got a feeling my other news is going to be a big relief for her too.

'Fill out the application, Sally. Just give it a try. You never know what's around the corner.'

She snorts again, and walks away, shaking her head. I smile at her retreating back and head off up to Edie's room. I'm all about spreading happiness today. Messing in other people's lives is much more fun that sorting out your own.

*

Edie is sitting up in bed when I knock on her door. She looks tired and older than usual. Some of her spark has gone, and I notice that she hasn't bothered putting on her strawberry lip treatment today. I pick up the slippers I bought her and take them over to the bed.

'Come on,' I say sternly. 'No lounging about on a weekday.'

She smiles tiredly and shakes her head. 'I think you can make an exception for me, can't you?'

'Well, OK. Just this once. But you have to let me give you a hand massage.'

Edie loves having her hands massaged. All the female residents of Twilight do, and I've managed to convince a couple of the men to give it a try too. But not many. They just can't take the ribbing. Which is a shame. Gender stereotypes survive well into old age, you'll not be surprised to learn.

I fill a bowl with warm water then pull up a chair and sit next to the bed while Edie immerses her hands.

'Did you mean what you said the other day, Edie?' I ask, gazing out of the window nonchalantly.

'Could you be a bit more specific?'

'About understanding why my family got involved in my business. Do you really think it's OK for someone to try and bring two people together if you can see that they are meant for each other, but the two of them are incapable of getting past a friendship, say?'

Edie wriggles her fingers and purses her lips. 'I suppose so, yes. I know it didn't work in your case, but sometimes people need a bit of a push, don't they? I used to be quite the matchmaker in my day, you know,' she says with a smile. 'That's the one good thing about being a spinster. You have loads of friends, male and female, and it's lovely to pair them off with each other.'

'Didn't you ever feel left behind?'

'Oh, Stella. You're such an old romantic. Life is what it is, my dear. Sometimes you just have to accept that your chances have passed you by. I don't cry myself to sleep every night, if that's what you're asking.'

With my head lowered over her hands, I pull a sceptical face. The tissues on the floor in the mornings tell a slightly different story.

'Have they been interfering again?' she asks while I dry her hands on a fluffy towel.

'Who?'

'Your family.'

'Oh, no. Not at all.' I start to massage lavender-scented lotion into her curled up hands. 'They are all behaving themselves beautifully. Listen, Edie. I know you're all organising something for my last day next week–'

'How did you know? Oh, Martha. Of course.'

'Anyway, I wondered if you'd like to have dinner with me that evening. Nothing special, and it'll be right here at Twilight, but I'd really like to say thank you for being such a great friend to me. If the weather's fine I thought we could eat in the gardens.'

'Why, Stella, that's a lovely idea.'

I lower my head again so she can't see my eyes. 'I thought I'd invite Franklin too. If that's OK with you?' There's no answer, but when I look up she's gazing out of the window, a tiny smile hovering about her mouth. 'I thought I could come up for you beforehand, help you get ready. Do your make-up or something. How does that sound? If you haven't got anything else on, of course.'

'Lovely,' she says, lifting up one hand to inspect it closely. 'That will be just lovely.'

As I get ready to leave, Edie turns her attention back to me. 'Stella, have you sorted things out with that man of yours yet?' I shake my head. Thinking of other people for a change has been a great distraction. But I do know I can't avoid it much longer.

'You know, Stella, he's going to be in your life forever now, no matter what. He's your baby's father. Sooner or later you'll have to come to terms with that, and if there's the slightest chance you could resurrect more than just your friendship, you owe it to yourself to give it everything you've got. There is nothing worse than having to see someone you love every day and not be able to hold them. Believe me, my dear, it's not something you want to experience.'

I could tell her that I have experienced it. Before Paul and I got together in the first place, that's what it was like for me. Seeing him every day, not able to tell him how I felt. But I get the feeling she's talking about someone much closer to home.

'What can I do, Edie?' I ask her. 'He doesn't want a family. I love him, that's never changed, and I know he'd make a wonderful father, and I know we could have had a wonderful life together. But he didn't want that. And now ... I just think it's too late.'

Edie looks down at her hands again. When she raises her head and meets my eyes, the hope there cuts right through me. 'It's never too late, my dear,' she says softly. 'You, of all people, should know that.'

Chapter 27

I'm getting to the stage now where I can't put on my own socks. Washing and drying my hair are mammoth tasks, as is taking a bath. This very afternoon I'm moving back into my own home, which is just as well: the stairs at Termite Towers are killing me. My belly is so huge I've had to buy a bump support, a stretchy strap thing that goes under my stomach and holds the baby up. I don't walk anymore, I waddle. Even my shoulders are fat. I'm enormous, I'm whale-like, and I'm loving it.

Walking around Willen Lake with Lipsy, pushing Phoenix in his buggy, soaking up the sun and watching the geese waddle along the footpath – the geese look like they're mimicking me – is just about the best fun I've had in ages.

OK, I really do need to get out more.

The only cloud on my horizon is what to do about Paul. Yesterday I remembered the letter I was about to write before Sharon came to see me and sent everything spinning; I'm thinking a letter is still a good idea. I can explain everything properly – no more misunderstandings, as my dad instructed – and then I can leave it up to him. If he wants me, when he knows how I feel and knows what's on offer, then he can damn well come and get me.

And if he doesn't ...

I can deal with that. I really can. Real life is not a love story. It's a series of tough decisions, disappointments and compromise. It ain't glamorous or fluffy, and it doesn't always have a happy ending. We live. And we learn. And sometimes that's the best we can hope for.

When we reach the far side of the lake, I stop, feigning tiredness. I am tired, but secretly I just need to stand here for a moment and let the memories wash over me. The scene of my impassioned last-ditch attempt to win Paul over; the setting for Paul's Christmas proposal. If I'm quiet enough I might hear the echoes of our love coming back across the lake.

There are no tears today.

'Mum,' says Lipsy, laying her head against my shoulder, 'do you still love Paul?'

I reach my arm around her, pulling her in for a sideways hug. It's the only way I can hug these days.

'More than anything else in the world, Lipsy. Except for you and Phoenix, of course. And the baby. And perhaps my sanity, which is seriously at risk if this doesn't get sorted out soon.'

Joking about it helps, but I don't think Lipsy's fooled for a minute.

'Jesus. How did it all get so complicated?' she says, gazing off across the lake.

Well, I was born and then ...

'It's just life,' I tell her, smiling bravely. 'But don't you worry your pretty head about it. It'll all work out for the best. You'll see.'

Wish I believed that. I don't half talk some shit at times.

*

The letter doesn't take long to write. Back at the bedsit, the tiny window open to the sound of boy-racers screeching up and down outside, out it all pours: every fear, every hurt, every wrong assumption and misguided decision. I tell him exactly why I called off the wedding, and writing it down reminds me that at the time, I really did feel it was the only option.

Now I can see about a hundred different options. Hindsight is a wonderful thing.

It's hard – my pride is just as sore as his, if not more so – but I also tell him how much I love him and how I wish it could have been different. Like, if he'd wanted a family with me. If he didn't think I was too old, and that families were dull and boring and a waste of time. OK, maybe he didn't say that exactly, but that was the impression he gave.

When the letter is finished, I reach into my make-up bag and pull out two objects I've been carrying around with me for months. The locket I hang around my neck like a talisman. I don't tempt fate by trying to slip the ring onto my finger – there's not the slightest chance it would fit anyway. Instead I wrap the letter around it and seal the envelope. Then I put the envelope in my bag and finish packing up the last few items left in the bedsit. I'll miss Termite Towers, with its piles of rubbish and odd, quirky characters. I've made no impression here; no one noticed me arrive and no one will notice I've gone. Except Stephan, perhaps. I've already pushed a card under his door with a ten pound note in it. Have a drink on me, it read. I think Stephan can have several on that.

Before I head home, I drive to the city centre and head for Silbury Boulevard. Working in Bletchley, I hardly ever come up here anymore. It seems busier. More people, all bustling about with their heads down, fixed on their own narrow paths. It's cool for mid July, but the sun is high and the sky is a deep azure blue. The mirrored buildings reflect the trees and the cars over and over again; the effect is mesmerising. I find a parking space not too far from Paul's office and heave my enormous frame out of the car.

Right. This is it.

Smart Homes. The facade hasn't changed, even though my dad said Paul is relaunching the business as something completely different. I guess he couldn't just open the doors and go back to how it was before. Going back isn't in Paul's nature. Ever.

Stop it, Stella. That way madness lies.

The office is in darkness, so I slip the letter under the door and turn to walk back to the car. That's when I see him. He's sitting on the floor facing away from me, surrounded by boxes and files. The one remaining desk, just to his left, is piled so high with stuff it looks likely to collapse under the weight. For a moment I picture this office full of life and people. A year ago, when I worked here with Susan and Joe and evil Loretta, there was never a dull moment. Who'd have thought we'd all have moved on so quickly, so resolutely. Loretta works for Smart Homes' arch rival now. Susan and Joe got married at Christmas and moved up the road to Northampton.

Stella Hill got herself knocked up and messed up her life big time.

Stella, you're doing it again.

I slip away before Paul notices the heavily pregnant woman spying on him from the street. Trudge back to my car and head for home.

When I arrive, Lipsy and Robert are running around like lunatics.

'It's OK,' I say for the hundredth time, 'you don't have to move out straight away, you know.'

If you don't mind sleeping on the sofa, I don't add, because at eight months pregnant I'll be damned if I am.

'No, Mum, it's all under control,' Lipsy reassures me, before turning away and shouting, 'Robert, you moron, you've packed all Phee's nappies already.'

'Phee?' I look at her, eyebrows raised. She shrugs.

'I like Phee. There's nothing wrong with it.'

'Well, I never said there was,' I start, but she's gone

already, racing up the stairs with Phoenix in her arms. Over her shoulder he smiles down at me, and I give a little wave. My grandson. Soon to be the number one playmate of my new son or daughter. Funny, there was a time when I couldn't get my head around that. Now it doesn't seem so very strange or complicated. Just different. And quite useful, in a way.

A pain pulls at my abdomen and I bend over with an oomph. Practice contractions, the midwife calls them. I had an appointment yesterday, where she measured my bump, yet again – and looked surprised, yet again – and told me what to expect for the coming weeks.

'Are you all ready for the birth?' she asked. 'Bag packed, birth partner lined up, breathing exercises under way?'

I nodded and reassured her that I was, definitely. Absolutely.

Bag? I'll throw a few things in my holdall when the day arrives: clean knickers, a bottle of water, a blanket for the baby and a big bar of chocolate for me. Breathing? I've been doing that for thirty-eight years. I think I've got it figured out.

Birth partner?

There's only one person I want as my birth partner, and I'm not holding my breath. No pun intended. But if it comes to it – and it sure looks like it will come to it – Lipsy will step into the breach. She's had recent experience, after all.

Bump kicks again, and I actually see the fabric of my top move. I love it when that happens. Then I'm doubled over in pain. It's like the worst period pain you've ever had, times a million. And these are only practice contractions? I'm in for a bumpy ride.

Chapter 28

'The red or the black? What do you think?'

I look across to where Edie is holding out two dresses. The red is a spunky number I've never seen before; the black is demure and screams classy. Both are lovely, but her face above the coat hangers is pinched with nerves.

'Which do you feel most comfortable in?' I ask. She pulls a face, then holds them up to her body one by one and looks at her reflection in the bathroom mirror.

'The black one. I think. But the red is just so … so …'

'Outrageous?' I offer.

'Do you think I could carry it off? Be honest, Stella. I don't want to look like mutton dressed as lamb.'

The expression has me doubled over with laughter. 'Oh, Edie, you kill me. My nan used to say that all the time. But worse than that was "mutton dressed as mutton".'

She smiles and slips the red dress off the hanger. 'Oh, what the hell. It's just a dinner with friends, right? And you deserve something a bit special, Stella, after everything you've done for me.'

I look away, embarrassed. I just hope Edie's not going to be too mad at me when she finds out what I've done. Before I came up here to help her get dressed I went outside to check how Sally was getting on. Everything was perfect. It's a beautiful evening, with the sun still shining on the secluded spot I've chosen under the arbour. There's a table laid with silver cutlery, and

Sally's offered to bring out the food herself. We lit candles and hung some pink heart bunting from the trees to the arbour. No one in the main house can see without walking right down to the bottom of the gardens, and no one's going to do that because they'll all be having their dinner too.

It looks so lovely, so special and glamorous, I wish I really was having dinner with them.

But the table is set for two.

I blow-dry Edie's fine hair into a fuller version of her usual style, and then I help zip her into her dress.

'You look a million dollars,' I tell her, and I mean it.

We slip out of a side door to avoid the main dinner crowd. As we round the hedges I can see Franklin waiting. Earlier, I had a quiet word with him. I kind of told him the lie of the land. Well, come on – Edie said herself she thought it was OK to get involved if you can see two people are made for each other, but they're just a bit useless at sorting themselves out. And if there are two people in this world who are made for each other, it's Edie and Franklin.

'Off you go, then,' I say to Edie now, giving her a gentle push in the direction of the table.

She looks startled. 'Aren't you coming with me?'

I shake my head. 'I wish I could, Edie. But it's my leaving do tonight, isn't it? And I've invited my mum and dad, and Lipsy, and I really need to go and make sure everything's going to plan.'

If looks could kill I'd be dead on the spot. 'Stella Hill, you planned this whole thing. You are incorrigible.'

'Yup,' I tell her, nodding. 'I sure am. Now you have a nice time with Franklin. Go on,' I say when she hesitates, 'or I'll tell Maude he's out here all on his own.'

That gives her the incentive she needs. I watch as she picks her way along the path, and stay just long enough to see Franklin's face light up when he sees her. He pulls out her chair, leans down, and gives her the gentlest of kisses on the back of her neck.

I slip away, satisfied. At least there's one happy couple in the world, about to make a go of it after years of messing about. I guess I'll just have to be content with that.

*

My leaving party is a sober affair, organised by the residents with a little help from Jean, Martha and Sally. My family add a festive element, and Lipsy is our token young person – it's so sweet how the residents crowd around her, eager for a piece of her youthfulness. Everyone's dressed in their finery; they love a party even more than youth. Violet is wearing a bright pink frilly dress that trails to the floor and keeps tripping her up.

'Be careful you don't break your neck,' I tell her as she hands me a glass of Buck's Fizz – which in my case is more orange juice than champers.

'What?' she hollers. 'What did you say?'

I smile and move on. Bump gives me a little press just below my ribcage and I stop and wait for him to settle down. Him? I'm convinced it's a boy. I figure I've done my time with a girl child and this time around I deserve to have a go with one of the male variety.

It'll be compensation for having no actual man of my own.

I haven't heard from Paul since I dropped off the letter. Knowing I took it to him with my own fair hands means I can't even blame it on the vagaries of the postal system. Mind you, it was only yesterday. Men take longer to react, don't they? They lack that necessary sense of urgency to jump in their cars and race around to see the one they love, begging forgiveness and promising that all will be well if they can only have just one more chance ...

Unless of course they don't love her all that much. Then it's fine to hang around and take your time.

Dinner's been cleared away, and the residents are gathered in the lounge to say goodbye to me. Martha calls me over and clears her throat.

'Stella,' she says, 'you left us once before, and we got you twenty pounds in gift tokens and a bottle of cava.'

'And a bed jacket,' Rosa pipes up. 'I knitted the arms myself.'

Martha nods. 'Quite. So Stella will have to take that off the value of this present, OK? We can't have people leaving and then coming back and then going off on maternity leave all the time. It just gets too expensive.'

'You're all heart, Martha,' Bernie shouts from the back.

'Thank you,' I say, taking a shiny red gift bag out of her hands. She winks at me, then slips away.

'Speech,' someone calls and I smile, embarrassed. I look out across the sea of faces, all so dear to me. It's great that my mum, dad and Lipsy are here, but it's the residents I'm focusing on now. With their funny ways and their stories of the war and their ingrowing toenails and hairs spouting from every orifice, I'll miss them so much.

I wasn't this upset the first time around, but I guess during the last six months I've gotten to know them so much better. And the good thing is, I know I'll be back.

'Speech!'

As I prepare for what I want to say, I see Edie and Franklin enter via the garden door. They are holding hands, and Edie's face is brimming over with happiness. A lump forms in my throat, and for a moment I can't speak.

'Thank you all so much,' I get out finally. 'Martha's quite right – you've all been very patient with my comings and goings, but this time I can say with absolute certainly, once this little one is old enough, I'll be back!'

'Like the Terminator,' calls Violet. I smile at her and nod.

'And, to that end, I've got one more surprise piece of news to share.'

'She's having twins!' This is from Franklin, who looks like he's lost a fiver and found a million dollars. He's still holding Edie's hand tightly. I hope he never lets it go.

'Triplets,' shouts my dad. I throw him a warning look.

'Very funny. No, nothing like that. But it is about babies. And children.' I look around the room and find Sally. She smiles and I keep my eyes fixed on her. 'There are lots of female employees here at Twilight who find it hard to pay for good childcare, and their work is all the harder for it. I'm going to be in the same position next year, so I decided to do something about it.'

Lipsy is looking at me with a new kind of respect. Of course, she's all sorted now she's got her grandma on tap – replacing me who she's had on tap thus far – but it's not that easy for everyone.

'You'll be pleased to know that the board of directors have agreed to let me convert the reading room into a crèche.'

I'm expecting cheers round about now, but all I've got is a bunch of confused faces.

'A crèche,' I explain, 'that will be staffed by volunteers, some working around their shifts, looking after all the children of the staff here, and providing a great place for the children of visiting families too.'

'I could help out in there,' Rosa pipes up. 'I was a teacher before I retired.'

'That's fantastic, Rosa, thank you.'

Sally's face is slowly breaking into a smile. I give a little bow and jump out of the limelight as quickly as I can. Well, they'll all be chuffed to bits when they see it in action. But right now, I've got other things to think about. My stomach has started up with those bloody practice contractions again; they're not too frequent, but they are getting progressively worse. I lean against the back of a wing chair and pause to catch my breath.

Sally walks over, still grinning. 'You know what this means, don't you?'

'Yes, I do. Get that application in pronto.'

She hugs me and fairly skips back to the kitchen. I close my eyes and wait for the contraction to pass.

'Some plan, Stella. What a brilliant idea.'

'Thanks, Mum.'

She lays a warm hand on my lower back. 'Are you OK?'

'I think so. It's just these practice contractions again. Like I need to practise! I have already been through it once.'

She smiles and shakes her head. 'It might be different this time around. You and Billy had totally different births. Billy was really easy, just popped right out, but you, you were –'

'A nightmare, I know. You may have told me once or twice already.'

Something else Billy did better than me.

'You know,' she says, gazing off above my head, 'I could come and help out sometimes. With the crèche, I mean. I could bring Phee with me. I'm CRB checked from my job at the school.'

I was kind of hoping she'd say that. So, finally it's all coming together. In the absence of my perfect future, at least I've managed to carve out one that is just about all right. And not just for me.

'Stella.' I sense her stiffening at my side and I look up in alarm. There's a look on her face that's somewhere between shock and joy.

'What's wrong?'

She shakes her head slowly, raises her arm and points. I follow her gaze.

Standing at the back of the room, holding the biggest teddy I have ever seen in my life, is Paul.

Chapter 29

I can barely see him over the top of the teddy. Really, the thing is quite preposterous, and if he thinks he can win me round by buying the biggest, best, most cuddly …

Just get yourself over there, you stupid woman.

For once, I'm listening to the voice in my head.

'Paul?'

He puts down the monster teddy and takes my hand. There is the slightest tremor in his, and I tell myself not to build up my hopes. This could mean anything – forgiveness, friendship, the softening of his heart. It doesn't necessarily mean what I want it to mean.

'Looks like a great party,' he says, looking over my shoulder. I've yet to take my eyes off his face.

'Hm-mm,' is all I manage.

Paul looks at my hand in his, then looks up into my eyes.

'Did they knit you another bed jacket?'

'No. But there's a bag of baby clothes over there that I think is coming my way pretty soon.'

'That's nice.'

My heart's pounding. I let out a breath and it sounds like a whimper. Paul looks down at his feet.

'What colour are they?' he says.

'What?' I follow his gaze. His shoes are brown, polished to a high gloss.

'The baby clothes. Are they pink or blue?'

If my heart keeps this up much longer I'm going to collapse.

'A mixture, I imagine,' I tell him, moving half a step closer.

'You don't know yet?' The hope in his voice is clear.

At least I got something right.

'Not a clue.'

'Stella,' he says, dropping my hand and taking hold of both my wrists, 'I've been such an idiot. I'm so sorry and I love you so much. I want more than anything to make things right between us.'

Wow. It *does* mean what I want it to mean.

'This has been the worst year of my life, Stella, but there's still time to turn it around. If you want to.' He's gazing at my bump reverently, admiringly. His hand twitches as if he longs to touch it.

I can't speak. My body is thrumming with emotion. I can feel it from my fingertips, through my wrists – still encased in Paul's trembling hands – all the way down to my swollen ankles. I'm a whale, an enormous tank of a woman, but next to Paul, with him looking at me this way, I feel like a fragile teenager all over again. And my mind is going round in circles.

My right hand escapes his and flies up to touch the locket at my throat.

Something old.

'Stella,' Paul says, going down on one knee.

Oh, my.

He fishes around in his pocket and then pulls out – my ring.

'Stella, will you marry me?'

A round of applause breaks out behind me. Oh, right – now they're clapping. Now I need them all just to disappear and leave me in peace, they're suddenly more interested in me than the TV. Typical.

'Stella?'

Paul is looking up at me expectantly. He's smiling, but it's a smile of anxiety, and I realise what this has cost him, to come here and risk humiliation all over again.

'Do you love me?' he asks softly.

'You know I do. But there are things we need to–'

'Talk about. I know. Definitely.' He nods his head furiously, nearly head-butting my belly. 'I've written you a letter, too. It's here somewhere.' He starts to root around in his trouser pocket again but then gives up. 'I think it's better to say it in person. I do want to start a family with you, Stella. You'll be a wonderful mother to my baby, and I'll do my best to be a wonderful father. You're not old, you're not past it. I thought I was, I thought ... But I was wrong. About so many things.'

'Is this a sudden change of heart?' I can't help asking. I need to know how deeply this goes. My entire future happiness depends on it.

I also wish he'd get up off the floor. It's making my neck ache looking down at him, and my abdomen is starting to contract again.

'When I spoke to your dad, he told me that pride nearly ripped your family apart.'

'And that's all it was? Pride?'

'It stopped me admitting how much I wanted a family. That and fear. Fear that it wouldn't happen for us. And I thought we had it all figured out, moving away, starting again. But I didn't listen to you, Stella. I didn't ask myself – or you – what we really wanted. We just went off on this ... tangent. We never really talked about the important stuff.'

He's right there. Which is all well and good, but someone has to break the pattern. Someone has to give in and be willing to take a chance.

And, in the words of my antenatal practitioner, in the end all it takes is one big push.

Or a leap of faith.

Trying to ignore the pain that is ripping at my belly, I bend down and whisper, 'Would you like to meet your new baby?'

He nods again, tears misting his eyes. I take his hand and place it gently on my bump.

'Oh, Stella.'

A cheer goes up, followed by another bout of clapping.

'Will you lot just sod off,' I say, turning to glare at them. I catch Lipsy's eye; her expression is one of almost unbearable hope. I'm just about to signal to her that I think this time it might really be OK, when another wave of pain hits me.

'What was that?' Paul says.

'Just a contraction. A practice one,' I add as he jumps to his feet and puts his arms around me.

'Ah,' he says, nodding sagely. I wonder if he has the slightest idea what a practice contraction is. He's missed out on so much. But, hold on, Bump wants to have his say.

'Feel.' I grab Paul's hand again and press it to the top of my stomach. His eyes go wide.

'It that the baby?'

'I sure hope so. Ooo!'

The pain is too much now, far more than it should be. My mother appears by Paul's side, and together they lean over me, concern clouding their faces.

'How close is she?' Paul asks her.

'She's got a few weeks to go yet. Stella? Are you all right, love?'

'It's fine,' I tell them, waving my hands. 'Fine. Just a little ... Ow!'

'Stella,' Paul begins, his voice husky with emotion, but then he looks down at my feet. My mother's eyes follow his, and I wonder for a couple of blissful seconds what is so interesting down there.

Then I take a look myself.

'What the ...?'

I'm standing in a pool of slippery liquid. My leggings are drenched through, and my shoes are slick with it. Paul's hands go slack and he drops the ring, just as another gush exits my body of its own volition.

But it can't be happening now, can it? I've got weeks to go yet. Haven't I?

'Stella?' Now my dad is in on the action, and I can see Edie and Franklin, their faces pinched with concern, hovering behind him.

Just before everything goes black, I see that they are still holding hands. It makes me so incredibly happy: a big wave of happiness washing over me as I fall into Paul's waiting arms and close my eyes.

*

When I come around again, I only have eyes for Paul. In the ambulance, on the gurney, along corridors and through crashing double doors, his face is all I see. He doesn't let go of my hand, not even when a nurse tells him to get out of her way so she can examine me. He moves to stand behind me, propping me up against his chest so I can see the top of her head as she moves her hands around under my clothing.

I'm beyond feeling whatever it is she's doing, and way beyond caring.

Or maybe that's the gas and air.

'Ten centimetres dilated,' she calls out to another nurse who is standing by just outside the room. 'I think we have a baby on its way,' she tells me with a smile.

I have a witty response lined up for this, and I'm ready to deliver it to the woman with her hands up my hospital gown. But just then the pain overtakes me once again and her face fades into nothingness. The only things I'm aware of are Paul's hand gripping mine and his heart beating hard against my back.

And the beep beep beep of my baby's heart as he fights his way out into the world.

Chapter 30

'Of course, I always knew it was going to be a boy.'

I'm sitting up in bed surrounded by my family – Mum, Dad, Lipsy and Paul. In my arms I'm holding ... well, a baby! That's what all this fuss has been about, after all. This tiny, helpless bundle of love. Astonishing that he managed to cause so much trouble, really.

'Our baby boy,' I say to Paul.

He smiles, a smile of such incredible love it takes my breath away.

'I know,' he says. 'And he's beautiful. Just like you.'

'He really looks like you,' I tell him. Paul pinks up with pleasure, and peers over my shoulder.

'He looks like you, too.'

'Only smaller,' I joke. 'And with a bit less hair.'

Lipsy hugs herself, and I wonder if all this brings back painful memories for her.

'Where's Phee?' I ask.

'He's at home with Rob. They're coming over later.'

'I'll be back on my feet in no time,' I say reassuringly. 'Don't worry – I'll still be able to babysit when you need me to. You won't have to rely only on your grandma.'

Lipsy rolls her eyes. 'Yes, Mum,' she says, 'that's all I'm worried about right now. Thinking of myself, as usual.'

My dad steps forward for a better look, and I send him a silent thank you. It's not just for putting Paul in the picture – I would have done that myself soon enough

– it's also for reminding me about what's important. Not pride. Not being right, or even being happy. What is important is to be clear, and understood. No more misunderstandings. Ever.

'Have you thought of a name yet?' my mother asks, wiping her eyes on Dad's hanky. I remember how drained I was after seeing Lipsy give birth, and my heart goes out to her. What a day. What a year. She'll need a holiday after all this.

Maybe they could go on honeymoon, I think with a smile, and I file that away to say to her later. There's a lot more I need to say besides. Like sorry. And I love you.

'Yes,' Paul says, nervously. 'Have you got any ideas for a name?'

'I have,' I say with a mischievous smirk, 'I'm going to call him Aiden.'

'Aiden?' Dad repeats. 'That's ... nice.'

'It means "little fire",' I add. And then I wait for it to sink in. But instead of hilarious laughter I just get a whole load of groans, and Lipsy reminds me that I said symbolic names were naff.

'Phoenix has brought me round to the idea,' I tell her, but none of them are fooled.

In a while I feign tiredness, and they take the hint and leave Paul and me alone. I am tired – I'm exhausted – but no force on earth could make me sleep right now. I'm too worried that I might wake up and find all of this has been a dream. That I'm still sitting in my grotty bedsit, staring out of the window and thinking about Paul, instead of sitting propped against hospital pillows holding a beautiful baby boy with curly blonde hair and a beatific expression, with the love of my life by my side, gazing at me like I'm the most incredible creature ever to have walked the earth.

'You were magnificent,' Paul tells me for the

twentieth time, and I give a little self-deprecating smile.

'I know,' I say, laughing. 'It was nothing, really.'

'Nothing? I thought I was going to pass out at the end there. And you, you just kept on going, and going ... Wow, Stella. I don't know how you did it.'

'But you're glad I did, right?'

The tears in his eyes tell me yes.

'I thought I'd lost you, you know,' he says, his voice breaking. 'Not when you called off the wedding. Not then. I thought ... I always thought we'd sort it out.'

'I can't believe you actually thought that I was–'

'Yes, well. Jumping to conclusions is what I do best, right? But what I found really hard was how you seemed so accepting of everything. Like you could deal with it either way. With or without me.'

This is the time now. The time for truths. I'm not basing our relationship on anything else from now on. Because it's not just us anymore.

Now we're a family.

No more misunderstandings. No more assumptions. And no more lies.

'I could, Paul,' I say softly, carefully. 'I could deal with it either way.'

His face turns from happy to confused to downright worried. I press on quickly.

'I guess I realised at some point along the line that I could live without you. That I wouldn't fall apart without you, that I'd manage, somehow. Not that I wanted to, you have to understand that. If I could have turned back the clock, made it all right again, I would have.

'But it was realising that I *could* live without you that made me realise I don't want to. Do you understand? I wanted us to be together all along, but I wanted it to be for all the right reasons. I didn't want to trap you into a life that wasn't right for you. I wanted our future to be based on the truth, on wanting the same things out of life. Not out of duty or responsibility. Or fear.'

I can see in his eyes that he doesn't quite get it, but that's OK. He's mollified by my words, and in time he'll understand. We'll be a normal couple, no dramas, no more grand sweeping gestures. Just the usual minor misunderstandings and silly rows. And then we'll get on with our lives. Me. Paul. And baby.

'I'd like you to name him,' I say, as we gaze down at our son together.

'Really? You would?'

'As long as it's not something crazy, yes.'

'David,' he says, so quickly I know he can't have just this minute thought of it.

'David?'

'It means "beloved".' Paul looks into my eyes. And then he says it again, and kisses my swollen mouth.

'Beloved,' I repeat. 'It's perfect. But how on earth did you know that?'

Paul puts his hand inside his jacket pocket and pulls out a dog-eared book of baby names. He also pulls out a slim volume about the stages of pregnancy and a leaflet on positive parenting. He shrugs sheepishly.

'I just kept hoping,' he says.

'David,' I whisper, holding my baby up to my face and inhaling his little puffs of breath.

'I'd like to give you this, too, if you'll take it.'

I look round, but Paul has disappeared. Then I see he hasn't disappeared but is kneeling on the floor on one knee. He holds out the ring I last saw swimming in a pool of amniotic fluid, and places it on the tip of my enormous finger.

'I hope you wiped it,' I tell him.

'I hope your fingers go back to their normal size,' he counters.

'Well?' he says. 'Will you marry me? Properly, this

time?'

I shrug, and snuggle David a little higher on my chest. 'Oh, all right then. I suppose I might as well.'

THE END

Acknowledgements

As always, I'd like to say a great big thank you to my husband, Jez, for his support and encouragement. Thanks to Chris Howard for another excellent cover, and to ace proofreader Jude White. I'd also like to thank my wonderful Beta readers: Emma Harrison, Dawn Hamilton, Marina Sofia, Vikki Thompson, Debbie Young, Lynsey James, and Pauline Wiles – you guys are the best.

Most of all, I'd like to thank the thousands of lovely readers who read and enjoyed *Can't Live Without*. Thanks for the great reviews and the messages of support on Facebook and Twitter – I hope you enjoyed *The Family Trap* just as much.

To find out more about my books, visit me at www.joannephillips.co.uk where you can sign up for my newsletter and hear about new releases, giveaways and special promotions.

Lightning Source UK Ltd.
Milton Keynes UK
UKOW05f2246250614

234069UK00004B/200/P

9 780957 309418